the
goodness gene

the goodness gene

SONIA LEVITIN

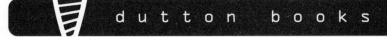

dutton books

DUTTON BOOKS
A member of Penguin Group (USA) Inc.
Published by the Penguin Group

Penguin Group (USA) Inc., 375 Hudson Street, New York, New York 10014, U.S.A.
Penguin Group (Canada), 90 Eglinton Avenue East, Suite 700, Toronto, Ontario, Canada M4P 2Y3 (a division of Pearson Penguin Canada Inc.)
Penguin Books Ltd, 80 Strand, London WC2R 0RL, England
Penguin Ireland, 25 St Stephen's Green, Dublin 2, Ireland (a division of Penguin Books Ltd)
Penguin Group (Australia), 250 Camberwell Road, Camberwell, Victoria 3124, Australia (a division of Pearson Australia Group Pty Ltd)
Penguin Books India Pvt Ltd, 11 Community Centre, Panchsheel Park, New Delhi – 110 017, India
Penguin Group (NZ), Cnr Airborne and Rosedale Roads, Albany, Auckland 1310, New Zealand (a division of Pearson New Zealand Ltd)
Penguin Books (South Africa) (Pty) Ltd, 24 Sturdee Avenue, Rosebank, Johannesburg 2196, South Africa
Penguin Books Ltd, Registered Offices: 80 Strand, London WC2R 0RL, England

LIBRARY OF CONGRESS CATALOGING-IN-PUBLICATION DATA

Levitin, Sonia, date.
The goodness gene / by Sonia Levitin.—1st ed.
p. cm.
Summary: As son of the Compassionate Director of the Dominion of the Americas, Will, along with his twin brother, Berk, has been groomed for leadership in a society that values genetic fitness, but he encounters information which causes him to question that society as well as his own identity.
ISBN 0-525-47397-1
[1. Genetic engineering—Fiction. 2. Cloning—Fiction. 3. Twins—Fiction. 4. Science fiction.] I. Title.

PZ7.L58Goo 2005
[Fic]—dc22 2005002143

Published in the United States by Dutton Books,
a member of Penguin Group (USA) Inc.
345 Hudson Street, New York, New York 10014
www.penguin.com/youngreaders

Designed by Jason Henry

Printed in USA   First Edition
1 3 5 7 9 10 8 6 4 2

FOR LLOYD, WITH LOVE

ACKNOWLEDGMENTS

My sincere appreciation to the following people:

Dr. Harold L. Karpman, M.D., cardiologist, Clinical Professor of Medicine, UCLA School of Medicine, Los Angeles, California, for discussions of brain damage, anaphylactic shock, allergies, and aging. As both friend and physician, Dr. Karpman has been consistently generous in sharing his expertise and support for my work.

Dr. Julie Korenberg, Ph.D., M.D., Vice-Chair of Pediatrics for Research, Cedars-Sinai Medical Center, Geri and Richard Brawerman Chair of Molecular Genetics, Professor of Pediatrics and Human Genetics, UCLA, for her kind and generous assistance in helping me to understand aspects of genetics, brain function, and behavior.

My son, Dr. Daniel Levitin, Ph.D., Associate Professor, Department of Psychology and Behavioral Neuroscience, McGill University, for his insight in both the scientific and humanistic arenas, and for his generous support for my work. I am particularly indebted to him for studies on Williams syndrome (used to describe Kiera's affliction in the novel), and for information on brain function and cloning.

My wonderful editor, Stephanie Owens Lurie, for her wise and expert suggestions and for being there whenever I needed an understanding partner in the creative process.

the
goodness gene

HAYLI'S CREED

THERE IS NO NATURAL LAW. That is a myth designed to keep people subservient to an invisible power that in reality does not exist. The idea of natural law or order was designed to prevent people from managing their own destiny. It forced them to think that their lives were ordained by some omnipotent force that knew the past, the present, and the future.

We will soon have the resources and technology to perfect the human race, to prevent every defect, to mitigate catastrophe, and in time even to control the weather. We will soon have the ability to prolong life far beyond our furthest expectation, to hundreds of years and beyond, even to immortality.

There is no reason why humans have to die.

HAYLI'S PLEDGE

HAIL TO THE GOODNESS, and to the *Supreme* Compassionate Director, most true, most powerful, most benevolent. To him we vow our allegiance and our love. To him we give the labor of our hands and the complete obedience of our will. We exist to please him. We long to serve him. Whatever he requires, we will do with gladness and joy in service.

CHAPTER 1

H E WAS CONTENT. And why wouldn't he be? His life was perfect. Everyone said so, and he knew it was true. Only the nights sometimes troubled him. There was a certain dream. He was cutting his way through thick wilderness, looking for Father.

By daylight, the dream-search receded, replaced by the orderly progression of his life. It was good. As the son of the Compassionate Director, he was respected by fellow students, servants, and even teachers. Beyond that, he was privileged to have a sibling—a twin—Berk. Thoughts of Berk reminded him of the puzzle he had just completed. Usually Berk finished before he did and phoned him with the news of his triumph. His brother must be slipping.

Now Will basked in contentment as he gazed around his living space, the neat nutrition center, the living area, and the sleep loft, all encompassed by the Screen. Just tonight, at the Pop Pageant, they had watched an old tape entitled *Family Living*. The audience had wavered between whoops of laughter and shuddering disbelief. How could anyone bear the constant sight, even the smell, of another person? There would be soapy residue and strange hairs in the basin, bits of clothing, even underwear left about, no matter how careful one tried to be. The film had shown a constant clamor of dissonant voices, people arguing, eating, laughing, screaming, and none of it could be switched off. "Alone, dearly alone," Will whispered to himself contentedly while from his canteen he selected the invigorating Nutra-green drink.

Will sat down with his drink and nibbled from a box of SNABS. He recalled the Pop Pageant with its flags and speeches following the film. Everyone was there, all his friends and acquaintances, and they greeted him with the proper enthusiasm and respect. Someone always saved him the best seat and watched for his reactions and copied him. He had leapt to his feet in a blind flash of love and patriotism at the sight of the cherished flag of the Dominion. He had shouted and clapped when Hayli's image appeared on the Screen, and everyone sang one of Will's own songs! How exhilarating it was to hear several hundred voices singing his words, "One heart, one blood, one unity!"

After the pageant, most of his friends had made their way to the Symsex. Not he. Will's entire being desired self-expression, oratory. Now he stood before the built-in camera that projected his image back onto the Screen so that he could see himself from every angle and perfect his oration.

Everyone agreed that Will spoke superbly—the other students in his form and even Father. In fact, copies of Will's speeches were often sent to Father at his special request. Later a servant would tell Will how the Compassionate Director had sat and watched Will's performance clear through, nodding, stroking his lips the way he did when he was enormously pleased. It was wonderful to see him gently repressing his brilliant smile so as not to reflect too much parental pride. On rare occasion Father sent a message, "Good job."

It pleased Will that Berk had neither the talent nor the interest for making speeches. Berk's was a straightforward, practical nature. People always compared the two of them. "Well, Berk asserts himself. Will is more thoughtful. A marvelous pair, they complement each other. The Two."

The implication was clear enough. Together, he and Berk composed a perfect whole. But leadership had never been shared in this Dominion of the Americas, not even before the Collapse. There always had to be one head of state, one chief.

If it troubled Berk, Will never knew it, but he wondered if Berk lay awake at night repeating the seemingly innocent remarks that always set one of them above the other. Did Berk wonder when the final choice between them would be made, and how?

Now, as Will watched his own shape turning and gesturing, heard his own voice rising, he was filled with a sense of power and control. He understood that a leader must know how to persuade the masses. First, establish the necessity. Next, propose a solution that brings good feeling. "We live from crisis to crisis," he declared, his fist raised, "from threat to threat. Dissidents abduct the innocent, pollute the environment, attack their neighbors. What can the average person do?" He paused. "Find happiness through service. Whatever your status, whatever your ability, go for The Goodness!"

He raised both arms, as if to embrace the invisible multitude. He brought a fiery expression to his eyes and showed strength by the set of his chin. His themes varied, but they always focused on enhancing The Goodness by better food production or increased vigilance and the importance of self-control and service.

He played back the sequence. Not bad. Not bad at all. Maybe Father would have it inserted into the Screen Banks. It had happened several times before, to Will's great delight. Past slogans of his hummed through Will's mind: "Before you can love, you must know what to hate." Somehow, words and slogans came to him, the way mechanics and numbers came to Berk. It was true, together he and Berk represented all that was good and successful. They had jointly inherited the brilliance of their father, Hayli. The thought that his father had helped to formulate The Goodness, the slow but steady unification and healing, filled Will with pride and awe. To become like Hayli was his overriding desire.

A flashing light and a simultaneous Incoming Message tone summoned him. Will pressed his wrist pad, and instantly his brother's image appeared.

"Will?" came his brother's voice. "Is that you?"

"Of course! You were the one who called *me*," Will exclaimed. "I finished the puzzle," he added. "Want to compare results?"

Berk hesitated, his eyes darting about. "Actually, I forgot to do it," he said.

"Forgot?" Will peered at his brother's image, so like his own, except that Berk's hair was shaggy and his gaze was rather truculent. "You are usually in such a hurry to beat me. What happened?"

"Can't a person make a normal mistake?" Berk said testily. "I'll get to it when I can."

"Fine," said Will. Lately his brother seemed irritable and often vague. "Are you all right?" he asked anxiously.

"I'm fine. I just got back from the Sym. What have you been doing?"

"Oh, I went to the Pop Pageant."

"How was it?"

"Lots of music and chanting, some great speeches. I was so energized that I—"

"Let me guess. You went back to your pod to work on some magnificent slogans, right?"

"I try," Will said. He could not gauge his brother's mood—was he being slightly sarcastic? He looked intently at the screen. "You look different. Are you shaving?"

"Starting to, and you?"

"Started a few weeks ago!" They laughed together. People often said they were identical. It wasn't true. Yes, they had the same features and straight dark hair, but just as no two pebbles dropped from the same boulder are an exact match, neither were they. Berk's eyes were brown, like Will's, but deep within lay a coldness that could border on cruelty. The set of Berk's mouth was taut, and his smile was swift and brittle. Will's smile was slow, almost shy.

"How was the Sym?" Will asked.

"Great. As always," Berk enfolded himself, his arms crossed over his chest in contentment.

Will felt a slight jolt of envy. Berk always enjoyed sex. He never complained or asked for anything more than the simulator offered. Will had tried, several times, to talk to his brother about it, but he could never follow through. Berk would get that cold, censuring smile on his face. It wasn't normal not to love the Symsex.

"You should go more often, brother," said Berk. "You are getting too serious."

"I'll do that," said Will.

A distinctive buzzing sound interrupted them, swiftly followed by a female computer voice: "Call. Urgent. Submit."

"It's for both of us!" Berk exclaimed. "From Father."

Indeed, the number 0101 was immediately displayed, and the name: Czeminhayli. Will chuckled. "Just like the old man," he murmured appreciatively. As if the Compassionate Director needed any identification other than his status initials, C.D., or his nickname, Hayli.

Berk's image became miniaturized, replaced by the Director's face, enormous not only in its screen dimensions, but by the powerful features: the thick, corded neck; firm jaw; and bright, piercing eyes.

"Good evening, my sons," came the voice.

Will took a step back, ducked his head. "Good evening, Sir."

"I am speaking to you directly," said the Director. "This is not a paternal tape. Do you understand?"

Will felt a pounding in his chest. He could count on his fingers the number of times he had spoken to his father directly. He glanced at Berk, who stood in profile on the screen, his throat pulsing.

"Six weeks from now will be a landmark event," their father said. "Do you know what that date signifies?"

"The anniversary," Will said loudly, "of The Goodness."

"Exactly," said his father. "Twenty-five years, Berk. How could you forget such a thing?"

"I apologize, Father, for being slow," replied Berk.

"Never mind. The Council is planning an anniversary pageant. Vital new policies will be announced. The announcements will affect your futures. I have arranged for both of you to be there. In person."

Will felt a jolt of excitement. He held his breath, bit his lips so that he would not interrupt.

"You will receive all the particulars on your Screens. Servants, both human and robot, will assist you, so do not worry about preparations for the journey."

Journey; it was a strange word, almost archaic, implying travel in devices with wheels and combustion motors. Will grasped the side of the air chair and sank down into it.

Hayli was smiling broadly, the same brilliant smile that graced countless stamps and seals and emblems. That look of kindness touched Will like a beacon. "We will meet on Mattelin Island for the ceremony of honor, conducted by the Great Council. All the Directors and Ministers will be there."

"Have they held the election yet?" Berk asked. His voice rose with excitement. "You're to be reelected, aren't you, Father? Hail to you, Father! Hail!"

Hayli chuckled appreciatively. "Wait and see," he said, but his tone, too, was exuberant, and Will wished he had expressed more enthusiasm.

Will cleared his throat; his voice cracked. "We are *meeting* you? Actually? We will all be together then? And Mara, too?" He had been to Mattelin Island only once before, when Hayli was named Compassionate Director, head of the entire Dominion of the Americas. That was ten years ago, when Will was only six. Will remembered how Mara had clutched his and Berk's hands as the parade went past. She had taught them how to salute and to shout, "Hail, Hayli! Hail The Goodness!"

"Of course Mara will be there. She is with me now. Yes, the Council has voted. I can tell you that they have compounded the honor."

"How, Father?" Will breathed.

"You will hear it at the anniversary pageant. I want you to be surprised, and to reflect that surprise for the media."

"An expanded term, Father?" Berk exclaimed.

"Hush. You'll see. You should know, I want you both to work directly in the Fifth Pillar from now on. There will be a brief internship period. Nobody must accuse me of nepotism. But rest assured, you will be performing vital work. You will be my right and left hands."

Will's heart pounded with amazement and joy. It was everything he had ever dared to dream, to live for.

"We will announce major changes at the anniversary pageant. After that, the two of you will travel to some of the distant colonies and sections. It's time for you to see the real world."

Will broke in, "We see news tapes of increased violence and sabotage, Father. They say the colonies are dangerous."

"Precisely," said Hayli, his countenance stern. "That is exactly why you need to be informed. A leader needs to taste and touch and smell the masses, so to speak. One can only go so far with the Vi-Ex. Don't worry. You will have protection, your own mentor, and, of course, your PAAR."

"Yes, Father," Will and Berk said together. "Thank you, Sir."

The Compassionate Director continued. "You have both been trained all these years to play an important role in public affairs. I hope you won't disappoint me."

Will called out, "What have you planned for us, Father? What role?" It seemed he had waited all his life for the chance to work beside his father, to see him in the flesh every day.

The Director answered soberly, "For a time you will serve in associate positions. You will write reports on various aspects of The Goodness. Berk, you will serve in the Security Sector. Will, you are best suited to the Information Section. Both are vital to The Goodness."

"Certainly, Father!" Will cried, standing at attention, though, in truth, it all seemed vague. He had hardly ever traveled beyond the district of Washolina, where he had been born at the Academy Gestation Lab, designated Status One from the first moment.

"I want both of you to prepare short acceptance speeches, to be given at the anniversary pageant. Everyone has to see that you are vigorous and competent, and that you thoroughly understand the principles of The Goodness."

Berk spoke up. "Father, I have been studying Security issues for several months. If it is not presumptuous of me, I would like to recommend—"

"Yes, I will want your recommendations, son," Hayli said warmly. "Will! I trust you have prepared some practical ideas on how to ensure cooperation. I don't want just a theoretical approach," he added with a hint of derision, "but something useful."

"Of course, Father," said Will, and, despite the climate control, he felt a flash of heat throbbing through his body.

"I expect you both to work hard to earn your positions," the Director emphasized. Back lighting gave his face a golden glow. His voice exuded strength and determination. "Nobody should ever say that favoritism played a part in your appointment."

"I'll do my best, Father," Will said ardently.

"You must call me Director. Never Father, never from now on."

"Yes, Director!" both boys chorused.

"And one other thing. I will arrange for you to witness an actual Compassionate Removal. I will expect a full report on the Compassionate Removal program, your experience with it, your assessment. Overall, it should be quite interesting. There will be pleasures," he said with a warm smile.

"Thank you, Father! Sir!" said Berk.

"Thank you, Director!" cried Will, his entire being attuned to his father's brilliant smile and to the glorious opportunity and personal touch he would soon experience.

CHAPTER 2

WILL TURNED TO THE SCREEN, certain that his image reflected the same amazement and delight that he saw in Berk's face. Both spoke at once. "Can you believe . . . we are actually going to meet Father, travel to Mattelin Island . . ."

"I can't wait to see the colonies. Do you suppose we can stop in the Great Desert?" Berk exclaimed.

"I'm sure not. It would be dangerous," Will objected. "I don't want to see those people, do you?"

"It will be part of our job to locate the dissidents," Berk said, "to root them out."

"How do we know there isn't anyone left from before the Relocation?"

"That was twenty-four years ago!" Berk exclaimed. "Surely they've all died out by now."

"We need to reeducate the dissidents," said Will. "If they knew the truth about The Goodness, they would want to cooperate."

Berk laughed. "You're dreaming," he said scornfully. "You have to accept the idea that some people don't want to change. They aren't fit to be part of The Goodness."

"Well, we have to try," Will insisted. "Persuasion is the best tool."

"That is why you are good with words," Berk said, "and I am better at action. I believe in separating the dissidents before they contaminate the others. I suppose eventually I will be in charge of enforcement. I always liked that game."

"You always won," said Will with a chuckle. He recalled all the tournaments they played together, using the miniature figures dressed in drab green with silver braid on their shoulders, copies of actual enforcers, their tiny rifles powered by batteries.

"When I become minister," Berk boasted, "security breaches will be a thing of the past. I believe in prevention, which begins with quarantine. I'm sure Father will agree."

"Security is your strength," Will said. He felt amiable, invigorated. He gazed around his pod, the sleek walls and immaculate furnishings, and suddenly he longed for something else, a crowd, a happening. Usually after pageant he felt satiated. Now his excitement for the future made him want something more. Feelings crept over him. Warm feelings, like those he had felt with Mara, when he was small.

"You and I," he told Berk, "will be together now, the way we used to be. We'll see each other every day, in person, when we are working with Father."

"Perhaps," said Berk, and glanced away, disinterested. "If there is time."

"Don't you want to see me?" Will asked, feeling hurt.

"It doesn't matter what we want," Berk said sternly. "We'll have our jobs to do. We're to be Hayli's right hand and left hand. We're the only people he can really trust."

Will frowned. "What about Mara? He has to trust Mara."

"You haven't learned even the most important lesson, Brother." Berk chided him. "Trust nobody."

"I trust you," Will retorted.

"I am your twin," Berk said. "That's different. We are nearly the same." He went on. "You know what the Director went through at the beginning, the betrayals."

"Of course. Don't tutor me, Berk," Will said sharply. "I believe I spend twice the time as you do at the history tapes. I know it all very well. But even Father had to trust Mara. And he had to have followers. He couldn't do it all alone."

"Come to think of it," Berk said thoughtfully, "we should be organizing our own followers."

"Do you think so?" Will asked anxiously. Yes, Berk was always one step ahead when it came to imagining the future. Even when they were very small, Berk had told him with great solemnity one night, "They are not going to let us sleep together anymore. You'll see. They will take you away."

As it turned out, it was Berk who was moved to another Academy, far to the north of the district. Then Will's dreams had started, the dreams of wild beasts.

"I suppose I have enough of a following," Will said stoutly. Mentally he counted his friends and the larger group that always gathered around him. "How about you?" The Screen flickered and buzzed. "It's the nightly tape," he said. "We'll talk later."

Every night the Screen projected the paternal tape, like clockwork. It was impossible to avoid or to switch off. One had no choice, except to designate maternal or paternal tape, or perhaps both parent-types together. Will had always selected the paternal tape.

Berk's face vanished. In its place was the image of Father dressed in casual clothes, sitting at a table eating supper.

Will leaned back, only half listening, responding automatically.

"How are you today, son?"

"Very well, thank you." He rubbed his fingertips absentmindedly over the rash on his arm, just above the elbow.

"Any pain or unusual symptoms?"

"No. I'm fine," Will said mechanically. Tone of voice didn't count. His responses were digitally recorded by the computer.

"Are you taking your daily supplements?"

"Yes, Sir." The small packet of pale blue powder appeared each morning on the outtake tray of his canteen.

"I have checked your Screen for bodily functions. Everything seems to be in order. You have gained three-tenths of a pound. Your muscle mass is slightly deficient. You must add ten minutes to your training starting tomorrow."

"Yes, Sir."

"Your brother surpasses you in muscle mass and endurance."

"I'll try to improve, Sir." Will frowned. His father had told them to refer to him as Director from now. Did that mean in actual conversation, or also in these paternal tapes? Unsure, he realized that "sir" was probably a safe response.

"How were your studies? What did you learn?"

"I reviewed half a dozen history tapes, concentrating on the wars. I also went to a Vision Experience about the Collapse." He shuddered. "It was very disturbing."

"Are you neglecting mathematics?"

"No, Sir. I realize that mathematics is vital. We need to learn how to project the effects of actions taken."

"And current problems?"

"Extreme pestilence in the African Dominion. Several abductions in Washolina." Will glanced over to the corner, where his personal anti-abduction robot, PAAR, reclined. It seemed incredible that people were stolen away right here in his own district, the highest security sector of all.

"What needs to be done?" came the question.

"Continual surveillance. Suspect everyone."

His recital apparently hit exactly the right note, for the tape continued. "Very good. Have you eaten?"

"I will program it now, Sir."

"I trust you will make nutritionally good choices."

"I often select the 170. Flavors from the Indian Dominion, fortified with hormones to build up the muscles."

"Good choice. Is your canteen fully stocked?"

"Yes, Sir. The yellow truck came just yesterday."

"Sleep well, then. Your Screen is set for eight hours rest."

"I—could I have an extra hour?" Will felt suddenly alive, excited. "I thought I might visit the Sym after dinner."

"Be back before midnight."

"Yes, Sir. I will. Good night."

"Wait! Before you retire, you must read at least a page from Mattelin."

"I will, Sir. Thank you. Good night."

He tried to get Berk again, but the Screen informed him that his brother was not available. Would he like to see a previous program? No.

Will shrugged, trying to remember when he has last seen his brother in the flesh. It had to be over four years ago, at the district-wide Pop Pageant the year they turned twelve. Then, they were already selected for leadership, known for their intelligence and stamina. As offspring of the Compassionate Director, they were, of course, Status One. The only remaining question was which ministry of the five suited them best, and even that was now resolved. Both would work in the highest, the Fifth Pillar, which governed progress, security, and information. Will hoped he and Berk could work together.

Will recalled those halcyon days when they were very young, the two of them sleeping in the same bed, nestled close all night. Even then, Berk was brave and very physical, while Will was more verbal, inclined toward stories and songs. He loved to argue, whereas Berk chose fists and feet instead.

From the Screen came a familiar voice. It was Mara, beautiful and articulate, as always. It was one of Mara's great pleasures to narrate the children's programs that were shown at this time of the evening,

". . . now our foods are scientifically created for maximum nutritional value and minimum waste. Imagine—it sometimes took more than an hour to eat a meal, and even longer to prepare it. Some people ate poorly and became grossly fat. There was no organization, no standard for eating. Everyone simply ate whatever he wished, and they would kill a cow, a sheep, or a pig and consume them. Other food they ate grew in the soil, absorbing all the filth and contamination of waste products from factories and thermonuclear waste and even human waste. No wonder the plagues came!"

Mara answered questions posed by children planted in the audience. Then she whirled to and fro, showing her robe of bright lavender. "People used to spend hours changing their clothes, depending on the weather. Now, of course, our robes and tunics contain temperature sensors." Mara laughed lightly. "I remember how it was before we had I.D. implants, the credit devices and licenses people had to carry, and the nuisance of . . ."

With a wave of his hand, Will closed down the Screen. From his canteen he took a bag of SNABS and munched several as he changed into a light leisure suit, white tunic and pants, and made his way outside. His PAAR followed at a discreet distance. Nobody liked to be reminded of the presence of these personal anti-abduction robots, but they were a necessity, especially for people of high status.

Will greeted the other people in his form. All were pursuing some late-night activity. Most were bound for the Virtual Experience Centers, or returning from them with that sleepy, soppy expression on their faces. Virtual travel always left its mark.

"Will!" called his friend Brodi. "Coming to the Vi-Ex?"

"No," he called back. "I'm headed for the Sym."

"I thought I'd do the Veldt again," said Brodi, coming closer. "Last time I actually felt the breath of a lion on my back. It was exhilarating, let me tell you, and terrifying!" Brodi laughed loudly. "This time I'm requesting elephants."

"Have you done the stellar gaze?"

"Half a dozen times," Brodi said with a nod. "I'm into Earth reality now. You know, a different phase for me. I've done three of the planets and the inner earth. Now I want to experience the animals. Every time, I'm thankful it's only a Vi-Ex. Can you imagine what it was like, with real animals roaming about?" Brodi shuddered.

"Yes." Will took a deep breath. "Those fangs and claws and horrible teeth. No wonder there was so much sickness."

"People used to eat them," Brodi said with a grimace.

"Some still do," Will retorted.

"Well, not anyone we know."

Will laughed. "We can be thankful for that!"

"We are thankful," Brodi agreed. For a brief moment they looked into each other's eyes. They had been together since birth, along with the others in their batch. But between Will and Brodi a special understanding had developed long ago. Whatever he did, Will knew that Brodi was his greatest supporter. They turned in accord, each with a quick grin and a wave of farewell.

Will recalled his last Virtual Experience, a flight to the moon and to space satellites. It was thrilling. Once again he was filled with a sense of Goodness, of patriotism and appreciation for his life. He felt the lightness in his step, the joy of anticipation.

He turned back and called out, "Brodi! Meet me later if you can."

Brodi stopped in his tracks and came rushing back. "Of course I'll meet you," Brodi said. "You usually retire early, so I didn't ask. What do you want to do?"

"We'll go to the pavilion. I spoke to the Director today. Things are happening. Big changes."

"Tell me now," Brodi said.

"Later. I'll pad you when I'm done. Bring Alberz, and few others, if you like." He needed a following. He must take a few people into his confidence, gather a nucleus of supporters, people who would be willing to do anything for him, as he was willing to do anything for Hayli. Yes, Berk had sized up the situation once again.

As he walked on, Will felt that strange confluence of desires. He wanted to be alone, yet he wanted people, hordes of people, all cheering, all looking upon him with awe and respect. He needed, needed— something he could not name, something warm and complete. Like the times when he was with Mara, and she held him and sang to him and said, "You are my lovely, my own. You are my best boy. Beloved." Remembering brought a flush to his face, embarrassment and pleasure combined. It seemed perverse to be so touched by a memory, especially now that he stood on the verge of true adulthood and the leadership he had dreamed of.

He felt unready. Oh, how he wanted to be strong and firm, commitment and competence shining from his very features, as Hayli's face radiated supremacy. Few people are born with that charisma, this he knew. But, Will wondered continually, can charisma be nurtured? Can it be achieved? Perhaps with age and wisdom it would come to him.

Now, came an alternate voice, mocking and tormenting, *what is the matter with you? Are you afraid?*

I'm too young, he retorted in his mind. Inexperienced.

Afraid, jeered the unseen tormentor. *Afraid to lead, afraid of contro-versy, afraid to make decisions, aren't you? Afraid to be wrong. Afraid to take a chance.*

No! He straightened his shoulders, accelerated his stops. Why, the Compassionate Director was only sixteen when he drew up his first plan for The Goodness. He had already formed The Five—Hayli himself, Mara, and three others who became the founders of The Goodness. They swore a blood oath, at sixteen. *Sixteen.* And from that core came every-thing. He, Will, could rise to leadership. He *would.*

Will took deep breaths of the purified air that encased Washolina. He swung his arms briskly. Slogans thundered in his mind now, and he matched his steps to the mantra: "The weak get eaten. The strong sur-vive. Man survives by means of struggle. Struggle is the father of all things. Before you can love, you must hate. Hate weakness. Hate doubt. Love your strength. Love yourself."

As he approached the hall with its columns and wide portals, music urged him on. He stepped through the doorway, and he heard sounds of tranquil water. Servants in white glided past him through the shimmering halls. The scent of lilies and roses enveloped him. His thoughts eased and fell away.

Will's steps slowed, and his breathing lengthened. Berk was right, he thought happily. I need to get away more. I've been much too serious. What I need is pleasure.

He saw the shadowy form of a girl gliding through the adjacent corri-dor. She was nearly as tall as he, and as she moved, he became aware of flowing robes of a thin iridescent fabric that flickered blue and silver-green. He left the soft air pull him into the Symsex, onto the fragrant air couch that received him in its embrace. He whispered his desires. And then it began.

CHAPTER 3

MUSIC ACCOMPANIED THE FRAGRANCES he had preselected. Fresh-cut watermelon, green grass, and pine. Music wove patterns in his mind, soft colors alternating, mingling with the touch, the ever increasingly tender touch. It stretched his emotions almost beyond endurance, bringing tears, delight, sweet, sweet solace. Every thought fled from his mind, and into this blissful vacancy poured all the feelings of which he was capable and more, the desire, in turn, to touch another. Will moved slowly, languidly, caught in the magic of the Symsex.

Slowly he extended his hand in yearning, hoping that his touch would be met, as indeed it was. Through the mist that separated the two chambers, the wall that allowed only this, the touch of a hand, Will felt his fingers meeting warm flesh. Music murmured and melted within him. Visions came with the music, indescribable, beautiful, and all the while *her* hand remained in his.

Was the hand real? Was it truly? Or was it only a simulation, part of his imagination being aroused and played upon, making him utterly helpless? Now it didn't matter, real or simulated, for his delight was complete. He groaned with pleasure, sang out! And then it was over. He drew back his hand, trembling from head to toe, exhausted and happy. It was a word he did not use lightly: happy.

When he awakened, Will was surrounded by the fresh scent of mint and pine, and now the music played a carnival of tunes. He got up, grinning at his satisfied image on the Screen.

But even as he walked through the shimmering corridors to the outside, the faint, nagging discontent seized him. The Sym was supposed to soothe away restlessness and leave him satisfied for several days, at least. Everyone else seemed entirely content with what the Symsex offered—pleasure without guilt or responsibility, happiness without a price. Will had briefly considered inputting his problem on the Health Advisor, but then he rejected the idea. If he were diagnosed as depressed or confused, a robo-servant would bring him a small packet on a tray. He had tried the drugs before. They left him feeling slightly out of body, and he hated that feeling of losing control.

Will padded his friend Brodi and walked outdoors to the canopy of stars and moons. From the corner of his eye he saw two girls and heard them talking. Their voices were filled with gaiety. Somehow, it bothered him that they should walk so freely, swinging their arms and their hair. One looked decidedly foreign. What was she doing here? An occasional outsider did attend the Academy on scholarship; they rarely lasted more than a year. But this girl seemed so confident! It irritated him. Her brown hair gleamed with golden lights, and now he saw that she wore a purple feather tucked in at her ear. Ridiculous! He wanted to look away, but he could not, as if she were a magnet and he a lump of metal. Will chided himself, astonished at the hammering of his heart. Unwittingly, he had lengthened his steps, and he could hear them talking.

". . . you've never been before? I can't believe it, Leora!"

"Well, there is always a first time, isn't there?" Leora's voice had a lilting quality.

"Did you enjoy it?"

"Who wouldn't?"

"Do you always answer a question with a question?"

"Do you?" Leora's laughter was full and musical.

They walked on, swinging their hair over their shoulders. It was Leora who wore the purple feather in her long, shining hair. Now she glanced back over her shoulder. Seeing Will, her brows lifted almost imperceptibly, but her mouth moved into a smile that was oddly mocking and almost inviting.

Will refused to meet her gaze or to smile. She was really too provocative! Of course, many girls were among his admirers, and sometimes he did speak to them and give a cool smile. A leader must balance friendliness with distance. But this girl seemed to know nothing of such matters, for her look was bold and direct, and she even tossed her head as if to say, "So what if he is the son of the C.D. It means nothing to me!"

"Will!" He turned at the call.

"Brodi! Alberz!" Relieved at the interruption, Will called out exuberantly, extending his arms in greeting. Brodi and Alberz looked gratified, especially since several bystanders stopped to stare. Alberz wore his tunic open at the throat, to expose his I.D. implant, decorated with rubies. It was a new fashion, and too ostentatious, Will thought. He wore only a modest gold stud at the center of his implant, with a tiny diamond winking from the center. He was pleased to see that Brodi had copied him. Someday, Will thought, all his followers would wear only a duplicate of his decoration. It would identify and bind them. *One heart, one blood, one unity.*

"How goes it?" the boys asked.

"Wonderful," Will said, smiling broadly. "I'm glad you could meet me."

"I guess you've been to the Sym," Alberz said with a grin.

"Indeed," Will replied. He turned, thinking he heard that lilting laugh, but he saw only the nondescript crowd.

"How about a drink, then? We can sit outside," suggested Brodi.

Will checked his pulse pad, a miniature version of the Scanner-Screen. "I have about twenty minutes."

"Plenty of time," said Alberz. "You are very organized," he complimented.

Throngs of young people were gathered at the bio-dome Café. Enforcers stood at attention around the pavilions, their drab green uniforms almost blending into the structure. Their expressions were bland, as if they were immune to the din.

The place was abuzz with music and the sounds of entertainment, light shows, dance pavilions, and food concessions. Will's PAAR joined the dozens of personal security robots lounging against a low wall. Their small, round heads and rectangular bodies were pocked with sensors. They might have been manufactured with humanoid features and the ability to speak, but it had been decided long ago that these men of metal must always be acknowledged as mere machines, incapable of thought, emotion, or real intellect. Their segmented legs were long and thin; they could cover vast distances swiftly. Their arms ended in hammer-like hands with a single rotating digit, like a thumb, that could clasp a throat in a death grip.

Will ordered his favorite "mocca-pro," a creamy beverage that delivered a powerful combination of proteins, stimulants, and time-release relaxants. The flavor was of real strawberries and almonds, delicacies that were the subject of many romantic songs. One of them, in fact, echoed from the Dance Dome at this moment:

> "Fields of berries
> Make us merry
> Sweet as the touch of a hand;
> The Goodness in the land
> Brings peace and pride
> All strife aside. All strife aside."

Alberz raised his glass. Will did the same. "The Goodness," both said together.

Something caught Will's eye at middle distance. The same two girls sat but one table away, nibbling nutria-cones wrapped in bright paper. They laughed and talked with great animation, their gaze resting often on Will and his friends. Will caught his breath. "Look at those two," he muttered. "What makes them think they can sit here? Don't they know the front tables are for seniors?"

"They're new," Alberz answered. "That one with long hair is on scholarship," he said. "I spoke to them at the pageant this afternoon."

"You spoke to them?" Will exclaimed. The one with the feather, Leora, gave him another glance, then she turned to her friend, whispering in her ear. Will felt an unexplained, rising irritation. He tried to dispel it with talk. "You can tell that one isn't from our district. Probably an outsider, don't you think? She looks a bit *dissy*."

"She's loud," observed Brodi. "Not only her talk, but the bold way she looks at you."

"Well, she must know who you are," said Alberz. "She's probably longing to meet you. Shall I introduce you?"

"Certainly not!" Will shot back. "What makes you think I need you for an introduction? You seem to think you have a priority on social graces—" He stopped, aware of the look of fear in his friend's eyes. Will took a long sip from his mocca-pro, seeking composure. In truth, he could not understand his own moods, careening from pleasure to irritation, growing so swiftly to anger.

"I'm sorry, Will," Alberz murmured. "You are right. The girl does look *dissy*. Hardly the sort of person that would interest you."

Will's PAAR, summoned by Will's outburst, had strolled up to the table. Now it turned back, clattering slightly as it moved. "Remember when we used to race our PAARs?" Will said amiably. He felt better now, in control.

"You always won," said Brodi with a nod. "You designed all those clever pitfalls and obstacles."

"We should do it again sometime," Will said. He noticed a small group of people moving toward them, hesitant, expectant. He was aware, always, that his presence stirred not only interest but desire. To be seen in his company was a definite plus for anyone. Several people stopped at the table where the two girls sat. In moments a lively conversation ensued, and a good deal of laughter.

"You said you met them?" Will asked Alberz. "Where are they from? What are they doing here?"

Alberz drew himself up, eager to provide information. "The small blonde one is called Cosma. She is a year or so behind us, from Lab Eleven, you know that batch. Some of them didn't even make Status One."

"And the other? The one with the feather?"

"Oh, Leora is from District Seven, the west," Alberz said. "She said she was wait-listed for three years. She adores our Academy. She won a scholarship to get in."

"You mentioned that already," Will grumbled.

"Most of those scholarship types never graduate," Brodi said hastily.

"She would have to be intelligent, wouldn't she, to be accepted?" said Alberz.

"Why are you so *dissy* about that girl?" demanded Brodi. He glanced conspiratorially at Will. "Are you thinking, perhaps, of partnering?"

The three laughed, and Alberz flushed deeply. Nobody partnered until they were at least in their forties. One saw old partners holding hands sometimes. Young people ridiculed them. Of course, a Director would have a partner, as Hayli had Mara. But that was different. They were colleagues. Mara had been one of The Five architects of The Goodness. Their full devotion was to the cause.

"I might be going out west," Will began pointedly. His friends gasped in astonishment.

"Really!" Brodi exclaimed. "How would you manage? I mean, do they even have Syms out west?"

"They're a bit backward," Will told him. "They have a few outdated Screens, nothing modern, I guess. Somehow we have to educate them. That will be part of my job."

"I've heard some of those people still keep animals," Alberz said. He glanced over at Leora. "I wonder what she eats."

Will frowned. "The Goodness provides food for everyone, even out in the remote colonies. I agree with you, Brodi, that most won't ever make Status One. But it is the Compassionate Director's desire that they be allowed to try. Of course, without all the advantages of birth and breeding—"

"But the births are all controlled, aren't they?" said Alberz. "There are laws."

"People don't always follow the laws," Will said sharply. Alberz was so dense! "We still have problems of people being born deficient, don't you know? Where do you think all the Abs come from?"

"I've heard that in some places people can't afford the labs," Alberz murmured. He glanced at Brodi, seemingly for support.

"There's no excuse for it!" Will shouted. "We are talking about morality! We are talking about survival!" He sprang to his feet, gesturing. "Look at the old Vi-Ex tapes, why don't you? People had packs of children, without any genetic monitoring." He felt wound up, agitated, unable to stop that raging from deep within. "The masses are like an animal," he said loudly, "that obeys instincts. They act out of selfish desires, no matter what the cost to society. Some people had four or five or even more children, even if they turned out retarded. If they couldn't earn a living, they just went on welfare. The gene pool got so horribly polluted it was a menace to the entire world!" He was breathing heavily; his face felt damp. About a dozen people had gathered around, listening, nodding. There was even a sprinkling of applause.

Will stopped suddenly and sat down. He wasn't ready to broadcast his ideas, not yet. He needed to hone his words, so that if he were quoted later, the Compassionate Director would be proud. "Sorry to have created such a stir. I do get carried away on this subject. This impurity, the misery it causes—it's the Director's main concern, and a matter of great concern to me, also."

The onlookers dispersed, to Will's relief. He did not like having an audience unless he was well prepared.

"We are all concerned," echoed Brody and Alberz in unison.

The three of them sipped their drinks. Brody and Alberz shifted uneasily in their chairs, seeming to have lost the art of conversation. At last Brodi again took up the topic of the girls at the next table. "She is a strange one," he said. "It must be the way she moves. Look at her hands." Leora was fondling her long hair.

"Compassion is one thing," said Will with finality, "and giving them opportunity. But that doesn't mean we have to mix."

They drank in silence for a few moments. The relaxant began to do its work. Will leaned back in his seat. "Listen, I have news," he began. "My father came to me and my brother tonight," he said, gratified by his friends' looks of envy and amazement. He used the term "my father" deliberately. "There's going to be an anniversary pageant. Berk and I will attend. In real time." Will waited for his announcement to sink in.

"Tell us! Oh, can you bring a guest?" his friends exclaimed.

Will shook his head. "You'll be able to watch the proceedings on the Screen. Father said there will be new announcements. Berk and I will be appointed interns in the Fifth Pillar," Will said. "If I need help, can I count on you?"

"Of course!" Brodi cried.

"Always," said Alberz. "I knew you'd be Fifth Pillar!" he exclaimed. "Someday you'll be Director, Compassionate Director. I hope you will remember your friends then!"

"You are much brighter than your brother," said Brodi.

"A rising star," echoed Alberz. "Please be sure to pad us after the pageant, so we can congratulate you."

"Of course," Will said. He basked in their praise, but immediately he wondered, would he really surpass Berk? All his life he had been in competition with Berk. Was there really a place for each of them? Or would one have to knock the other out, as in ancient time? He remembered the games of their youth, one in particular, the maze, with its vicious rats and the loops and dead ends, and tower at the center. Whoever first reached the tower was rewarded with showers of praise and lovely sweets. The loser clung in panic to the spiked iron fence, until the proctor came, laughing wildly, as he released the desperate child.

Will heard the girls' laughter, and he felt stung by it. They were probably talking about him. Abruptly he stood up and strode over to the small table. Startled, Leora, the one with the little feather, drew back. Cosma, the blonde, looked flustered.

Two enforcers immediately approached, their shoulders squared menacingly. Will waved them away. "I can handle this," he said.

Will rested his hands possessively on the table. "Perhaps you are not familiar with the rules," he declared, "but these tables are reserved for Seniors."

"Oh, pardon us!" cried Cosma, quickly gathering her cape around her shoulders.

"I suppose you want us to leave," said Leora. She stood up, and her eyes were nearly level with his, smoky blue eyes, unwavering.

"That would appear to be obvious," Will said stiffly.

"Come, Cosma, I was getting bored here anyway." Leora swung her cape over her shoulders. The silver design glittered. It was the Academy emblem. It infuriated Will.

"I would like to see your I.D.," Will said sternly.

Leora never took her eyes from his as she slowly unbuttoned the top of her tunic, exposing her implant. Will read the I.D., a blue tattoo, devoid of any ornamentation. FMC-2289-09. Like all I.D.s, it included location, birth year, and batch number.

Will gave her a stern look. "Do you know who I am?" he inquired.

"You are the son of the Compassionate Director," she replied, unflinching.

"I expect that you will learn and follow the Academy rules," he said. "I won't post it on your record this time."

"Thank you, oh, thank you," said Cosma, ducking her head. She gave Leora a slight nudge.

"Thank you," said Leora, at last looking down. But about her mouth a slight, sardonic smile remained. It was nothing that Will could identify, nothing he could claim as outright rudeness or disrespect. Yet it left him feeling confounded.

Abruptly he turned back to his friends, checking his pulse pad as he went. "I'm clocked," he said, making his tone breezy. "Good night." He paused, then turned back and pointed at Alberz. "I would prefer to see less dazzle at your throat."

Alberz bit his lip. "I'm sorry," he said, covering the gems with his hands. "I will change it tomorrow."

Will stepped away, circling around the motion path to the perimeter. He needed a brisk walk. Swiftly his PAAR followed. A sudden stitch in his side, deep down, made Will slow his steps, and he regretted not having taken the easier way. The night air was clammy. It made him itch, especially the patch of raised skin above his elbow, and another on his right hip.

Back in his own quarters, Will shed his clothes and put on a soft robe, savoring solitude. The pain in his side subsided. He felt gratitude for everything that was his. And now he looked forward to the anniversary pageant, to seeing Mara and Hayli and his brother, Berk.

There were few twins in the world. Will had learned, early on, how to react when people stared or questioned him about it. When they were little, the children in their form used to giggle and ask, "Were you cloned?" Then a sharp slap on the mouth stopped them, along with the admonition, "There are no clones. Only a *dissy* would say that. Clones have been outlawed for years."

"But—but," the offender would stammer, "there are two of you! T-t-twins!"

"The egg split in the lab, that's all. We both have the same parent DNA; it simply split in half, and so we are twins. Now, lose yourself, or I'll set some animals on you!"

Never mind that there were no real animals in all of District One; the threat always did the job, and the tormenters ran away, frightened. Added to which Berk, even at the age of four, was a powerful opponent, with kicking feet and swinging fists.

It was this strength of both boys that, even when they were mere embryos, allowed them to come to maturation. Splitting eggs were not so very unusual. But letting both mature, instead of sacrificing one to benefit of the other—that was exceedingly rare.

The twins were inseparable until they were five years old. Then the proctors recommended that they be parted, so that each boy could "achieve his utmost potential." The first night, when Will lay down to sleep, he felt the agony of cold aloneness. Tears flowed down his cheeks. He could not stop them. Instantly the Screen projected images all around him, terrifying images of wild beasts and large flapping birds with sharp beaks and piercing talons. They flew at his face. "The weak get eaten," came the words beneath the roars, while the Screen showed victims being torn apart, eyes pecked out, leaving bleeding holes. "The weak get eaten." He lay there trembling, screaming.

Mara had come to him with her song. Softly, softly she sang,

"Fear no evil,
Shed no tear
I am with you
Always near . . ."

It was a strange song. He never quite understood it, but its gentle rhythm always made him calm. Mara's arms around him were warm and soothing. Did he remember rightly that she held him close and kissed him? And did she murmur to him, "You are my sweet, my own, my little love." He wanted that again, even as he knew it was impossible and errant. Nobody of right training desired touch, human touch, did they?

The lights went down to a low amber glow. "Sleep, sleep, sleep," came the whisper from his Screen. Music filled his quarters. The temperature fanned down to a cool comfort level, while gentle currents led him to the bed. Will lay down, deeply relaxed. The words of Hayli's pledge filled his thoughts, marking the end of the day. "Hail to The Goodness, and to the Compassionate Director, most true, most powerful, most benevolent. To him we vow our allegiance . . ."

His thoughts moved from the pledge to Hayli's various words of wisdom emblazoned on banners and sweeping continually across the Screen. "There is no superpower or force that pulls the strings of the universe. There is no reason why humans have to die."

Soothed and comforted, Will fell asleep.

CHAPTER 4

Like a constant luminous presence, thoughts of the anniversary pageant accompanied Will on his daily routine. He imagined it all—the pomp, the excitement, the trip itself, taking him to unknown regions, fabulous possibilities. Soon, so soon he would begin his rise toward leadership.

But change also brought uncertainty and apprehension. Away from the Academy, how would he fill up his time? How would he know what to think? He would be forced to interpret things for himself, and more. His ideas would be transmitted to others; they might even become law. It was a huge responsibility. But Hayli thought he was ready!

His acceptance speech would be a test.

As he settled down to work, Will reviewed his previous speeches. "A leader needs nobody. A leader is self-sufficient, sublime." He had composed that in honor of Hayli's twentieth anniversary, five years ago. Not bad for an eleven-year-old, he thought. But now it seemed flawed. After all, Hayli had Mara beside him, always. Now Will pondered their relationship. Was it in any way physical? Certainly not! His face burned at the thought. Everyone knew that Hayli and Mara were the ideal, working together for the common cause, without regard for personal pleasure or gain. They never touched, but walked side by side, like two dignitaries, like the strong leaders they were.

Will tried to imagine such a relationship, that perfect unity, but all he could think of was the Symsex, overlaid with Leora's face, that half-arrogant smile, those smoky blue eyes. He took a drink from the canteen, a pink drink designed to cool the body and eliminate subversive thoughts.

Will paced back and forth in front of the Screen, seeking ideas. Usually an idea or a phrase sprang to mind, unleashing a flow of words. Now he was stuck.

Will reviewed the few paragraphs he had composed. Trash. Brittle and unimaginative. He crumpled the paper cup in his hand, tossed it down onto the gray, spongy floor, together with several empty boxes of SNABS.

"Cleanup!" he shouted. A small, squat robotic sanitizer whirled out from its alcove and consumed the refuse. Will glanced around his pod. Untidiness always made him uncomfortable. But everything was in order, antiseptically clean. Shelves were neatly sealed away, with nothing to detract from the constant flow of the Screen with its reminders and mantras. "Hail Hayli! Seek The Goodness. Power-building class at five. Sublimate selfishness. Pageant at seven . . ."

Will stood before the Screen, fighting his impulse. He argued with himself. He had no good reason for finding her. He most certainly didn't intend to speak to her! Of course, he might find her face repugnant. Then he could be done with these thoughts. He shouted the order, surprised and also irritated that her I.D. number had fixed itself so indelibly in his mind. "FMC-2290-09."

In a moment her image appeared, mouth serious, gray-blue eyes staring straight ahead. Cool relief swept over Will. He read the words that accompanied the Screen voice:

"Given name: Leora Jasper Jurraine. Turned out 2290, western colony of Fresmofield, Middle-Caligoria. Male donor, food production manager; Female donor, medical technician; Gestation Laboratory, District Seven. Personality/ Genetic Quotient: Highly intelligent, adaptive, analytical, curious. Status Two, eligible for promotion. Recipient Academy Scholarship. Interests: Ancient and contemporary history, government, information processing, cult activities, The Manifesto of J. Thomas Mattelin . . ."

He was astonished that anyone outside the Academy had studied The Writings. Mattelin had been Hayli's mentor and teacher. *The Manifesto* was Hayli's favorite book.

Will sat back, stroking his lip, deep in thought. Perhaps Mattelin was required reading for people seeking Status One. That made sense. Will had no idea what tests were required to gain investiture to Status One. He didn't know anyone who had risen so, though he was aware that thousands of people aspired to this exalted state.

Will studied Leora's image on the Screen. Her face was intelligent, with a wide brow and calm, clear eyes. He would have imagined that Status Twos had that *dissy*, confused look. Obviously, Leora was an exception.

"Continue," he ordered. "Background, writings, scholarship materials."

The information swept across the Screen. Leora's candidacy had included an essay entitled "On a More Perfect World."

Will beamed Leora's essay into his pulse pad for future reference. As he read, his breath quickened, and his hand trembled slightly. Amazing, he thought. This was exactly the kind of report Father had requested. Intelligent. Provocative. Original. He could imagine himself saying these very words at the anniversary pageant. New phrases leapt out at him, and he marveled that a female could come to such thoughts. But perhaps it was precisely this femininity that accounted for the graceful phrases. "Sweet persuasion . . . universal longing for . . . perfection is but a state of mind, depending upon the beholder. It is the task of a benevolent government to find ways to lighten the daily burden not merely with physical rewards but with words. Words of praise can be a powerful tonic, invigorating the body, stimulating the mind. People want most desperately to be noticed, to belong, to be given credit."

"Audio," Will prompted, and he closed his eyes, listening to Leora's words:

"Do not feed information to the masses. Provide only enough to encourage the people so they will perform their tasks gladly. Only superior persons of Status One can process whole truths. All others care most for their own basic needs for food, work, peer approval, and pleasure. The intricacies of government are beyond them. Social planning does not interest them. Given too much information, they will only become frustrated. Frustration leads to discontent, to strife, revolt, anarchy."

Will stood up, dazzled by the essay. His face felt flushed with excitement. *Yes!* he cried inwardly. This was the beginning he needed, with the further instruction on how these theories were to be implemented. Taking Leora's preamble, he could develop this into a memorable oration.

He faced the Screen, spoke her I.D. number, and said, "Visual contact." She appeared, sitting in her quarters, eating a nutri-cone.

"Hello," he said. "Is that all you ever eat?"

"Is that why you contacted me? To watch me eat?" she responded, licking the cone. "Why don't you try it? Lilac lorbean. Delicious. Also, it sharpens the memory."

"I've heard," Will said. He moved away from the Screen and sat down so that he could see her better. Still impertinent, he thought, appraising her posture, reclining in the air chair, feet up on a stool. He was perplexed. All other females he knew would lower their voices and their eyes when they spoke to him. And now this girl, this Status Two from a backward outpost, would challenge him, would drive him mad with her voice and those compelling eyes.

"I looked you up on the Screen," he offered.

She laughed, and the sound of it, like music, enveloped him. "So now you know everything about me," she said teasingly.

"Do you have Screens out west?"

"Of course. What did you think, that we are primitives?"

"I've never been out west, except in a Vi-Ex. I don't know what goes on there."

"Well, what goes on," she said saucily, "is pretty much the same as here. We work, we eat, we take some pleasure, and some of us are chosen to rise in status. Actually," she admitted, "we don't really have many source codes for the Screen. Being here is overwhelming."

Will smiled. He was beginning to feel relaxed. "How were you chosen for the Academy?" he asked.

"My aptitude test came out at 99.8 percent. My proctors sent in my dossier, and here I am!" She spread her arms as if she would fly on wings of her own. "Then, of course, there were lots of tests. Most of the candidates give up from fatigue. Some of the tests last for fourteen hours. A Status One," she said archly, "is supposed to be resilient."

"Well, we are bred for that," Will said. "I read your essay," he continued. "Very interesting."

She said, "Are you surprised that a Status Two from a colony out west can write something intelligible?"

"I have never known a Status Two," Will admitted, "or anyone from outside my district."

"What a shame!" Leora exclaimed. "Don't they ever let you out of Washolina?"

"Not often," he said. "There's no need to leave. Everything I want is here."

"You mean you have never been anywhere? Not to any other states or colonies?"

"Most are not very safe," he said.

"Ah, and you have to be preserved. You are slated to follow in your father's footsteps, after all. Aren't you curious about the real world?"

"Certainly, but everything in its due time. I'm scheduled," he said proudly, "to see a Compassionate Removal, and to visit some of the colonies. I might even go out west," he added.

"You should see the ocean while you're at it," she said. "It's wonderful. And the forest, too. There is a special smell to it that once you have inhaled it, you never forget."

"Aren't there wild animals in the forest?"

"No, not really. Nothing to fear. And the beach is—well, it's wonderful. I went swimming in the ocean. Maybe someday you'll try it."

"Ha! Not until the Time of Perfection!" Will exclaimed, "I suppose someday it will all be decontaminated."

"Or else," she said, "we will learn to live with a certain amount of contamination."

He felt stuck, at a loss for conversation. Usually he was so articulate.

"Would you meet me at the Café?" he suddenly proposed. "I want to talk to you about your essay."

"Now? You want to meet now?"

"Yes. At the same place where you sat the other night."

"But I am not allowed," she said teasingly. "I am only—"

"You will be with me," he said with finality. "Please come."

She nodded. "I'll leave right away."

He watched as her image receded. And it struck him, in that moment, how dense he had been. He needed to branch out, to find true followers, both male and female, intelligent, original. Such were Hayli's supporters, The Five. He must emulate Hayli! Now it was clear.

Will hurried out. Students, workers, many shadowed by PAARs, moved in every direction. A maze of motion paths dissected the Academy grounds, taking individuals to their destinations. As they moved, flowing messages alternated so swiftly that they hung at the very edge of awareness, like the distant music that repeated the theme:

> *"Do not condone a clone, a clone*
> *Rather be alone, alone*
> *Nobody can atone*
> *For a clone . . ."*

Sung in a melancholy key, the song recounted the horrors of cloning that, because of The Goodness, were now ended. Unauthorized cloning had provided the last thrust needed to bring about reform. The Collapse, with its plague, nuclear fallout, and almost total anarchy, had also allowed experimentation to go unchecked. Psychopaths created duplicates of themselves in home laboratories. Pseudo-scientists manufactured drone clones, subhumans with near-vacant brain cavities and immense strength designed for labor or for aggression. One of Hayli's campaign promises had been to rid the Dominion of clones. He was elected by a resounding majority.

As Will moved on he thought of Mara. He wanted to see her. Mara would understand his mixed feelings about leaving, about Leora, about his emerging leadership. Had Mara been here he would have taken the path to her rooms. But she was with Hayli, preparing for the anniversary pageant.

Screens along the motion path projected images of the Compassionate Director congratulating men and women as they visited their namesake embryos in the Gestation Labs, receiving food and pleasure stamps, rewards for service.

Will stepped off and walked toward the pavilions, all filled with people, mostly students. A few recognized him and waved. He nodded in reply. He walked on, scratching his arm, just above the elbow. That particular spot nearly always itched, especially when he became anxious. Maybe she wasn't coming. It was a hot night. Perhaps the Environmental Dome was malfunctioning. His tunic stuck to his chest. Will pulled off his cape and hung it over his arm. Loud music from the Dance Dome pounded in his head. The singers were always too frenetic, gyrating, drenched with sweat.

Then Will saw her, dressed in a blue turbo-suit of the new style. It was a lively, energetic look, wide pants and sleeves, with climate sensors woven into the elastic cuffs. Leora stood leaning against one of the bars, eating something from a small bag. She smiled when he approached.

"Hello! What on earth is that?" he asked. Happy music rang out from the Dance Dome. Will tapped his feet to the lively sound.

"Peanuts," she said. "My father grows them. It is only a hobby," she added quickly. "Want some?"

A slight shudder went through him. "No, thank you." It was hard to imagine how different her life must be. Maybe she was involved with her parents on a daily basis, even living with them. And they actually ate food that they grew.

Leora peered at him with a curious smile. "Have you never eaten things that grow?"

"No," he said abruptly.

"Not even eggs from a chicken?"

"Certainly not," he said. He still felt uncomfortably warm.

"I wouldn't eat these," Leora assured him, "except that my father has perfected them. He is contracted, you see, by the regime. Obviously, food from the silos is healthier."

"Certainly," Will said. "Nutritionally perfect."

Leora tossed the remaining shells into a receptacle, and they were immediately pulverized. The grinding sound alerted Will's PAAR. It stood up, circled, and then retreated again to sit cross-legged on the ground. Leora stared. "Doesn't that thing get in your way sometimes?" she asked.

"No. I'm used to it. It's like a shadow, that's all."

"What's that sound it makes?" Leora moved closer to the PAAR, her head cocked in curiosity.

"That's its cooling system. Ventilation. See that trapdoor in back?"

Leora nodded. "Yes. What's that for?"

"That opens up into the controls, in case it ever needs adjustment. Actually, I've never had to do any maintenance. It's designed to be self-repairing and self-lubricating."

"And it's your bodyguard?"

Will nodded. He felt embarrassed to have to explain, but it also amused him. "The PAAR is only a defensive fighter, not like an enforcer. It will never attack, unless I'm threatened."

"How would it know?"

"It's tuned to my implant like a radio beam. If anyone gets too near my implant, the PAAR will strike."

"So I guess nobody ever touches you," Leora said.

"Not without my permission," he retorted. The conversation was becoming uncomfortable. Will was glad when Leora changed the topic.

"What do you do all the time?" she asked. "You look so serious."

"I study. Seriously," he said. "I'll be attending the anniversary pageant in a few weeks. I have to prepare a talk. Actually, I've been stuck, sort of, because—well, I'll be speaking in front of all these dignitaries."

He paused, waiting for her to speak, but she stood silent, watching him intently. He felt self-conscious, uncertain, but he continued. "I wanted to use some of your ideas—with your permission."

"Does the son of the Compassionate Director need anyone's permission?" she asked in her teasing way.

He flipped his cape over his shoulders. The silver fabric molded itself to his shape. "Shouldn't the son of the Compassionate Director be ethical?" he countered.

She nodded, looking up. "Of course you can quote me. I'd be honored." She paused, then asked, "Is anyone going with you?"

"My brother. Berk."

"Oh, yes. You are the famous twins. I looked you up," she said shyly, "even before I came to Washolina."

"Then you knew who I was the other night, when you—"

She ducked her head, her lips compressed. "I'm sorry I was rude."

"I forgive you," he said grandly. It rather pleased him that she had looked him up, and perhaps even hoped to meet him.

"I have never known another twin," she said. "Even siblings are rare. I have a sister," she said hesitantly, as if she were admitting to some flaw.

"Really!" He wondered whether in the western colonies such things were the norm. "Is she your age?" he asked.

"Younger. I teach her and play with her. She is very sweet and laughs a lot. What is it like being a twin? Are you exactly alike? Are you inseparable? Do you love each other deeply?"

Will was aghast at the question. It was intrusive, outrageous. Stiffly he replied, "I hardly see him. Berk goes to Academy in a different district. Our proctors thought we should be separated so that we wouldn't compete."

"But of course, you still do," she said, gazing at him, as if she could see through him. "I mean, can you both follow in your father's footsteps?"

Her words struck him like a blow to the chest. How dare she smite him with his very own fears? Never before had anyone questioned him, forced him to face unpleasant truths.

Quickly he bade Leora good night. After this, he doubted that he would see her again.

CHAPTER 5

BACK IN HIS POD, Will still felt unsettled. He wished he had never met Leora. She was disturbing, with those blue eyes drilling into his. She raised questions that he had been pushing aside for years. They emerged only in his dreams, phantoms that disappeared whenever he got close. Always, he was looking for Father.

Will paced around his pod, desolate. He took no comfort in being alone, as he usually did. He wanted—what was it he wanted? Uncertain, he stood before his canteen, surveying the possible foods and drinks. But he wasn't hungry or thirsty.

He wished Mara were still in Washolina, but he knew she had already left for Mattelin Island with Hayli. When he needed to talk, it was always Mara whom he went to, and she was always ready to receive him with her smile and her wisdom. As a child, when he hurt himself, it was Mara who took him to the medic. When he was defeated by Berk in one of the warrior games that often left him humiliated and despairing, it was Mara who soothed him. "You have the power to persuade," she would say. "The greatest leaders fight not with weapons, but with words."

Will stood before the Screen and gave the command. "Mara."

Immediately her image appeared. She was reclining on a lounger, wide awake. Her head was wrapped in a purple turban, matching her robe. Around her neck on a thick chain was a gold medal, encircled with diamonds, embossed with the words "For Service To Humanity." Only five such medals had ever been struck.

"How lovely to see you, Will!" Mara moved toward him, and her Screen image expanded. "Are you well? Hayli says we will soon meet in person."

"Yes. I'm so glad. Mara, I have to talk to you."

"So serious!" she chided, spreading her hands, as if to enfold him.

"Mara, how come Berk and I are twins? Why were both of us allowed to survive? Father needs only one successor."

She replied patiently, "Your father won't need a successor for a long, long time, Will. What he needs are people loyal to him, assistants to carry out his plans."

"For that he didn't need sons," Will argued.

"Look, you and Berk will work together. The sum of your efforts will be all the greater, because you have been raised to do the same service. Think what that will mean to The Goodness! I'm going to be so proud of you, Will."

Proud. That word, always and forever. It was one of the primary reasons that people donated reproductive cells, to take pride in their offspring. Also, they were rewarded with extra food and pleasure stamps.

"Why so many questions, Will?" She looked worried. "It isn't like you to dwell on the past. Have you checked your health monitor?"

"I'm fine," he replied with a heavy sigh. "I met someone. A *dissy* girl from District Seven. She asked me all sorts of questions. It was . . . unsettling."

"How in the world did you meet someone like that? What is her status?"

"Status Two. She's here on scholarship. I don't suppose she'll last long, but—"

"Those people are not like us, Will," Mara said evenly.

"I know that. I know that, but . . . When I am with her," he groped for words, "I remember things. Like when I was small. Remember how you used to hold me?"

Mara nodded. "Of course. You know I was always interested in gestation. I held many babies, Will, as they were turned out."

"For years," he said, "when I was frightened or upset, when the animals came . . ."

"What animals?" Mara asked with a puzzled look.

"Maybe I was only dreaming, but I remember I was terrified, and then you came to me. You sang that special song."

"I don't remember that," Mara said. "Are you sure you haven't been overexerting yourself, Will? You seem fatigued and confused."

He held up his hand against her protests. "Did you also go to Berk when he was frightened? Did you hold him, too?"

Mara tossed back her head, laughing. "Berk never liked to be held," she said. "From the time he was first turned out. If someone tried to hold him, he would kick and scream. You see, people are different. Even twins. You always wanted to be held. I remember, you grasped my finger and put it into your mouth."

Will smiled to himself; it was true. Berk was tough and rugged from the start. By the time they were two, Berk had outgrown the Cuddle Corner that was built into every nursery, a brightly colored cocoon that offered soft cushions and fuzzy cones for little children to embrace. Will used the Corner until he was four, the usual age for weaning.

"This Status Two I met," Will went on, "talks about her parents, mother and father . . ."

"Well, some people still use those terms," Mara said. "It doesn't mean anything. If she stays at the Academy she will outgrow it." Mara continued, speaking in that lecture tone she used for her nightly education sessions, "Motherhood was not really the ideal the old diaries make it out to be."

"Yes, I've seen some of the old tapes," Will said. Motherhood meant pain from childbirth, constant worry. He had, in fact, dwelt on that subject so much that his proctor questioned his choices, and he was warned against being obsessed with the past. Still, Will had wondered and wondered about parenting and donors. Now he asked Mara outright, "Who was my female donor? Was it you?"

Mara retreated, arms folded across her chest. "No, I am not your donor," she said with great scorn. "If you weren't told, it means you are not meant to know. It is most improper of you to ask such questions. Now, get some rest. You're sounding quite *dissy*."

"Yes. Of course. Good night, Mara."

Will hoped Mara wouldn't tell Hayli about their conversation, about his foolish questions and doubts. Hayli would think he was weak. And as he well knew, *the weak get eaten.*

As the days went by, Will battled against the weakness that kept him looking around when he went out, listening for her laughter, hoping for a glimpse of long brown hair flecked with gold. Then, without warning, he began seeing her everywhere. At the evening Pop Pageant, she might be sitting just behind him. He caught glimpses of her at the pavilions, just ahead on the motion path. Often, Will wanted to call out, but he was always with his friends, engaged in conversation, and, in truth, he did not know what to say to Leora.

Walking out one evening from an Africa Vi-Ex, and feeling a little queasy from the experience, he saw her again. It was late, and he was alone. On impulse, Will called out, "Leora! How did you like the Vi-Ex?"

She turned to him, breathlessly exclaiming, "I never imagined anything so exciting! The animals, the tribesmen, and the savannas—it is so beautiful!"

They followed the crowd out of the Vi-Ex hall.

"*Was*, you mean," Will said. "It is all devastated now. The people have been busy killing each other and dying of disease."

"You sound very cynical," she said.

"No, realistic," he said.

"The Vi-Ex is superrealistic," she said.

"Don't you have them in your district?"

People dispersed. The night was pleasantly cool and fragrant. The constant hum of atmospheric machinery sounded comforting, almost like music.

Leora shrugged. "We have a few. Most are about the rise of The Goodness, showing current projects. I did Washolina several times before I actually arrived. It's very different in reality," she said. "So modern and clean and very secure." She looked around at all the conveniences, the pulverizers, motion paths, the silent enforcers. "I can understand why you never want to leave Washolina."

"Now that you're here," he said, "you can do any Vi-Ex you like. We have thousands of them, every dominion, every experience, both past and present, and even projections of the future."

"I love the Vi-Ex," she said. They walked toward the glittering pavilions, Leora gazing up to the Atmospheric Dome with its artificial constellations. "Have you seen actual stars?" she asked.

"Of course," Will replied, amused. "We have a wonderful planetarium. I have even seen African animals in the actual zoo, not that I choose to go there."

"Do you often do the African Vi-Ex?" she asked.

"My first time," Will admitted. "I'm not fond of such things."

"Then why did you go? Oh, I know. It must be part of your lesson plan. The son of the Compassionate Director has to be exposed to everything." She gave him a mischievous grin. "Even to an ignorant Status Two."

"No," he said lightly. "That is my own choice. Besides, you are not ignorant, only inexperienced." Tonight, her questions and comments were refreshing.

They walked on toward the Café. "Are you thirsty?" he asked.

"Very," she replied. "After all that virtual hunting in virtual heat."

"Would you like to drink something?"

"I thought you'd never ask!" she said playfully, and they sat down together talking and laughing, and Will forgot that he had been angry with her.

"Are you working on your speech?" she asked.

"Constantly," he said.

"Are you nervous?"

He hesitated. "Yes." She had a way of getting into his mind that was disturbing and also engaging. Her questions freed him to express feelings he usually would not claim.

She only smiled. "I will watch you on the Screen," she said.

"It would be better if you could be there in person," he said. It was unlikely, as they both knew. Attendees were carefully selected.

She asked, "What will you wear?"

He was startled. "It doesn't matter," he said.

But the next day as he stood in front of the vast Outfitter, Will labored over half a dozen choices. None seemed right, though the small crowd that had gathered around him murmured approvingly every time he tried on a new garment. "Very regal, quite the thing," they enthused. Whatever he selected, dozens of people would soon copy him, and purchase the same thing.

He glanced around. There was Leora, watching. He called to her. "Leora! Come and help me, please."

She stepped forward through the onlookers. Reluctantly they parted a path for her. She glanced at the pile of discarded garments. "How many have you tried?" she asked.

"About a dozen," Will said with gesture of helplessness. "Can't seem to find just the right thing."

"Here comes another!" she exclaimed as a package slid from the Outfitter tray.

Will opened it. The mauve fabric glittered. He pulled the jacket on over his tunic. "What do you think?" he asked.

"Gorgeous!" exclaimed several onlookers. "Very regal."

Will shook his head. "I don't know." He turned to Leora.

She pressed her lips together, as if she were struggling to hold back, then she blurted out, "That color is terrible on you. It makes your skin look almost blue."

He broke out in a laugh. "You are absolutely right!" he said gleefully. "What do you think would be better?"

"White," she said instantly. "Pure white, with some gold strands at the cuffs. To match the gold in your implant."

Will surveyed his so-called friends and followers. Did any of them really care about him? Or was he only a status symbol? He slipped on the new suit and turned to thank Leora, but she had vanished into the crowd. Moments later he saw her moving away on the upper motion path. She waved to him, but he kept his hands down at his sides. It seemed undignified for the son of the C.D. to be so demonstrative.

Back in his pod, Will prepared several drafts and rehearsed them, complete with gestures. Will sat back, watching his own oration. It was good—quite the best thing he had ever done. He was thrilled to hear the ardor and authority in his voice, and to see the strength of his movements. How the people would cheer! It would most likely be inserted into the Screen Banks for posterity. Yes, he was good!

He sent the final draft to Leora. He waited for her response, pacing back and forth. At last it came. "Not bad!"

He laughed to himself. It was perfect, but of course, Leora would never say that. He wished she could be there to hear him give that speech. He would seek her out from the audience, see that look of amazement on her face. Of course, she could watch the anniversary pageant on the Screen, along with everyone else in the Dominion. But it would be so much better to have her there, actually there.

If he invited her . . . no, it was not appropriate. If he invited her . . . how could she pass Security? If he invited her . . . she would embarrass him with her Status Two questions, her flaunting smile, her ignorance.

But it would be interesting. It would be *fun*.

He had never done anything purely for fun, not that he could remember. Even the Symsex was used in answer to psychological and physical needs, prescribed by the medics for occasional tension release. But fun? Fun was something spontaneous, frivolous, and yes, selfish, indulged in by those of low status.

And yet . . .

Will strode up to the screen. "Mara!" he demanded.

She appeared, full bodied, bustling about at some huge display surrounded by tall columns and Screens. "Will! We are all frantically preparing for the anniversary pageant here. When are you coming?"

"In three days," he replied. "I have a favor to ask you, Mara. This girl I told you about from District Seven . . ."

"The Status Two?"

"She is well on the way to becoming Status One, I think. She is very bright. I want her to attend the anniversary pageant. Could you clear it with Hayli?" His heart was pounding, as if he had been playing a warrior game.

"I don't know, Will." Mara frowned. "You know that the guest list must be approved by Security. How would she behave at such a function?"

"She manages quite well here at the Academy," Will said. "You could look her up. Leora. FMC-2290-09."

Instantly Mara checked her Screen. "Ah. Pursuing investiture, I gather. I suppose, in a way, she could be a good supporter for you."

"Exactly."

"Someone needy," Mara mused, "but intelligent. Impressionable. She will owe you her investiture."

"What do you mean?"

"Don't you know that a candidate needs referral from a Status One involved in the regime? You hold the key to her rise."

A terrible thought made Will's breath stop. He felt nauseous and clung to his air chair. It must be for this that Leora had sought him out—to win his favor, to guarantee her rise.

"You look suddenly ill," Mara said. "What is it? Are you afraid the girl is using you?" She began to laugh. "Oh, Will, grow up. Of course people will use you. You are the son of the Compassionate Director, the most powerful man on the planet! They will use you, but you will use them more. You have every advantage. Now, don't worry. I'll see to it that your friend is invited. It will be interesting to meet her."

The approval came within minutes, and Will contacted Leora on the Screen. She met him at the entrance to the park, where artificial trees and fantastic statuary were formed into benches where people could sit and talk.

Will watched her face as he told her of the invitation. "My father has approved it," he said, purposely using the familiar term. "I might even introduce you to him."

For the first time, Leora was speechless. Her eyes brimmed with tears.

At last she said softly, "I'll be the first in my entire colony to have such an honor. You have no idea what this means to me." She reached out to take his hand and quickly retreated as his PAAR approached.

"Oh, I'm sorry," she cried. It was an unspoken rule, like a wall between them, that the son of the Compassionate Director must never be touched without his consent.

She took a deep breath. "I'll be able to see you give your speech," she said. "Listen, Will, I've been thinking about it. Don't give me credit for my few phrases. This is your important speech. Don't dilute it by mentioning anyone else."

They walked to the motion path. She stopped and turned, standing so near that he could easily have touched her cheek. She stepped onto the path, and in a few moments Leora was out of sight, and Will stumbled back to his quarters, wrapped in confusion. He could not remember when anyone had given him anything without asking for something in return.

Mara's words haunted him. *"They will use you."*

Leora was different, wasn't she? Or was he incredibly naïve?

CHAPTER 6

"THANK YOU, THANK YOU, THANK YOU!"

The Compassionate Director stood at the dais, acknowledging the applause that erupted from the audience. From his place on the stage, Will could see his father's image on the Screens surrounding the amphitheater. Hayli was magnificent, a glowing face and strong, massive shoulders—magnificent. Behind him hung a huge banner for the Dominion of the Americas, of which Hayli was the Director. The other flags were for the Dominions·of Africa, Europe, Middle East, Asia, India, and Island Nations.

"Directors, Ministers, and Deputies," Hayli's voice rang out over the assembled dignitaries, and carefully selected workers and students, "Twenty-five years ago, we were overwhelmed by the disasters of famine, war, pestilence, and the consequences of nuclear waste. We were barely beginning to extricate ourselves from a Collapse more devastating than any the world has ever known. Today, thanks to the efforts of all assembled here, we have made enormous strides. We have brought The Goodness not only to our own Dominion, but it has become a model for the entire world."

The sun struck the bronze panel behind the Compassionate Director. His face shone with a golden glow. Strength emanated from his features; his thick neck suggested permanence; his eyes were ablaze with commitment and passion.

The Director continued, his voice rising over the multitudes, reproduced in a million factories, schools, and offices. Surely the whole world was watching. "In the Dominion of the Americas, we have solved many problems. We have quarantined the Great American Desert. We have, in a massive and complex system of relocation, created districts of safety for our inhabitants. We have virtually eliminated birth defects."

Will glanced at the row of interns who sat with him on the stage. Everyone knew the history, but it needed to be retold. Many of these young people's grandparents had been relocated when the chemical levels reached the danger zone. It was a stunning migration. Within two weeks, masses of immigrants were gathered at collection points and taken on government trains, with only the few goods they could carry, to the coastal areas or to the mountains, where they would begin new lives. He had seen it all on the history tapes, along with the mass graves of people who died of various cancers and other viruses, so swiftly that often the corpses were simply burned.

Will forced himself to sit still, to ignore the annoying itch on his arm and his backside. The white tunic was new and irritating, but he dared not show any sign of discomfort, sitting at the head of the row of eleven interns. Beside him sat Berk, with eleven more interns seated behind him. Will glanced at Berk. His brother's head seemed to nod. Was he falling asleep? But suddenly Berk turned, meeting Will's gaze with a smirk.

Hayli continued, "Although we have made great progress, we still face worldwide shortages of food and water. Pollution threatens every aspect of our environment. Pollution of the gene pool threatens our future as human beings on this planet and beyond. In our own dominion and abroad, dissidents and malcontents threaten to destroy The Goodness. We *will* not let them win."

Great applause, especially from the foreign dominion dignitaries who wore various headdresses, flowing scarves, and curtained hats as a defense against contaminated air.

"These malcontents spread superstition and regressive ideas. They would move us backward to that terrible time we have all gladly left behind. *They must not be allowed to continue.*" Hayli's hands cut through the air, a strong chopping motion that Will often copied when he spoke. "We are in danger of losing everything we have gained in the past twenty-five years."

Huge Screens surrounding the stage depicted the latest acts of the rebels. They invaded towns, burned silos, terrorized the peaceful occupants with hatchets and knives. When the Bumblecops came, some rebels were caught and set aflame, but others managed to escape to the Great Desert, where they lived underground to avoid detection.

The film sobered the audience. A large world map came into focus on the Screens. Hayli continued his review. "The European Dominion is in chaos. Each country coins its own money, jealous of its resources, unable to agree on anything except mutual suspicion. Vandals plague the Middle Eastern Dominion. The remnant population of Africa is still heavily diseased and lacking industry. In our own Dominion of the Americas we still suffer from radiation sickness, and airborne viruses that seem to defy all intervention. We can predict that famine and disease will continue for decades, *unless firm measures are taken now.* We are in the first stages of a reorganization designed to resolve these problems. In the next few weeks I will outline my plans for the immediate future, with new policies and further welfare programs to enrich and expand The Goodness."

A huge cheer erupted over the multitude. Flags sprang up everywhere, the yellow, red, and green flag with the seven interlocking triangles representing the seven districts of the Dominion of the Americas.

This was the moment. One of Hayli's guards, Sileus, gave Will the cue, and he stepped up to the dais. In his excitement, he had barely heard the introduction, and now phrases echoed back in his mind . . . *son of the Compassionate Director, bred for leadership . . . genetically superior . . .*

Will had memorized his speech and the accompanying gestures, the lift of his head, the full release of his voice when it came to the strongest portion. His remarks were brief. Into them he wove Leora's words: "Everyone deserves to live in a perfect world. Words of praise can be a powerful tonic . . . sweet persuasion is better than punishment . . . Happiness lies in sacrifice. The rewards of serving The Goodness are life and health and happiness."

For his finale, Will placed his hands at an angle on his brow. "Hail to The Goodness," he began, and instantly the crowd joined in the pledge, all hands lifted, ". . . and to the Supreme Compassionate Director, most true, most powerful, most benevolent. To him we vow our allegiance and our love. To him we give the labor of our hands and the complete obedience of our will. We exist to please him. We long to serve him. Whatever he requires, we will do with gladness and joy in service."

A burst of applause followed Will to his seat.

Berk spoke briefly about Security, the importance of vigilance within their own Dominion. Returning to his seat, Berk stumbled. A faint gasp came over the audience. Will felt a pang of embarrassment for his brother. Berk sat down, unconcerned. Since childhood, Berk never admitted a mistake. Nothing seemed to faze him.

Now seven bands stationed throughout the amphitheater struck up the anthem, "Goodness Forever!" Hayli shook hands with each of the new interns. Then he drew Berk and Will close and exclaimed, "With young people like these in service, we shall enjoy one thousand years of The Goodness!"

The spokesman for the Great Council strode up to the dais with his official proclamation. "We, the Directors of the Seven Districts of the Dominion of the Americas," he said, "have cast our ballots. I hereby report to this assembly that the vote is unanimous. Czeminhayli, our Compassionate Director, shall be elected for another term of office. Moreover," continued the official, "the Great Council has voted to increase the term of office from ten to forty years."

Cheers followed the announcement. From outside the dome, Will heard isolated shouts of protests. He heard the roar of Bumblecops and saw the flashing flames. In moments the protestors were gone. Will glanced at Berk, who sat with his arms crossed over his chest, smiling slightly.

"These are desperate times," cried the official. "Our Dominion needs consistency. Commitment. Courage. Only one man can provide us with wise leadership. And who is that man?"

The crowd responded. "Hayli! Hayli! Hail, Hayli!"

Will leapt to his feet. The other interns followed. They clapped and cheered. Will felt as if he were being borne away on a tide of joy.

Again Hayli took the podium. "With gratitude and deep humility, I accept this position."

"Long live Hayli!" Will shouted. He was gratified when the shout was taken up first by the interns, then by the multitude.

Forty years! Hayli had already spent more than half his life in public service. How long might he yet live? Some of the Directors were well into their hundreds, rejuvenated by artificial organs and implants. But the shortage of organs, even artificial ones, was severe.

Now Hayli's life story was projected on multiple screens placed strategically through the huge amphitheater. The narrator began:

"He was an orphan, abandoned in a box on a street corner. The note pinned to his ragged blanket said Hayli. The vagrant who found him added a portion of his own name and the name of the town, to create Czeminhayli. If nobody knew his exact origins, then he was destined to be, truly, a child of the world.

"From the beginning, one thing was certain: Hayli was extraordinarily gifted, physically powerful, intellectually superior. He was, above all, a survivor.

"By the age of seven Hayli knew mathematics and the basics of computer science and physics. Three years later he became the ward of one of the most brilliant and versatile scholars of our time, J. Thomas Mattelin. Mattelin found the boy one evening, browsing through the local archives. He took him in. Hayli became his assistant. He studied Mattelin's notes. He organized, synthesized, listened, and learned."

"And so I decided," came Hayli's own voice now, "that the best way to serve was to educate myself in history and science, especially biology, physics, and genetics. Because I knew, even as a child, that the world was a cauldron of opposing and evil forces—human greed and the propensity toward violence, combined with rampant disease and pollution. In the vast Heartland of our country, water was not fit to drink, and the soil could not nourish plants. Farms were abandoned. Domestic animals went wild. They began to attack in towns. The Eastern District had most of its infrastructure destroyed by terrorist attacks. The western coastline had receded alarmingly, reducing thousands of acres of fertile soil. Fish from polluted water carried their own poisons. Trees were stunted. And always there was the menace of unchecked plague.

"Something had to be done. I gathered a team of scientists and advisors, young men and women, all dedicated to what we came to call The Goodness. We gave ourselves to the cause without hesitation or regret.

"We five, together with our spiritual leader J. Thomas Mattelin, formulated a plan: first the country needed to be reorganized, people relocated into safe areas, and random reproduction halted. Because each year more and more children were being born with physical and mental deficiencies. I personally have seen monsters so appalling that their own mothers drowned them in buckets of water minutes after birth. Their own fathers buried them alive. This must never be allowed to happen again. By following our guidelines, people will never bring monsters into the world."

Hayli made his signature gesture, arms out wide, fingers together and thumbs up. The gesture embraced everyone. "We must be brave. We will persevere. Nothing can be accomplished except with hard work and sacrifice. One of the original Five is still with us today. Mara, please stand and be recognized."

Beautiful, elegant Mara rose from her seat, beaming and bowing. She was met with resounding applause.

The film replayed, the images were reflected and repeated from half a dozen screens three stories high. Hayli, the Compassionate Director, stood in the shadow of the dais, not onstage, but down on the same level as everyone else, to greet the people.

The receiving line stretched for nearly a mile. Will and Berk stood beside Hayli, murmuring greetings, shaking hands. And then, suddenly, there was Leora.

"Hello, Will," she whispered, all traces of impertinence and levity now gone. "You were wonderful. Thank you for giving me credit, for using my name."

"I told you I would," he replied, and in the next moment he felt Hayli's hand on his shoulder.

"Who is this?"

"Leora . . ." she whispered. "A student from District Seven. On probation, Sir, for Status One."

"An honor student, Sir," Will put in, "on scholarship at my Academy." He saw that she was trembling.

"Yes! You quoted her in your talk. Very good. We need young people like this in our organization." The Director smiled, and his face became radiant. "I also had such a friend when I was your age. Mara and I have worked together all these years, and it has profited both of us and, I might say, the entire Dominion."

Hayli continued to gaze at her as he clasped Will's arm, and said, "Will, I am appointing my man Sileus to assist you. This is your travel and training itinerary. You will report on your experiences and make recommendations. First, you are to witness a Compassionate Removal in District Seven, which happens to be where your friend comes from."

Hayli bent toward Leora. "Would you like to go along? I understand that you are on probation for Status One. It might be interesting for both of you to share the experience."

Will felt dazed, astounded. Leora bent her knee in a gesture of humility, eyes lowered, as she exclaimed, "Yes, Sir. Oh, yes, thank you, Sir!"

From across the mass of people, he saw Mara smiling at him and nodding, with a swift gesture of victory. She mouthed the word "Congratulations!"

Will's mind was a blur as he struggled to compose himself and appear nonchalant before the cameras. Leora was to go with him! And Mara was congratulating him. He was following the very path of the Compassionate Director. It must mean that he was the front-runner!

He saw that Berk was surrounded by a throng of admirers, among them half a dozen enforcers, warrior types. His brother would not take second place without a fight. He must remain vigilant.

CHAPTER 7

I T WAS GLORIOUS. Will had never felt so alive. The dignitaries bent toward him, took his arm, sidled up to him with an air of benevolent familiarity, peering into his face as if to seek traces of his father's attributes.

"Young Will! Gratifying. Your progress! Internship now, Fifth Pillar!" they exclaimed, as if they had been following his progress for years, and perhaps they had. Words rolled off their tongues like beads, all strung together. "Pleasure, not surprised, talent, genetic predisposition, like father like son, chip off the old . . . great future, call on me, need anything, if you ever . . . my boy."

Sileus remained beside him all the while. His entire appearance was disturbing, his nervous gestures and that enormous head, far too large for his body. Sileus had small, black eyes, like onyx buttons. And Will wondered, What was his real function? Was he an assistant, a security guard, or a spy?

Will looked over at Berk. He had been assigned his own helper, a giantess of a woman called Cullah, with wild hair and lips tattooed a bright blue. She looked powerful enough to pick Berk up and carry him away.

Hayli took Berk and Will by the arms as they made their way out of the amphitheater. He told them, "Go where your curiosity leads you. I expect you to send twice-weekly reports to your director at the Ministry. Do not fail!"

"Yes, Sir!" both said together.

"I will personally review those reports," the Compassionate Director continued, loud enough for the retinue and the microphones to pick up. "Assess the people. Are they efficient? Are they loyal? Report any breach of Security, any breach of loyalty. Also, report any extraordinary service. The Goodness rewards the faithful."

Then Hayli lowered his voice, drew Berk and Will close. "Listen to me. Don't let anyone become too familiar with you. A leader must inspire both awe and fear. Keep a certain distance. Don't let yourself be betrayed!"

Will braced himself against the tides of emotion that he always felt when he was with Hayli. Did Hayli think he was weak?

They reached the pavilions designed for every pleasure, food and drink, exotic Vi-Exes, Symsex experiences, music and dancing. Hayli stopped for moment to listen to a young singer. He touched her forehead. "Angel voice," he murmured and signaled to Rondo, his chief guard. "Get her name." The girl might have been eleven or twelve, with fair hair and a pale complexion. She was very thin, and for an instant Will saw in her eyes a look of weariness and pain.

Will murmured, "Are you ill?"

She did not reply, but shrank back, and Will was borne away by Hayli, who muttered, "Don't waste your time on such creatures. You are too soft and sentimental!"

The rebuke stung, and Will dared not look back.

Amid the din of celebration, Will was surrounded by dozens of people congratulating him, patting his shoulder, smiling. It was both exciting and, after a while, stifling. He saw Berk, arms folded over his chest, basking in the attention. At last Will spotted Mara and went to her. She was seated on a low couch in a sheltered alcove, her satin robes about her, looking like a queen of ancient time. She drew Will toward her. "Sit down, Will. How wonderfully well you spoke! I am so proud of you."

He sat down, glad for the respite. "When are you leaving?" she asked.

"Tomorrow we go to Caligoria to witness a Compassionate Removal," Will replied. "On the way back we'll stop at some of the colonies before visiting the other dominions. Hayli has planned some exciting experiences for us," he said. "Actual experiences."

Mara nodded. "A leader needs to experience realities," she agreed. "But be careful. When you are in the colonies, don't take any chances."

"Don't worry, Mara. I'll have my PAAR," Will said.

She waved this aside. "Things are very different in the colonies. You need to be on guard. You'll find that not everyone is loyal to The Goodness. This girl, Leora, what do you really know about her?"

"Only the facts from the Screen," Will said, "and a few conversations. She seems committed. She has good ideas. Hayli thinks she will be a good supporter for me."

Mara nodded, though her eyes showed skepticism. "Yes. She is young and bright, and it does help to have the female viewpoint. But don't tell her everything. Never reveal yourself completely to anyone."

"In other words," Will said soberly, "trust nobody." The sounds of celebration contrasted sharply with his foreboding. "But you and Hayli trust each other," he said. "Surely a leader has to confide in someone."

"Hayli and I are different," Mara said, lifting her head and her shoulders. "You cannot compare yourself and this girl to us."

"I didn't mean . . ." Will stammered. "It's just that I sometimes need . . ." He did not know how to express his need, even to himself.

"You need to keep control of yourself," Mara said sharply. "When you're in doubt, focus on The Goodness. You are not like other people, Will. You are superior, bred for leadership, the son of the Compassionate Director. Be strong, Will. The Goodness needs you to be strong."

"Yes, Mara, I will be strong!" Will breathed, infused with confidence.

Mara drew closer, her eyes intent on his. "We are on the verge of a new era," she said. "There will be enormous changes. You and Berk are standing on the edge of a new universe. Man was not meant to die. It is more than a slogan, Will. Immortality, the hope that has eluded mankind from the beginning, is about to become a reality."

"How?" Will asked. He was trembling. "What do we have to do to make it happen?"

"We have to live every aspect of The Goodness. We are entering the Time of Perfection," Mara said in her low, throaty voice. "First we have to improve the other dominions, bring them into The Goodness. Perhaps you already know that Africa is going to be quarantined. Hayli will announce it in the next few days."

"Quarantined!" Will echoed, his eyes wide. Quarantine meant withholding food and supplies. Already weak from disease, the people would die out quickly. "I thought that we were sending aid, and persuading the people to change their habits."

"We tried persuasion and relocation," Mara said. "Sometimes, stronger means must be used. It sounds cruel," Mara said, "but ultimately it is for the best. You understand that, don't you, Will? The Goodness must provide the greatest good for the greatest number. We must see things in larger perspective."

"Of course," Will breathed, though in truth he did not understand. Hundreds of thousands of Africans would die without aid from the other dominions. "What will happen to the land?" he wondered aloud. "Will Hayli claim it for our Dominion?"

"Can you imagine it?" Mara exclaimed. "Think of all the people who can settle there. We will rehabilitate the land," said Mara. "The Africans have squandered their resources. For centuries they have had intertribal wars. They refused to industrialize."

"So it is their own fault," Will said slowly.

"We can start fresh," Mara said eagerly, "developing all those resources—oil, gems, grains . . ."

"And we will distribute them equally to everyone," Will added, feeling relieved.

"It is for the good of the many," Mara said warmly.

"Survival of the fittest," quoted Will.

"Survival of the fittest," echoed Mara. She fingered the large medal at her breast, the emblem of The Five. "We have all had to make sacrifices, Will," Mara said gently. "We Five were continually forced to make difficult choices. But we made them, and now"—she spread out her arms— "you see how far we have come."

"What happened to the others of The Five?" Will asked. "There isn't much about the others in the history tapes. I only know their names— Taroo, Farleen, and . . ."

"Taroo died in a horrible accident," Mara said. "Farleen committed suicide. She was a genius, but"—Mara lifted her hands—"psychologically disturbed. Poor Felix has acute dementia. Don't look so stricken! They lived full lives. They are well remembered. Now, let's not talk about that anymore, Will. Come! It's a party. We need to celebrate. There's a time for everything, you know, and now we celebrate your induction and Hayli's election and—"

"The Goodness," Will exclaimed, happy beyond anything he had known. "Hail! Hail to you, Mara!" he suddenly cried out.

"And to you, Will."

Everyone was satiated with pleasure by morning, when the tube-transports came to take the dignitaries back to their dominions, and the students to their destinations. Will and Berk were scheduled to go together to District Seven for the Compassionate Removal. With them rode Sileus, Cullah, and Leora. In the back, two PAARs reclined, bodies folded up to conserve space. The hum of the transport blocked out all but the most direct conversation. Will was glad to be free from Selius's fierce, examining gaze.

When she heard the destination, Caligoria, Leora exclaimed, "That's just north of my home colony, you know."

Will tried to fathom her excitement—what was so good about home? Surely it was not as safe or as interesting as the Academy. Berk was staring at her, too. He leaned forward and asked abruptly, "What did you say your name is?"

"Leora!" Will answered, surprised. It was not like Berk to forget a name.

"Is she in the Information Ministry?" Berk asked.

"No, I'm only a student," Leora replied.

"Of course, of course," Berk said with a nod.

"I can't believe I'm going," Leora said excitedly. "I can't believe that the Compassionate Director himself chose me. I've only been on a transport twice before—first to go to Academy, then to this anniversary pageant."

"Where did he say we were going?" Berk asked.

"Caligoria," Will said impatiently. "To witness the Compassionate Removal," he added. "What's wrong with you, Berk?"

"Nothing!" Berk snapped. "You are always finding fault with everyone. Ever since we were children. You always tried to turn Father against me."

"How can you say such a thing?" Will asked, aghast and embarrassed.

Leora shifted uncomfortably. "Tell me about your childhood," Leora proposed, making peace. "Were you always at the Academy?"

"Always," Will said, trying to calm his irritation. He glanced at Berk. His brother seemed to have forgotten their exchange. His head lay on his chest, as if he had fallen asleep.

But Berk looked up suddenly. "Oh, Will used to get into plenty of trouble," he said. "Once he ignored a summons and—"

"I didn't hear it," Will said.

"The enforcer came and dragged him away."

The memory sickened Will. The enforcer had dragged him along the path, his back scraping against innumerable sharp pebbles. Blood seeped through his tunic. That night Mara had come and sung to him until he fell asleep.

The transport took off. A panorama of color spread out below, where settlements hugged the shores and dotted the eastern and southern fringes of the continent. Beyond, for a seemingly endless expanse, lay the vast arid plain, a brown stain that, like a cancer, had eaten away every cell of healthy, green growth. No sign of habitation broke the dull monotony, only an occasional strip of white, where once a road had led to a town, or perhaps to a running river or lake. Now, waterways seethed, heavy and still, overlaid with sludge.

"We came from there," murmured Leora beside him.

"Not Berk and I!" Will exclaimed. He wished now that she had not come. She was unsettling, *dissy*, with her ignorant comments and questions.

"I mean, my parents. They lived in what used to be called the Heartland. They were part of the relocation. What about you?" she asked boldly.

"You heard the story of our father's life," Will said. "He was an orphan."

"But your mother," she began, then looked away, nervously fingering her hair. "I meant, your female donor. Aren't you given the history of your donors?"

"No need," Berk retorted. "Status Ones are usually quite uninvolved with their donors. They go immediately to the nursery, then to Academy."

"I know that," Leora stammered. "I . . . of course, I know that. I only meant—"

"Don't you have nurseries out west?" Will asked. He was beginning to dread his journey even more, imagining all kinds of low-status children running wild.

"Of course we do!" Leora retorted. "But we are given our donor history so that we can understand our genetic disposition. In my case, both my donors were scientists, extremely bright. So they were allowed to educate me."

"Your donors *educated* you?" Berk exclaimed.

"Not entirely, of course," Leora said quickly.

"Look," Will interrupted. "We're coming to the coast. I can see the ocean!"

Leora drew near to the window, her shoulder almost touching Will's. "Oh, I do love the ocean!" The sound of her voice filled the small cabin, and Will found himself smiling again. "I've heard that before the Collapse, people used to travel all the time. They just got onto airplanes and went wherever they liked. It must have been wonderful."

"It was a security nightmare," Berk put in. "It had to be stopped. Besides, who needs real travel? You can go anywhere with the Vi-Ex."

Will looked down at the ocean. "Hayli says we will soon desalinate the water and have plenty to drink," he said. "No more thirst, ever." Leora looked up at him, and he felt suddenly powerful and wise. "Father says we are going to accelerate the Compassionate Removals. That will ease congestion in the cities and speed us toward the Time of Perfection."

"What happens to the Abs? Where do they go?" Leora asked.

"*You* know," Will said. "They are transformed, healed."

"I know what they say, but how—"

A robo-servant interrupted, offering a tray of nutri-cones, SNABS, and beverages. They had only time to eat their cones and finish the drinks when a computer voice announced the landing.

Even before they touched down, Will could see the line of people waiting. Those bound for Removal stood on a red carpet, marked off with satin ropes, entwined with artificial garlands. Friends, relatives, and well-wishers were gathered all around them, waving small Dominion flags.

All his life Will had heard about the Compassionate Removals. There were songs about them, songs of praise at the glory of Removal and relief from suffering. Will had never seen an Ab in the flesh. Of course, he had seen tapes of those beings, creatures so strange that whenever the tapes were shown the audience hooted and laughed and then chanted, "Rehab an Ab . . . Rehab an Ab!"

The moment the transport touched down, Will and all the others rushed out. They ran toward the crowds. The capsule gleamed silver in the hazy sunlight, and from it came music, beautiful music. Friends and relatives pressed as close as they could, waving and calling out their farewells. "Don't forget your poor friends back on Earth. Send images of your new life! Maybe we'll fly up to join you." That brought chuckles all around. The expense of such transports made visiting out of the question. Only the government could afford to offer these benefits.

A layer of filmy gray heat hung over the area. Will fought a sudden feeling of claustrophobia brought by lack of clean air. He was accustomed to the purified air of Washolina. He glanced at Berk. His brother, too, was holding his hands over his mouth, as if to filter the foul atmosphere. But the people who were gathered here seemed not to notice. Indeed, they laughed and talked in a celebratory mood.

A loudspeaker spilled out announcements in a constant cacophony. "Welcome! Welcome! Visitors, please stand back. You will receive refreshment and food stamps and pleasure stamps after takeoff. You must show your certificates of relationship in exchange for the stamps. Repeat: Be ready to show your certificate of relationship in exchange for the stamps."

Leora had run ahead. Now she came back to stand beside Will. In her hand was a paper cup containing a frothy drink of pale green color. She drank deeply. "Mmmm. Want some? There's a dispenser over there." She pointed to a long, gleaming bar on which stood a dozen large dispensers and cups. People jostled one another, hot and thirsty, eager for refreshment.

The loudspeaker voice boomed out. "Travelers, one at a time, please, no pushing." Enforcers in their dull green jackets trimmed with silver braid came up to assist them. Those without feet or a missing leg were carried. Some without arms were simply given a pat on the back, a steadying hand. Many had to be pushed in small, portable wheelchairs that would later be discarded, of course. Some lolled their heads aimlessly; others trod on their toes, like drunken puppets. They rolled their eyes. One boy's mouth hung open in a drooling grin. "Are you happy, Chomsey?" yelled a man's voice, and the grinning one nodded vigorously, yes.

On they went, along the red carpet, up the ramp, and then the doors were slammed shut and locked. The countdown reverberated over the land. Everyone stood transfixed, looking skyward. The whoosh of rockets left behind a blazing, smoking trail, and a great cheer went up from the spectators. A woman cried out, "Oh, he'll be so happy there—normal and productive."

"Yes, my Tillie went last year. We got back the images—so improved she is, nearly whole again. Her message was joyful, let me tell you."

"It is our most unselfish act, letting them go."

And as Will watched, he felt Leora's shoulder close to his. He heard her breathing, a gasp of emotion that matched the thumping of his own heart. Oh, how beautiful! The thought sang through him. He spoke rapidly into his pulse pad, making notes for his report:

"How ennobling it is to see these wretched creatures, the trash heap of humanity, being transformed into joyful, hopeful people moving to a new destiny. If only you could all see their faces, not on the Screen, but in actual reality, glowing with that hope. Instead of infirmity, they will know health. Instead of disability and dependence, they will become useful members of society."

Images and messages from former Abs were projected on huge Screens

for the spectators. Faces, once distorted, were now healed. Heads dispro-
portionate, eyes glued shut, noses missing—all were transformed. Bodies
formerly twisted and deficient were now whole.

Along with the images, voice messages rang out. "Thank you for sending me to Compassionate Removal! I have never known what happiness
is until now. Don't worry about me. I am busy and productive. Take care
of yourselves; we have everything we need."

Will turned to Leora. She and Berk stood together, Leora watching,
her eyes wide. Berk was working on his pulse pad, muttering to himself,
glancing up now and then to watch the slowly disappearing comet tail.

"What are you doing, Berk?" Will asked, still smiling, amused.

"What do you suppose it costs to keep them at the Removal? First, to
transport them to the satellite, then to house and feed and rehabilitate . . ."

"A lot," said Will. "I couldn't begin to calculate it."

"I can," said Berk. "It's too much. Exorbitant." Berk shielded his eyes
from the haze and the smoke. Together they watched the last trail of
smoke from the rocket.

"What are you saying?" Will wiped his face. The echoing roar from
the rocket oppressed him. He felt flattened from the heat, parched.

"It is cost prohibitive, Will."

He was interrupted by a blast of music and overwhelming echoes from
a dozen amplifiers. "Celebrate! Celebrate! Free refreshments for all.
Dancing! Celebrate their freedom and your Goodness!"

Will and Leora ran with the others to the refreshment stand. The
pale-green-colored drink cooled his parched throat. It had a sweet mint
flavor, such as Will had never before tasted.

"It's delicious," Leora said, reaching out to refill her cup. "What do
you think it is?"

"Something wonderful," said Will, as his thoughts cascaded one into
the other, like tumbling water, cleaning out every worry, leaving him on a
cloud of bliss.

CHAPTER

I T WAS YEARS since they had slept in the same room. Nor was this really a room, but more like a tent with a view to the sky, and walls of some opaque material that offered privacy, temperature control, and security. Through the walls Will could see the shadows of their PAARs, looking flat, two-dimensional.

"So, now the old man's got it all," Berk said, in a low, sleepy voice.

"What do you mean?" Will asked. "Father has always been in charge of the Dominion, more or less."

"This is more." In the deep bluish light, Will saw Berk raise himself on his elbow. "Whoever controls reproduction and information," Berk said, "controls everything. Ultimately, the whole world."

"Father isn't interested in control," Will argued. "He only seeks the greatest good . . ."

"Yes, yes," Berk replied. "But you can see that he must expand his reach. Everything either grows or shrinks. There is no standing still."

"Sounds like a good slogan," Will said lightly. In truth, his own thoughts seemed shallow, and he wished he had a better grasp of things. Berk saw ultimate ends, understood consequences, while he—he seemed stuck, always, in the moment.

"Listen," Berk said, "be realistic." Berk turned, reaching over to scratch between his shoulder blades. "It's enough to control the Dominion of the Americas. The rest depend on us for leadership—Asia and India lack industrialization. The African Dominion is doomed.

Europe is in constant conflict, just like the Middle East, so they are no threat to us. Let them consume each other! When they are done, we can move in and harvest their resources and—"

"And bring them The Goodness," Will said.

Berk grunted. "Exactly. The Goodness."

"Our father," Will said, "will probably be the most powerful man on earth."

"And he will pass that on to us," said Berk. "Unless he lives forever."

Will laughed. "What do you mean by that?"

"Hayli has no intention of dying," Berk said soberly. "He's gotten himself installed to rule for forty years. After that . . ."

"How long can he live?" Will said. Mara had talked about immortality, humankind's eternal dream. Was she serious? Immortality, like the Time of Perfection, was not really attainable, was it?

"It is possible," Berk said, "to live forever. At least, in theory."

"Well, we're pretty far away from it, then," argued Will. "There's still the problem of organ rejection, of premature aging from duplicated cells."

"Yes, yes," said Berk. "When human cells are duplicated, the DNA retains its own age. But once that problem is solved . . ."

"A pretty big problem," said Will. "Every part of a person would have to be replaced if he were to live forever!"

"Well, in theory," Berk insisted, "it's possible. And then there's Hayli's Creed." He quoted, and Will joined him, their two voices blending, "There is no natural law. That is a myth designed to keep people subservient to an invisible power that in reality does not exist. . . ." until the last two lines: "We will soon have the ability to prolong life far beyond our furthest expectation, to hundreds of years and beyond, even to immortality. *There is no reason why humans have to die.*"

"Not to die," Will mused. Every child memorized Hayli's Creed, but rarely was it discussed. Will had not really thought about the implication of those words. Now he mused, "What makes a person who he is? If someone were replaced bit by bit, who would he be? His head? Brain? Body?"

Berk laughed and lay back on his cot. "Who cares? As long as he could enjoy himself." He paused, then asked, "Do you take pleasure in your work, Will? Making speeches? Managing information?"

"I suppose I do," Will admitted. "I hadn't thought in terms of managing."

"Filtering through facts," Berk said. "Truth is relative, isn't it? Depending on your goal."

"I suppose so," Will said. Surely each person saw the truth in his own way, according to his own needs. He lay with his eyes open wide, as if he might memorize the intricate pattern of stars, the never-changing pattern. His mind wandered. "What do you think of the new turbo-suits?"

"*Dissy*," Berk replied. "Those high-neck things, you can't even see an implant."

"Some people look good in them," Will said.

"You mean Leora, don't you?" Berk snapped. "She talks about *parents* all the time. It isn't normal."

"Not all the time."

"Must you always be so literal? Go to sleep!"

Berk sat up, rubbing his back again.

"You itch?" Will asked.

"Sometimes."

"Me, too," Will said, scratching at the rash on his arm and hip. It wasn't an agonizing itch, just an occasional twinge, like a reminder from his body.

They were silent for a minute or so. From outside Will heard the thudding, cranking sounds of the PAARs doing their self-maintenance.

"Her parents are probably naturals," said Berk.

"So what?"

"That means *their* parents did it."

"Did what?" Will retorted, though he knew.

"Sex. The old way."

"You're disgusting!"

"You don't know anything."

"Shut up, Berk!"

"Sorry, sorry, didn't know you would be so defensive about her. She's just an Outsider."

"I'm not defensive."

"You are, too."

So this is what it's like, Will thought heavily, to be with a brother all the time. Hang it!

After a silence, Berk raised himself up again. His voice sounded unsteady. "Have you talked to Father?"

Will did not answer, feigning sleep.

"I saw him walking with you. What did you talk about?"

"Nothing. It was only for a moment," Will lied.

"If we don't send the right reports," Berk said, "what do you think will happen to us? What if we don't measure up?"

Will smiled to himself. Berk was nervous, worried about *him*. "I don't know." Then he asked, "Are you afraid of Hayli?"

"Yes," Berk said softly.

"Me, too."

They laughed together, a nervous laughter, soon ended.

In the morning they parted. Berk and Cullah and a few other students and aides took a transport headed for the southern districts to witness a security check. "Dissidents and criminals are constantly crossing the borders from the Great American Desert," Cullah explained. "Abducting people, you know, especially Status Ones."

The illegal trade in superior brains was said to be highly lucrative. Renegade scientists promised successful brain transplants for an outrageous fee. With brain transplantation, even a dull person could become a Status One. Of course, it was highly problematic, since the brains in question had to be stolen.

Berk's excitement was obvious. His eyes shone, and he paced in a tight circle, waiting for the transport to be ready. "Father said if I contribute to this program, I may become assistant minister within the year."

"We are not to call him Father, don't you remember?" Will said irritably. He had not slept well. All night their conversation had swirled through his thoughts—immortality. Living forever. What would his agenda be, if he knew he'd live forever? And Berk's comment that Leora's parents were probably conceived in a sexual way. The very thought was shocking. He had heard of people doing that in the past, before the Collapse. Sexual intercourse spawned diseases. Babies born from such unions were often deficient or maimed. It was rumored that the dissidents who roamed the Great Desert engaged in sexual intercourse. They and their offspring posed the greatest threat to The Goodness.

"You are probably right about the dissidents, brother," Will had finally admitted. "Those people have to be eliminated. There's no other way. Evil habits are ingrained in them." All night he had been bothered by visions of the Great Desert, with its vandal hordes planning their raids, and the sterile land itself, with piles of bleached bones and birds of prey circling overhead.

Now Berk put out his hand in farewell. "Brother," he said, "let's plan to meet soon. Where are you headed?"

"Indian Dominion," Will replied. "To assess their information management."

"Take precautions," Berk advised, "against contagion."

"Of course," Will said.

"I'm taking the transport to Africa," Berk said.

"Will you actually touch down?"

"Of course not. I'll view the animals and the populations from the transport; we will hover down. I can make some electro-sketches."

"You've done some beautiful sketches," Will said with a smile. Competition was forgotten; it felt good to be here together, standing in the sunshine. "It is a talent."

"No more than yours with words," Berks said. They clasped each other's arms, and Will felt the strength and warmth of his brother's body. "Pad me once in a while," Berk said.

"Sure. You, too," said Will.

Sileus was waiting for him. "You are to proceed to the transport that will take you to the Indian Dominion," he said. He fixed his small onyx eyes upon Will. "We can bring the girl," he said. "The Director was impressed with her, and he said you need—"

"Followers," Will completed for him, as the man spoke with annoying slowness.

"Be sure," said Sileus, with a brooding look, "that it is clear who is the leader and who the follower."

Fury shot through him. This deputy had the nerve to challenge him! He was only a messenger, after all, doing the work that any robo-servant could do better, without that beady stare. "Someday," Will said heatedly, "that will be crystal clear, my friend. And you will be the first to know it."

Sileus seemed to stiffen. His black eyes bulged. "I have been with the Compassionate Director for thirty years," he said. "From the beginning. I would give my life for him!"

"Then you also owe me your respect," Will said, his voice rising. "And your loyalty." He was gratified by his own tone, demanding and firm, but without ire.

Sileus ducked his head. "Yes. Certainly. You are right." He did not meet Will's eyes again, but shuffled toward the transport, extending his arm as if to guide and protect. "Transport programmed, sir," he reported, having checked the robo-pilot's instructions. Will's PAAR stood at the side of the transport, waiting to board.

With a new sense of ease and authority, Will climbed into the transport, taking the head seat. Leora followed, and he indicated the seat beside him. She buckled on her harness and said excitedly, "This is my fourth time on a transport! I never thought I'd be able to travel."

"Travel is not for the masses," Sileus said in a sullen tone. He sat down opposite Will in the jump seat.

Will nodded, gazing out at the vast desert that now appeared beneath the transport. An occasional ridge of color showed against the drab brown land, indicating where a mine had once been or a missile landed, puncturing a deep cavern into the soil. He leaned against the window, looking in vain for movement or for the hills of bones that he had seen on a Vi-Ex. But the ground below was too far away. Just as well, Will thought. He wondered why the regime had not simply eradicated all life-forms with flames and poison gases. He supposed it was his father's compassion, the hope of reforming even the dissidents, that prevented such extreme methods. And yet, now they were to quarantine Africa. Old lessons reverberated in his mind: *There is a time for compassion and a time for strictness. The greatest good for the greatest number.* He felt ashamed of his doubts, his lack of loyalty. Surely the Compassionate Director, in his wisdom, knew when to persuade and when to force, when to punish and when to reward.

"Firm he was," Sileus continued in his monotone. "Betray him once, and never again. He caught a guard listening in behind the Screen one time. That man never heard anything again."

Will nodded. He must review more of the history tapes to strengthen his own resolve. "Firmness is important," he agreed.

But Sileus seemed mesmerized by his own voice. "Born to lead, was the C.D. They say that as a child he had a dream. He was standing on top of a mountain with a sword in his hand. Imagine! A sword, like in ancient time. And with the sword he sliced off seven heads. Now, that's a sign. He was destined to rule the seven dominions, don't you see?"

At last Sileus's voice trailed off, and he began to nod and snore in fitful, irregular bursts. And Will was left alone with his thoughts. He looked back at Leora, her hands clasped under her chin and knees drawn up, fast asleep. She looked so innocent and meek, and he wondered whether her flashes of arrogance and quick repartee were only a game. She was obviously devoted to The Goodness, eager to rise and be of service. Still, he remembered Hayli's and Mara's admonitions. He must not allow anyone to know his innermost thoughts. His life was filled with purpose. He thought again of the Compassionate Removal and Berk's comment, "It is cost prohibitive . . ." Berk was obviously mistaken in his analysis. Whatever the cost, the Compassionate Removals would continue and even increase. For wasn't the regime intended to spread The Goodness to everyone, even Abs? Will felt lulled into a state of love and gratitude; how kind, how farsighted was the Compassionate Director. As he began to doze, Will recited the pledge in his mind: "Hail to The Goodness, and to the Supreme Compassionate Director, most true, most powerful, most benevolent. To him we vow our allegiance . . ."

A scream hurled Will to consciousness. It was his own voice, responding to pain, terrible pain. His abdomen was on fire, as if someone had twisted a knife into him. With a cry he bolted up, feeling the harness straining against his flesh. The pain mounted, utterly claiming him.

"What is it?" Leora cried. Extricating herself from the harness, she rushed to his side. "What's wrong, Will? Are you hurt?"

"My . . . stomach," he groaned through clenched teeth. "I . . . can hardly . . . move." He doubled over, chest to his knees, feeling as if he were about to explode.

"Sileus!" Leora screamed. "Sileus! Help!"

The man flung himself at Will's feet. "Poisoned! He's been poisoned! Oh, oh!"

Will shook his head, unable to catch his breath. The pain from his abdomen spread to his chest, like a monstrous hand working deep into his bowels.

"He needs to get to a clinic," Leora said. "Quick. Call in to reprogram this thing!"

"Where?" Sileus's hands flew to his head, as if to crush it. He rocked from side to side. "Son of the Compassionate Director—in my care— what will become of me if—anything should happen—where can we go?"

"Fresmofield," Leora shouted. "My home colony. It's not far. Hurry! Turn this thing around. My mother works there at the clinic."

"Your *mother!*" Sileus paled. Will glimpsed his face, the trembling lips.

"Hurry," Will rasped. He broke out in a sweat. Weakness held him immobile. His chest felt crushed, and as blackness seemed to curl at him from the edge of things, he pushed at the pain, thinking, *So this is how . . . it feels . . . to . . . die.*

CHAPTER 9

BRIGHT LIGHT BECKONED from a great distance. A long, hollow tunnel stretched out before him. Faces crowded around the opening, all illuminated from some invisible source, as if a lamp burned inside each person. And they came, an assembly of people he had never seen before, looking as if they existed in quite another time frame, with tousled or high-piled hair and old-fashioned clothes, the women in skirts, the men wearing belted trousers and thick-soled boots. They stood over him, murmuring. Their faces broadcast a range of feelings, from pity to fury.

He heard phrases, disembodied, as he himself felt disembodied, his head seeming to grow larger and larger, like one of those atmospheric balloons he had seen on the Screen, floating over the earth, retrieving messages. *Kill him . . . oh, he's just a boy yet . . . son of the Director . . . malevolent narcissistic tyrant . . . Kill him! How can we let him in? Dying, dying, we ought to say something . . . but he is certainly agnostic . . . while he is weakened . . . move him out of here . . . no! Not a hair of his head! Stupid. Could provide . . . vital . . . unprecedented opportunity!*

Slowly, slowly, the haze lifted. Then there was blackness more total than any he had ever known, and with it a dome of iron lay over his head, his entire body, so that he could not move. Only his mind remained alive, and then, only a whisper saying over and over again, *I am. I am. I am.*

Will began to emerge. Light stung his eyes. Strange odors crept into his lungs and his mouth, making his nauseous. He tried to sit up. His arms and legs felt as if they had been tied down. His head whirled. From his mouth poured a stream of vomit.

He thought he saw faces at the window, the same faces that had crowded into his reverie. Were they real? Had his fantasies emerged into tangible form? He shook his head, as if to banish this absurdity. The movement brought a searing pain settling over his eyes and down into his throat.

A man in a white coat came to him. He was followed by another, dressed in a green tunic, with startling green eyes and large teeth that stood out too far. With them came Sileus. His hands clasped the sides of his large head, his eyes bulged with fear.

The man in white sat down at Will's side and adroitly checked all the vital signs with a single monitor laid upon Will's chest, head, and groin. "It's all right." The man mopped Will's face and held a sliver of ice to his mouth. His eyes were deep set, framed by thick white eyebrows. His face was lined in a way that one rarely saw, except in old Vi-Exes. It made him look distinguished and also a little frightening. But his voice was soft. "There, lie back," he said. "I'm Dr. Varton, Thad Varton, your father's physician. No problem, no problem." He rubbed his hands together. "You're going to be fine. We had a bit of a scare, that's all."

"What happened?"

Sileus stepped forward. "I contacted the Compassionate Director at once. He sent Dr. Varton to attend to you." Sileus nodded, as if to reassure himself that he had not failed, that he was, in fact, a hero. "His own physician. You are in the best possible care."

"You've been quite ill," said Dr. Varton. "They tell me your white count was astronomical." The doctor held a tiny light to Will's eye, lifting the lid, asking, "Any changes in vision? No?" The doctor's breath was an affront, but Will felt too weak to turn aside. Besides, it would be insulting. Hayli's own physician! He endured the dreadful breath. "Any sleep disturbances? Lack of appetite?" The doctor lifted Will's arm, briefly squeezed Will's bicep, let it drop again onto the bed. "Any noticeable muscle weakness? Lack of coordination? No?"

To everything Will shook his head, trying to remember how he had felt before his body was assaulted by . . . what?

"What happened to me?" Will asked. Sileus still hovered, his anxious face bent over his valuable protégé.

Dr. Varton stood back, appraising Will. He touched Will's abdomen. "Have you been feeling any pain here in the last few months?"

"No. Well, sometimes, when I was walking fast. Or in the night, I got a pain in my side."

"And you ignored it!" stated the young medic in green. His large, prominent teeth gave him a comic/vicious look.

"I have been taught," Will whispered, "not to complain."

"But what about the 'ternal tapes?" asked Dr. Varton in astonishment. "When you are asked for your physical condition?"

Will shook his head. It brought a shooting pain spreading from his eyes to his forehead. "The weak," he whispered, "get eaten."

The medic flashed the doctor a mocking grin. "Ah. A brave one."

"Well, you nearly died," said Dr. Varton sternly. "There are reasons for the daily reports. Your health is of concern, not only to yourself, but to the Compassionate Director. You are expected to do your part in promoting The Goodness. This you cannot do," he said harshly, "if you are dead!" He massaged his hands vigorously.

"Dead!" echoed Will. The light, the images had indeed been like ghosts. "What's wrong with me, Doctor? What are you going to tell my father?"

The doctor packed up his monitor and stood looking down at Will. "There's nothing basically wrong with you at all, my boy. I'll tell your father what I'm telling you. This was one of those odd accidents. A burst appendix. Lucky you got here to the clinic when you did. You must rest and regain your strength. You are in good hands here, Will." He patted Will's hand reassuringly. The sudden warmth brought a swelling feeling to Will's throat.

The doctor frowned, moving his fingers up on Will's arm to the rash above his elbow. "How long have you had this?"

"I don't know," Will said. "It doesn't really bother me."

"Same thing on his backside," offered the medic, quickly silenced by the doctor's stern countenance.

"It looks like . . . I could give you a topical cream, something like . . ."

The medic leaned forward eagerly. "Have you ever seen such a thing in a young person?" he asked excitedly.

"No," said Dr. Varton. "But one must always be ready to learn something new."

"Yes, indeed!" said the medic, looking chastised.

"It doesn't really bother me," Will repeated. "Thank you. And please give my regards to Fa . . . to the Compassionate Director, and thank him for sending you."

"You are his son, after all," said the doctor, smiling as he turned to leave.

Will basked in the moment. His father had sent his own personal physician; his father was concerned about him, cared about him.

The medic in green took over as Sileus walked to the door with the doctor. They paused in the doorway, and Dr. Varton turned back. "You must be sure to continue your daily supplements. I've brought extra packets, and I am entrusting them to Sileus." He pointed his finger and said sharply, "Do not forget!"

The medic took over, fussing with the pillows. "Your appendix must have been inflamed for months," he said. "We've pumped you full of antibiotics, but you still have to rest. Your white count was drastically elevated, and your platelets . . . For a few minutes here, we thought you would bleed to death."

"So you operated?"

"After we stabilized you. We had to do it, even before Dr. Varton arrived. We scraped out, sucked out all that infection." He seemed to relish the thought, licking his lips.

Will lifted his head slowly. A window came into focus. Beyond it he saw vast expanses of empty land, with faint tufts of greenery and an occasional tree, where plants were just starting to evolve, fringing the edges of things with color.

"Where am I?" he asked.

"District Seven, in a colony called Fresmofield."

"California?"

"Middle-Caligoria," said the medic. "There hasn't been a California for years."

"Of course. Middle-Caligoria." He glanced about. "Is this a hospital?"

"We are part of a large compound," the man answered, "with facilities for research and a few wellness beds in this section. You were brought here because your companion insisted upon it. She is in line for Status One, you know. Her female donor works in one of the labs."

Will lay back. "Thank you," he said weakly.

"Your companion has been asking about you. She's just outside. Shall I call her in?"

"Yes."

Leora looked pale. Her hair was disheveled, eyes red, as if she had not slept. "Hello," she said, "Welcome back. We thought you were gone. Sileus was beside himself. He was camped outside your door the entire time."

"How long have I been here?"

"Two days. You went into a coma. They operated yesterday morning. We thought—we so were worried. Afterward, you were screaming something about birds and faces. Hallucinating, I suppose."

Will tried to sit up. He fell back on the pillows. "I remember the birds," he said. "I remember the faces."

Leora said, "You're supposed to take your time recuperating. You can stay here and, when you're feeling better, explore the district. Nothing too strenuous."

"And you brought me here? The medic says you've been here the whole time. Watching over me? You look terrible. Why didn't you go to sleep?" It wasn't what he meant. It wasn't the way he wanted to sound—cross and ungrateful. He could not understand his own outburst.

Leora's expression changed from concern to annoyance. She flipped back her hair, as she had done the first night they met. "Well, I guess it wouldn't look good for me if something happened to the son of the Compassionate Director and I didn't try to get him some help."

He sighed and leaned farther into the pillows. "Quite so." He watched her for a few moments, her eyes downcast. He said, "You told me this is your home. You must know people here."

"Yes, I know people. And everyone knows about you, the son of the Compassionate Director, here in Fresmofield. It created a big stir. You're a celebrity, you know. And since I came with you, that makes me a celebrity, too."

"Do you like that?" Will asked.

She bit her lip. "No," she said curtly. She hesitated. "We thought you would die."

"And that would create a problem for you," he stated. He composed the Screen message in his mind, tried it out aloud, "Son of Supreme Compassionate Director killed in Fresmofield. Young girl taken into custody. Found *dissy*—wears a feather in her hair . . ."

Leora laughed. Will felt light-headed, rewarded by her smile. "Would you care if I'd died?" he asked, half teasing.

"How can you ask?" Leora exclaimed. "You think I have no feelings?" she began, but she was interrupted by the appearance of a woman wearing a green lab coat and pants, her head bound in a kerchief. Her eyes were large and smoky blue, like Leora's, with the same steeply arched dark eyebrows. But a sharp line was etched between them, giving her face a perpetually worried look. She was gaunt, as if she had known hunger all her life.

"Senna!" Leora exclaimed, and she bounded up guiltily.

"Leora! You must not tire him," Senna said in a voice of complaint. In her tone Will sensed layers of unresolved arguments. The woman snatched up a cloth from the bedside stand, glancing at Will without meeting his eyes. "Ah, you are awake. Are you in pain?"

"No," said Will. He tired to focus on Senna's face. Now her features seemed wobbly. Nothing stayed in place. It hurt to breathe. "A little," he admitted.

"Well, they have sedated you. You will sleep," Senna said. She took Leora by the arm. "Come outside. Let him rest. I need to talk with you, Leora."

She turned to Will, plucking at her kerchief with nervous fingers. "What do you eat? We have food in our silos. Original packaging."

"I'm not really hungry," Will murmured. He felt himself drifting. "Anything. Later. Please." It took all his resolve to get the words out, and to brace himself against Senna's penetrating stare. *Original packaging,* Senna had assured him. She thought he feared being poisoned. The remark only accentuated his sense of strangeness.

Alone again, Will felt like an alien, transplanted into a hostile corner of the world, a world where lights blinded him, people hurried past and asked him innumerable questions about how he felt. He felt rotten. He felt as if his insides had been taken out and put back together—wrong.

He tried to rally. He was, after all, Status One, son of the Compassionate Director. He must send a report to Hayli, fulfill his mission, get to know the people here, and, above all, be continually on his guard.

Hayli and Mara had both warned him about enemies of The Goodness. And now here he lay, weak and vulnerable. The walls, faint yellow in color, seemed to press in upon him. He glanced to the window, seeking escape, finding it difficult to breathe. His back itched, and also the scabby patch above his elbow, but he felt too weak to scratch, tired and confused. His harsh breathing echoed back at him, an exaggerated, prolonged sound. Again the faces leapt up at the periphery of his vision. Dreams and fantasies wove their way in and out of the reality of this room, the breeze from the window, the buzzing of equipment.

From a distance he heard voices. They rose and fell in argument. Was it real, or part of the dream?

"How could you bring him here? What in the world were you thinking? I never thought you'd be so stupid . . . thoughtless . . . you've put us all in danger, the whole colony."

"What was I to do? He was sick. You wanted me to befriend Status Ones, and he is the son of the—"

"What do you really know about him?"

"Son of the Compassionate—"

"No. He is not."

"Are you saying he's an imposter? You are always criticizing me. I met the Supreme Compassionate Director! I shook his hand. I thought you'd be proud of me."

"Someone is using you, Leora. Making a fool of you. As usual, you failed to analyze—"

"Why are you yelling at me? Leave me alone!"

"Listen to me! He is an imposter. He is not Hayli's son. He is a clone."

"Senna, that is absurd. How can you—?"

"I have proof, Leora. Scientific proof. Why would I invent such a story?"

"It isn't possible. All the clones were killed."

"Not this one. Leora, you have put us all in danger. Don't you realize what happens to people who harbor a clone?"

The word clanged in Will's head like a bell: *clone, clone, clone, clone.*

CHAPTER 10

O F COURSE, it wasn't true. Will lay on the special air bed designed to comfort the sick. Air pockets cushioned the body to minimize pressure and pain. But the wound in Will's belly seemed to tighten and blaze, as if the word *clone* had the power to cut.

For some reason Senna had told this horrible lie to Leora. What could it mean? *There are no clones around, not anymore.* This truth he knew, like a mantra burned into his skull; everyone knew. Human cloning had proved to be such a massive and unmitigated failure that every state and dominion legislated against it. He knew from the history tapes that cloning was supposed to be for the ultimate good, to help repopulate the earth with the best and fittest people, and provide bone marrow and healthy tissue to regenerate diseased organs. But it got out of control. Everyone began making clones—governments, private companies, even single entrepreneurs, working in makeshift labs. They created ghastly creatures, copies of copies, designed for special functions, mindless, sometimes featureless mutants. Many got diseases of aging when they were only in their teens. Others wandered about aimlessly, subhuman trash. Most died out. Then, during the worst years of the Collapse, vigilante committees hunted them down, killed them in the streets, like vermin. With the advent of The Goodness, cloning was outlawed forever.

Yes, there were still laboratories that cloned isolated tissue to use for organ repair. But that was carefully regulated by government clinics. Then there was the black market in brains, smart brains, or parts of brains to be transplanted and fused, giving the recipient exactly what he wanted in talent and I.Q. Of course, most donor brains were obtained by force, through illegal means, except when the donor had recently died. But that had nothing to do with cloning.

Why would anybody want to make a clone? It was obviously a mistake. Some stupid lab assistant thought he made a great discovery. Of course, any imbecile could determine a cell's age with a simple test. When DNA is cloned, the donor cells retain their age and pass it along to the copy— basic genetics that everyone learned in grade two. If the cells were older than the subject, it proved that he had been cloned. Some lab assistant obviously decided to test a piece of Will's hair or skin, just for fun, just because he wanted to investigate the son of the C.D. A foreign bit of matter must have gotten into the mix. The assistant was probably a stupid Status Three, trying to make a name for himself. In future, lab assistants must be restrained from doing anything beyond their specific orders. Will would write it into his report.

Clone! Clone! All day the word, the accusation accosted him, growing stronger, more oppressive as the sedative wore off. He told himself over and over again that it was a mistake, sheer nonsense. He couldn't be a clone. He was Status One, son of the Compassionate Director. Everything about him, his entire genetic makeup, had been carefully monitored from the moment of retrieval of sperm and egg. Even before that, the physiology of both donors was checked, Hayli being the male donor and a superior Status One providing the egg. Conception was achieved in a petri dish, nurtured with precise temperature controls and chemical analysis. The director of the Gestation Lab, Washolina Branch, would personally have monitored every step, from fertilization to cell division and subsequent incubation. Sexual preference was easily achieved. Hayli's child had to be perfect. And everyone said that Will was a fine specimen, capable, talented, intelligent.

In his mind Will repeated the praises of his proctors and his associates, until he was nearly convinced. He could not be a clone. It didn't make sense. Still, something smoldered inside him. He must erase all doubt.

Will waited until it was dark. The medic came to check him, lifting his arm, letting it drop, for Will made himself limp, feigning sleep. The medic's hand was cool. His touch was perfunctory. They might have been two machines interacting in the darkness.

When the medic was gone, and the night drifted into itself, and everything hummed in waiting for the dawn, Will knew it was time. Painfully he lifted himself off the air bed, bracing his hands beneath him. The movement brought a clutching at his middle, as if iron hands were squeezing him, hard. A surge of weakness made him stop. His legs hung down over the edge of the bed. He took several deep breaths, gulping air as if it were food, and he realized he had not eaten in days. The I.V. bubble was attached to his arm, a self-contained pouch that moved with him. Whatever nutrients it contained, it did not alleviate weakness or hunger. His belly felt twisted and empty.

Carefully, slowly, Will slid down from the bed and crept out into the hall, his PAAR following silently. Useless shadow, Will thought grimly, unable to protect anyone from the worst things, from pain or sickness or lies. Surely it was a lie, filthy lie, this clone accusation. Like the children who used to dance around him and Berk . . .

And suddenly he wished Berk were here. Berk would put these ideas to rest immediately with some firm logic. Berk would confront that woman, Senna, and let her know that accusing him of being a clone bordered on treason.

Will crept past Sileus, asleep on a narrow cot with his arms locked under his enormous head. Sputtering snores erupted from his throat.

He would call Berk later and tell him about this preposterous accusation. He should warn Berk that both of them needed to be on guard. Leaders, he thought, are in constantly jeopardy of sabotage and betrayal. This was just one more example of the sort of thing Mara had warned him against.

Will realized, with a pang, that he had been too trusting. He must make himself more like Berk, suspecting everyone, not only for his own sake, but for The Goodness. And he must deal with this young lab assistant appropriately, as Berk would do. He would send the enforcers. Let the people of Fresmofield understand who was in charge!

Will moved past the supply rooms, the control rooms, into the laboratory section and the gleaming door marked BIOMEDICAL LAB. Standing here in the darkness, Will felt his aloneness not as a curse, but the way a space rider must confront the vastness of the universe, floating outside his craft on a cable, above it all, the master. With his desperation, oddly, came a sense of control. He would trust nobody, seek answers only from himself.

He swayed, nearly stumbled. Probably the medication accounted for this light-headedness, this preposterous unraveling of thoughts that for one moment seemed brilliant, and the next moment evaporated into scattered bits of nonsense. *Do not condone a clone, rather be alone—if you are a clone, you will be alone. Or dead. People hunt down clones, like wild animals, residual foxes, possums, bears. It is right and good to kill a clone, good to kill a clone.*

Noiselessly Will moved into the lab. He motioned for the PAAR to come in so that it might blend into the darkness. The PAAR flattened itself against the wall. There stood the machine, no larger than a small meter, the kind designed to check blood pressure, body fluids and blood composition, and genetic makeup, all routine. The technician would insert the sample, then indicate what tests were desired. Simple truths came out, such as the age of the DNA, proof positive for determining a clone, if the DNA were older than the subject—himself.

Will pulled several hairs from his head. He laid them onto the small tray, clamped them down, and slid the tray into the machine. A tiny green light glowed for a moment, while the analysis was done. On the small screen, green letters printed out the results, the final one gleaming into Will's eyes, imprinting itself into his brain: Cell age: seventy-two years.

His heart pounded, drumming in his ears. No. It had to be an error. Frantically Will bit off a sliver of a fingernail and inserted it into the meter. In moments the test was complete. Cell age: seventy-two years. Desperately he scratched off a flake of skin above the sore patch on his elbow. The results were the same: Cell age: seventy-two years.

In shock, Will stumbled back to his room. His PAAR followed. For a moment Will wanted to hold on to the robot, take its cold appendage into his hand, that appendage resembling a human arm with a hammer-like fist attached. He wanted something to hold, but the thought of embracing iron left him desolate.

Will made his way back onto the bed, and he lay motionless, until the pain began to subside a little. *Clone. Clone.* He could not rid himself of the thought. *Clone.* He stared up at the blank ceiling, recalling the dome of stars he had seen just three nights ago, when he and Berk were together.

Thoughts of Berk brought new questions spiraling through his brain. The two of them were utterly bound now by this new reality. If he was a clone, then so was Berk. Their cells were old, seventy-two years old. Then why hadn't he felt the signs of aging? Why was he still able to run and leap and work for hours without getting tired? How come he and Berk had just begun to shave? If their cells were old, why were they just now approaching adulthood?

He summoned Berk with his pulse pad. Berk's voice sounded odd.

"Where are you, brother?" Will asked.

"In transit. Over Africa. It's stunning!"

"Berk, I've been sick."

"Yes, I heard. I meant to contact you, but—"

"I've discovered something about me. Actually, about us." He took a deep breath, holding back the word *clone.* It would be too shocking, too sudden. Berk wouldn't believe him, would call him *dissy.* He must proceed slowly. "What causes aging?" Will asked, his heart thumping. "You studied more science than I."

"Oxidation of cells," Berk said. "Look, this is not a good time for me."

"Not for me, either!" Will cried.

"Look it up," Berk said. "Really, I've got to go. We're coming down over an interesting area. Later. Later."

Will's pulse pad went blank, and Will was left alone to ponder this thing, like a disease or a curse. Oxidation of cells, like metal corroding. Might his aging suddenly accelerate, like a ball careening downhill, causing instant collapse and death at, say, the age of twenty-five? Or did cells somehow regenerate when they were cloned, so that a brand-new being was created from old stuff, much as a new shoot sprouts from an old tree?

He simply did not know enough about gestation or genetics. He had never needed to study the sciences with any depth. Now he wished he had.

His entire body itched, the spot on his arm and his hip felt raw. Now Will remembered Dr. Varton's remark, "Strange skin aberration for one so young . . ." Whatever was happening to his skin, it must be a sign of aging.

Maybe he was already beginning to disintegrate. What kept him going? Panic held him down, motionless, feeling as if he were about to break into a million pieces.

As the first light of dawn seeped through the window, Will sat up, startled. The sun was barely creeping over the edge of the horizon, spreading paths of light and color over the earth. In that first moment of wakefulness, again the shock swept over him. His entire life had been, in a moment, shattered. His very existence was false; he was not Hayli's son. Hayli had lied to him. His entire life was a lie.

Will looked at his fingers. He pressed his hands to his abdomen, feeling the pain from the operation, a reinforcement of his humanity. *I am. I feel pain. I think. I act. I am the same now as I was yesterday and the day before. But—who am I?*

A hollow ache lay at the pit of his stomach. He had been manufactured from a single cell, merely duplicated. If that were true, there might be hundreds of others exactly like him. Why not? If you are duplicating people, why stop at two?

No! he cried inwardly. He was unique. Even he and Berk were not exactly alike. Circumstances, small genetic quirks, had made them different.

He marveled at how stupid and trusting he had been! It should have been obvious. There was no resemblance whatsoever between Hayli and his sons. Will had assumed that he had inherited his brown hair and dark eyes from his female donor. Hayli's eyes were blue, and his hair was a light golden brown. Obviously, he was not cloned from Hayli's DNA. Now another question accosted him. If Hayli wanted a clone, why didn't he have his own DNA used? Why somebody else's? And whose was it?

Miserably it came rushing in now, how all his life Will had struggled to find Hayli's traits within himself, the intellect, the energy, the charisma. And all the time he was lacking, because he was only a clone. Whose? *Whose?*

Will's mind halted. His thoughts were scattered. *If I am not the son of the Compassionate Director, I am nobody.* But that's impossible, argued his rational mind, everybody is somebody. Somebody made me. But *why* did he make me?

He slept, exhausted from his ordeal. When at last he awakened, the day was bright, the sunlight slanting into the window. He heard a voice from the hallway, a delicate voice. A girl was singing. A child.

The girl's voice was vibrant and lilting, the tune a simple melody, the words strange.

> *"I will give you honey*
> *Honey, honey, honey from the rock . . ."*

It was a beautiful song, completely unlike the songs one heard in Washolina. New melodies and lyrics appeared periodically at the Dance Dome or along the motion paths, but these songs always contained messages, cautionary or commanding.

This song was haunting and soothing, like a lullaby. He thought of Mara's song, her soft voice sheltering him from pain and from fear.

"I will give you honey . . ." The girl's voice reached through to his very core.

The song made no sense, getting honey from a rock. But it brought tears to Will's eyes. This time, no evil animals rose in his mind to punish him for this weakness. He wept until the pillow beneath him was damp. At last he went to the window.

From the distance he could see a single line of people, all dressed alike. As they approached, they seemed to bob up and down, and Will realized that they were children.

He leapt back into bed, pulled the covers up, and turned so that he might appear to be sleeping. But there came a reluctant tapping at the window, and then a firm knock, and the round, smiling face of man in teacher's garb, the familiar black gown and red sash. "Son of the Compassionate One—oh, the children have come to pay their respects, if they may!"

The medic rushed out, scolding and swaggering pompously, and in a moment he returned, looking embarrassed yet proud. "This teacher humbly requests that you allow the children to visit. Just for a few minutes. They have heard that the esteemed son of the Compassionate Director has come to our colony. They beg to pay their respects."

So, the medic knew nothing of Will's real status. But how long could it be kept hidden? Maybe Senna had already told others in the colony. Someone would come in the night to kill him; there might even be a bounty on the head of a clone. He didn't know, but it was plausible, just as an occasional possum or fox killed in a field brought a handsome reward.

Will sat up, looking about. He smoothed down his hair, straightened his nightshirt. He must continue to behave like the real son of the Compassionate Director. He must continue to believe that he would inherit the Dominion.

Will made his voice stern and forbidding. "Very well," he said loudly. "Five minutes, no more."

Next thing he knew, some twenty children had formed a straight line in front of his bed. They stood as still as statues, their hands clasped over their narrow chests, boys and girls alike dressed in pearl gray tunics, the symbol of their age and status, along with the insignia on their sleeves. They were Status Four, ages ten and eleven, that age when their careers were determined and the matter sealed. Their faces all wore the rather blank looks of below-average intelligence, as required for factory workers of the lowest grade, those who fed and cleaned machinery, carted away waste, and responded to emergency signals by bringing in needed equipment, too dangerous for those of higher status to attempt.

They stood gazing at Will as if he were an apparition. One girl swooned; she swayed, dropped to her knees, weeping. Immediately the teacher pulled her upright and administered a small electric prod to her cheek. She jolted, winced sharply, her face red. "Respect!" the teacher hissed. He bowed to Will. "My apologies. They can become quite emotional, these Fours. That is why they are given few choices and programmed precisely to their tasks."

"Indeed," Will said sternly. "But even a Status Four must learn to obey. Obedience is the hallmark of patriotism!"

The teacher gave a quick half bow. "Two hours of every school day are spent on the principles of The Goodness," he assured Will. "And still we try to improve." He rapped a boy sharply on the head with his knuckles. "Stand tall!" he snapped.

"The children would like to recite for you," said the teacher, and he stepped back, clapped his hands three times, and nodded approval as the students began to recite in studied unison:

"Hail to The Goodness, and to the *Supreme* Compassionate Director, most true, most powerful, most benevolent." In accord, they lifted their hands over their eyes, symbolizing clarity of vision. Most of the children had remembered to insert the additional word *supreme*, though a few did falter. "To him we vow our allegiance and our love. To him we give the labor of our hands and the complete obedience of our will. We exist to please him. We long to serve him. Whatever he requires, we will do with gladness and joy in service."

Listening, Will stroked his upper lip as he had seen Hayli do hundreds of times. When the recital was finished, the children bowed swiftly in unison.

Will sat up. "Thank you, children," he finally said. "That was very good. Very good indeed."

"They have been working on this Pledge for many weeks," said the teacher. "When they heard you were here, Your Excellency, they were happy to practice all day so that they could recite it for you."

A leader bestows punishments and rewards to assure Loyalty, Will thought. "You will be rewarded," he said loudly. "A box of SNABS for each of you! I will command the local silos to dispense them tomorrow."

"Thank you! Thank you!" the children bobbed their heads. A few of the girls ducked down on one knee.

"Remember The Goodness," Will said grandly. Hayli would surely ask some questions of the teacher. Such things were expected from a leader. Will asked, "How many classes are in the school?"

"Only five," replied the teacher. "We go up to Status Three—most of those become office drones, and down to Seven, the sweepers and scavengers."

The teacher paused momentarily, then he smiled a saccharine smile. "Next week, Your Excellency, we are celebrating the Grand Release. We would be greatly honored if you would attend."

Sileus rushed in, flapping his hands, scolding, "What are you doing here, bothering the son of the Compassionate One! How dare you? Get out! Who said you could come here?"

"It was my decision to let them visit!" Will said sternly. He must, at all costs, retain control. Did Sileus know he was a clone? Was he, for some reason, keeping that secret? But—cloning was illegal. Hayli would never admit he had done such a thing. But *someone* had to know. Whoever had done the actual cloning would know.

First things first, Will told himself, fighting the urge to wipe the sweat from his neck and brow. First he must see to it that his secret went no further than Leora and Senna. And he must continue to appear composed and competent. He must continually herald his own celebrity.

"Wait!" Will called to the teacher. He lifted both hands, as he had seen Hayli do, and he intoned Hayli's own farewell, "Go with The Goodness!"

"The Goodness!" the teacher and students echoed with great enthusiasm.

Will watched as the children marched out. The girl who had been punished with the electric prod walked more stiffly than the rest. Will put his hand to his cheek; he could almost feel that pain again, as it has been administered to him when he was young.

CHAPTER 11

LIES BEGET LIES. That thought played through Will's mind as he lay on the air bed. If his birth was a lie, was anything else true? True: *I am a clone. A clone is the lowest form of humanity. It has no status at all.* Who in the Dominion would help him? Alberz or Brodi? Certainly not. Mara? Perhaps. But without Hayli's support, Mara was impotent. She might not even believe him. She would ask Hayli. Hayli could deny it. Hayli could have Will punished, even killed. Did Sileus know he was a clone? What was his real mission? Was he sent as a protector or as a spy? Maybe he was under orders to kill Will if anything went wrong.

Of all his floating thoughts, the most compelling possibility seemed to be to tell Berk. They were brothers, twins, possessed of the same beginnings and the same destiny. Or were they? Berk always had his own agenda. Will was glad now that he hadn't confided in him.

He managed to keep his composure when the medic came in to check his vital signs. Sileus came to his bedside with the blue powder mixed in water, and stood there watching while Will drank.

"You look well rested," the man said, his dark eyes gauging Will's demeanor. "In my morning report I can state that the son of the Compassionate Director is healing from his surgery and feeling quite well."

Was the man serious? Will had never felt more dispirited in his life. But he played the role with caution, swinging his feet out of the bed and standing up. "Yes, I'm quite restored, Sileus," he said. And then, summoning an authoritative tone into his voice he went on, "I want you to order a box of SNABS for each of those schoolchildren, and do it immediately. They must learn that the son of the Compassionate Director is scrupulous in keeping his word!"

"Certainly, sir," said Sileus with a half bow, his eyes still intent upon Will's face. Will met his gaze, unflinching. If he were the Compassionate Director, nobody would dare to initiate or keep eye contact with him. His position with regard to Sileus was still ambiguous.

"Do it now!" Will shouted, summoning all his strength, and the man fled from his sight.

Will lay back down. He felt exhausted. How long could he go on pretending that he had power? How long might it be before everyone knew he was an imposter—and then? Perhaps he should flee. But where could he possibly go? Anyone would recognize him. Hayli would put out an alert. No, it was too preposterous. Besides, he could hardly walk from weakness. His best chance was to stay here and pretend . . . what? That he hadn't heard.

He saw Leora standing in the doorway, hesitant, pale. She had been watching him, he supposed, assessing his condition. She remained in the doorway, biting her lip, all bravado gone from her manner.

"How are you feeling?" she asked softly.

"Better," he said.

"Did they give you something to eat?"

He pointed to the yellow-and-black carton on the bedside tray. "The medic got me this," he said. "Number 37. It's supposed to enhance tissue repair and also promote energy."

"Did it?"

He almost smiled. She was always so direct! "No," he admitted.

She walked toward the bed. Now he saw that she carried a small basket.

"What's that?" he asked skeptically.

"Figs," she said, showing him the oddly shaped purple things. "My father—Antone—grows them."

"I wish you would stop saying such things," he grumbled. "It's anachronistic, you know."

"What?" she asked, startled.

"Father."

"But you call Hayli your father," she objected.

"That's different," he snapped. "Hayli is the father of The Goodness."

"I see," Leora said, with the same mocking expression that had so irritated him when they first met.

"It's regressive," Will snapped. He peered at the purple fruit, picked one up, and held it cautiously by the stem. "I don't eat things that grow," he said brusquely, tossing it away. "You should know that."

Leora sighed as she took the basket from him. Still standing at the bed, she said softly, "I'm sorry. Antone, my male donor, thought they might strengthen you."

"Why would he think so?" Will demanded.

"He is a biologist," Leora replied, "head of one of the silos. In his spare time he works on land restoration and crop renewal. He has a permit."

"I'm really tired, Leora," Will said with a dismissive wave.

"You want me to leave," she stated.

"Yes. And if you see Sileus, tell him I want to rest." He could not meet her gaze, though he longed to see himself through her eyes. She must think him disgusting, contemptible. But her voice was the same as ever, lilting, almost teasing. And he had hurt her with his abruptness. He wished he could take it back, and he bit his lip, as if the spoken words could be retrieved.

They spoke at the same time, he saying, "I'm sorry," and she, "You heard Senna, didn't you?"

"I don't know what you are talking about," Will said, turning away.

"Last night. We thought you were drugged." Leora reached for a small chair and pulled it closer to the bed. "But you heard. I know you did. You are different. Frightened. I can hear it in your voice, and see it in the way you look at me."

"I'm not afraid of anything!" Will cried, alarmed. He scanned the room, saw that the door was ajar. "Close the door," he said. "Please," he added.

She did so.

"Sit down here," he said, indicating the chair. "Look," he began, "you're right. I heard you. Obviously, it's a mistake. You can't really believe that your equipment here is reliable, can you?"

"It is reliable," Leora said, looking into his eyes as she had done that first time, so that he felt a sinking sensation. "We checked it several times. The question is, What are we going to do?"

"We?" he exclaimed. "I am going back to Washolina, as soon as I'm able to get out of here. I'm telling Sileus to get the tube-transport ready—"

"You need to rest," Leora said. "You nearly died, Will."

"And who would care if I had?" he shot out.

"I would!"

He lay very still, absorbing her words. He wanted to believe her, but how could he? Maybe, as Mara had suggested, Leora only wanted to use him. He looked up at her face, flushed with feeling, her eyes so blue, so sorrowful.

Leora whispered, "Will, listen to me. You can't go anywhere now. You're too sick. Nobody knows, except for me, Antone, and Senna. And her assistant. We're not going to tell anyone about this. Why would we?"

"People talk," Will said. "After all, Senna told you."

"That's different. I'm her daughter. And you're my friend."

"Why would you protect me?" Will asked. "Assuming, of course, that I need protection!"

"Oh, you'll need it," Leora said, her voice low. "When they first brought you in, there were some people who wanted to let you die. They were going to kill you, just for being Hayli's son. It would have been easy, just by pressing a pillow over your head. You were only semiconscious. But then you blinked and you called out . . ."

"I remember," Will said reluctantly. "Bright lights and faces. And people were saying things, arguing about me. Someone said I was dying. Someone else said they should get rid of me, son of the Director, malevolent narcissistic tyrant. I remember those words."

"But Senna persuaded them to leave you alone."

"Why?"

Leora hesitated "Even if you're a clone, you still belong to Hayli. You are our responsibility. Senna says we can't let anything happen to you."

"What does Antone say?"

Leora shook her head, flustered. "He only worries about me. He didn't even want me to go to Washolina."

"Was he one of the ones who wanted to kill me?"

Evasively she asked, "Do you think it's all right to kill people?"

"It's all right to kill a clone," he said.

"I don't think so. A clone is a person, too."

"Everyone says a clone is fair game."

"I'm not like everyone," Leora said, her chin thrust out, eyes blazing.

"I can see that," Will said. "You will even condone a clone. Why are you different from everyone else?"

"Maybe because I was raised here. Maybe because I'm only Status Two."

"No," Will said. "Don't look away. Come here. Let me see you, your eyes. There is something else about you . . ."

From outside came the delicate voice, that strange song, "I will give you honey . . ." Will let his mind focus on the voice, the song. "I will give you honey . . ." What did it mean? Honey was sweet. How could anyone possibly get honey from a rock?

"Who is singing?" he asked

"My little sister, Kiera."

"Why does she sing?"

"She is talented in music. She makes up songs."

"Why?"

"They comfort her. Do you like it?"

Will nodded, blinking away the sudden emotion that threatened to overwhelm him. More than anything he wanted to give voice to his thoughts, to tell Leora how it felt to be nobody, worse than nobody, a clone, an outcast.

Sileus appeared, nodded obsequiously. "I have done as you asked," he muttered. "Ordered the SNABS."

"Thank you, Sileus," Will said. "I will call you later, when I have prepared my report on the Compassionate Removal."

"Sir, do you feel up to it?"

"Are you implying that I am not capable?" Will snapped in his harshest tone. "That I am weak?" The man shrank back. Will continued to glare at him; not for a moment must Sileus detect any weakness.

"No, no, forgive me! I will be just outside, when you need me," said Sileus.

"And close the door!" barked Will.

Leora sat beside him, hands in her lap, her face troubled. "You sound so fierce," she murmured at last.

"Are you afraid of me?" he asked.

"Sometimes," she said with a slight smile. "Usually not. You pretend to be so stern. Actually, you can be"—she paused—"nice."

"Nice," he repeated. He thought for a moment. "Leora, do you have a Screen?"

"Antone has one. But it's limited. We don't have all the codes."

"I can start here. But I need to get back to Washolina. Maybe talk to Berk. Make some inquiries. In truth, I hardly know where to begin."

Leora said, "Whoever cloned you would not want you to know about it, would they?"

"Probably not," Will agreed. "The fact is, Hayli lied to me. All my life I've had to live with lies."

"Are you sure Hayli was the one who . . . had it done?"

"Yes. Nobody else would have the power and the means. He wants the world to think Berk and I are his sons."

"And maybe there are more," Leora said.

"Yes," Will said, imagining himself replicated a dozen, a hundred times over. How would he ever know? How could he accept the idea that he was not unique? "Why?" he gasped. "Why would anyone want to do this?" He began to tremble, felt the vibration in his knees, even along his jaw. His teeth were clenched.

Gently Leora said, "Why do you assume it is for something evil?"

"Cloning is evil. The law says so. Everyone says so. Your own donors don't want me around. You can't pretend that they do."

"Antone is upset," Leora admitted. "But Senna thinks maybe Hayli is trying something new. She's involved in research herself. A clone is a rarity."

"So she wants to keep me alive," Will said bitterly, "as a rare specimen."

Leora shrugged. "Maybe there are new techniques, and Hayli wanted to prove their worth, and what better way than to create a clone and monitor it from the start?"

"You said 'it,'" Will pointed out, hurt.

"I'm sorry, Will. Truly, I am. This is strange for me, too."

"And when do you think Hayli was planning to tell me the truth?"

"Maybe never. Maybe people don't need to know everything."

"That's what you wrote in your essay," Will said heatedly, leaning forward, bracing himself against the pain. "But this is personal. This is me, my life!"

"When you find the truth, you might not like it," Leora said. "Senna told me how clone-people used to be persecuted and killed."

Will flinched. "That's what I've been telling you. Why should I be any different?"

"Because you're special. You belong to Hayli. Besides, when people get to know you, they find out that you're just like everyone else." She smiled and brushed aside her hair. "A little cranky and very bossy, but just a regular person."

"Is that supposed to be a compliment?" he grumbled, but he also felt a certain lightness, as usual with Leora when she was teasing, making him feel so different, so *real*.

Senna rushed in, her arms outstretched. Her hair was bound in the same kerchief. She wore the green smock of a laboratory worker, including skin-tight gloves, which she now pulled off and stuffed into her waistband.

"Good day!" she said, too brightly.

"Hello," Will responded.

"He knows, Senna," Leora said softly "He heard us talking. And he checked it out himself in the lab," she added with a hint of pride.

"Oh." The woman seemed to crumble, her shoulders sagging. She pulled the kerchief from her hair and shook her head, so that the lights caught various shades of gold and brown. She looked younger now, and vulnerable.

"I can leave right away," Will said. "There might be trouble, and I don't want you involved. I have to work this thing out for myself. There's no reason for me to stay."

"We want you to stay," Senna said, moving toward him with firm, determined steps. "You are not strong enough to travel. You're supposed to rest for two weeks, at least. Dr. Varton was very firm about that."

"I am feeling stronger," Will said.

"If you left suddenly," Senna argued, "it might seem that we were not taking proper care of you. It would put us in a very bad light." Her voice rose with anxiety. "We would seem unpatriotic, almost as if we were opposed to The Goodness."

"But what if people here find out about me?" Will argued. "'Do not condone a clone!'" he quoted.

Senna held up her hand, warding off arguments. "Please. You aren't in any danger here. Nobody knows, except for Leora, Antone, and me."

"What about that lab assistant?"

"Chip?" Senna glanced away. "He won't cause you any trouble."

"Why not? He ran to tell you right away, didn't he?" Will argued.

"He . . . died," Senna said reluctantly.

"He died?" Leora echoed incredulously.

"Well, we think he was killed."

"How?" Will demanded. "Who killed him?"

"We don't know," Senna said reluctantly. "Daran came to the lab this morning to tell me. They found Chip—what was left of him—in the refuse pit outside the silos."

"Who would do such a thing?" Leora gasped.

"I don't know," Senna said. "Daran didn't say. He's the chief enforcer here, and he doesn't give out information."

"Was there a witness? What happened?" Will's head throbbed.

"Somebody must have thought he knew too much. I don't know who, Leora," Senna said sharply. "I didn't kill him!"

"I never said you did!" Leora objected.

"I have to go to work. And I have to think." Senna's movements were vigorous as she knotted her kerchief tightly onto her head. "Go and look after your sister," Senna told Leora. "She is waiting for you under the jacaranda tree. Antone wore her out, taking her salvaging so early in the morning."

Salvaging? What did she mean? The woman was a puzzle, a conundrum. She obviously couldn't bear the sight of him, yet she asked him to stay. To save her own skin, probably. And that thing with the assistant. Who would have killed him? Why not Senna? Someone had to plan the murder and carry it out. And as Senna and Leora both admitted, nobody knew about the cloning thing except for the two of them and Antone. Was Antone the killer? Will's mind moved from the deed to the victim. Chip, only a name. He couldn't tie a face to the name, only the fact that his body was in a refuse pit, probably stinking and oozing.

Will had never seen a dead body. Nobody had ever been killed because of him. Now guilt gnawed at him. He wished he had never come here. He wished he had stayed in Washolina. But that wouldn't have altered the fact that he was a clone, that something was terribly wrong.

Fatigued, Will slept again, and when he awakened his first thoughts were of the report that he must file. Everything had to be done as usual and on schedule. From his pulse pad, Will checked his notes. For a long time he lay motionless, pondering. He recalled Berk's words, said with such certainty: "It is cost prohibitive."

Will spoke into his pulse pad, "Berk." A brief search, static, and then his brother's face appeared.

"Where are you?" Berk asked.

"Fresmofield. And you?"

"Back home. Washolina. Indian Dominion is getting new protocols for Security." Berk sounded so official, as if he were already in charge. "African Dominion is in a dismal state. No need to investigate further.

Father has put the quarantine in motion. I suggested we just firebomb the place and let it burn down. What have you been doing?"

"Nothing much," Will said carefully.

"Are you feeling better?"

"Yes. I've been thinking about the Compassionate Removal. I think it's a lie, brother. What do you say?"

Berk laughed heartily. "Welcome to reality," he said. "I thought you'd never get here!"

CHAPTER 12

OVER AND OVER AGAIN, Will replayed that scenario, the Abs walking onto the red carpet, into the rocket, blasting off, and Berk's words: "It is cost prohibitive."

Of course, it was impossible for the regime to transport and maintain these people forever. Supposedly they were kept on an asteroid, living in comfort. How preposterous! If those Abs were somehow healed, why wouldn't they simply be returned to their colonies? The very words *Compassionate Removal* actually meant euthanasia. How could he have been so blind?

Will recalled those moments just before the frothy green drink had lulled him into blissful passivity. He had never questioned Hayli or The Goodness.

Now Will fixed his total concentration on his report. He would tell Hayli what he wanted to hear. Hayli expected him to pinpoint the truth, and then to help promulgate the lie. That was the cornerstone of keeping power.

Will reviewed the notes he had taken at the site of the Compassionate Removal.

"How ennobling it is to see these wretched creatures, the trash heap of humanity, being transformed into joyful, hopeful people . . . instead of infirmity, they will know health . . . they will become useful members of society . . ."

He called Sileus, set the pad to audio, and watched Sileus closely as the report was given. *"The above is intended for dissemination to the masses by every possible means of communication—the Screen, the history* tape, the Vi-Ex. It is essential that the myth of the Compassionate Removal be maintained. Indeed, the common person feeds on myth. He requires it to sustain his energy and his passion. Only those of superior Status One can function fully without myths and imaginary support systems."

Sileus's onyx-black eyes seemed to flicker with a new intensity.

"To the Director: I found the Compassionate Removal to be efficient and thorough, accomplished without incident, the participants willing, witnesses cooperative and supportive. Recommendation: Continue program of persuasion, rewards, and follow-up propaganda."

Will paused. "Comments?" he asked.

"Brilliant," said Sileus.

"In conclusion, the Removal, as a program of euthanasia, is a brilliant solution to the problem of genetic pollution and costly rehabilitation. Furthermore, it is no doubt understood, at least on a subconscious level, that Removal means annihilation. To meet the psychological needs of family and friends, a benevolent fabrication is provided and happily accepted by everyone. Evaluation and Recommendation: The Compassionate Removal is an innovative program achieved with little cost and great benefit to The Goodness. It should be maintained and expanded."

"Go now," Will ordered. "I want to rest."

Sileus stepped out, walking backward, projecting a look of awe tinged with fear.

When the medic brought Will another meal in a black-and-yellow carton, he pretended to be asleep. The thought of food, whether synthetic or grown, left him nauseous.

He slept intermittently, awakening to flashing images of wild beasts, old memories that he had thought were forever gone. He imagined himself a small boy again, screaming, and Mara coming to his bedside, holding him in her arms and singing her song:

"See no evil,
Have no fear.
I am with you,
Always near.

Like a shepherd in the wale,
I will keep you, never fail.
Lead us to the better way,
At evening now we play."

Will sat up, startled. His bed felt as if it was on fire; he was drenched with sweat. How many more Abs would march trustingly to their death because of his recommendation? No, no, he was not responsible. Hayli had already decided to expand the program. He recalled his private meeting with Hayli right after the anniversary pageant, just four days ago. It seemed impossible that his entire world had changed since then.

Will had felt a jolt of surprise when Hayli led him away. With PAARs and human security surrounding them, they walked beyond the amphitheater to a long, narrow compound of cool, sleek steel. Doors opened at Hayli's touch. Crystal fixtures lit the walls, like inner suns. Will knew that the gleaming mirrors could be transformed with the flick of a finger, for Hayli always surrounded himself with transforming images.

"Sit down, Will," Hayli had said. He motioned for the several PAARs to flatten themselves out of sight. Rondo, Hayli's primary security guard, stood at the window, arms folded over his chest, his expression as impassive as a piece of furniture. "Don't worry about him," Hayli said in a pleasant tone. "He hears nothing."

"You mean, he does not repeat what he hears?"

"I mean, he does not *hear*. And he is not permitted to look at us while we are conferring, so he cannot read our lips."

The air of secrecy brought a delectable shiver across Will's back, while he wondered over and over again, why me? Why not Berk, too? Why has he chosen me?

A robo-servant brought a tray laden with circular finger sandwiches, tiny nutri-cones, and a basket of SNABS. Hayli indicated the stack of crystal plates. "Help yourself, son," he said.

Son. The word glowed inside him, and Will dutifully took several of the sandwiches and a handful of the synthetic-nut-and-berry-snacks, the

SNABS that were so popular at the Academy. How did Hayli know his favorite foods? Will had asked him.

"It is my business," said Hayli, "to know everything about you. I know, for instance, that you are diligent in your studies, more so than your brother, Berk. I know that you spend less time idling and indulging in pleasures like the Symsex and the Dance Dome. I see that you try to perfect yourself, spending time alone in rehearsal, never simply shooting off your ideas without first analyzing and practicing."

"Not always, Sir. I'm afraid that I am, at times, impulsive."

Hayli stretched out his legs, half reclining on the soft couch. His image was reflected back a hundred times in the maze of mirrors that surrounded them. "Impulse can be a good thing," he said with a smile. "Swift action, immediate decisions are often the best, before enthusiasm is drained away. Isn't it so?"

"Yes, Sir!" Will surged forward, grasping the small plate in his hands. "That is so true. My best speeches seem just to flow out, and if I go with the impulse—"

"You have to rely on your instincts," the Compassionate Director told him. "But first, do your homework. That is where Berk often fails. Never undermine yourself, do you hear? Never admit to weakness, not for a moment. A leader must always radiate strength! You do not make mistakes. Do you understand what I mean?"

"Yes, Sir, yes," said Will. These moments were precious. He set down his plate, having eaten only two of the sandwiches, reluctant to dilute this opportunity with such a base act as eating.

But Hayli picked up the plate and handed it back. "Eat. Do you eat everything?"

"Yes."

"Nothing makes you ill?"

"No, Sir."

"Eat, my son."

Nourishment, more than from food, came from his father's gaze, and from his father's gesture of love. And Will ate, as much to please Hayli, to obey his every wish, as to satisfy himself.

"You realize, of course," Hayli said calmly, "that most people want to be led. The masses have neither the stamina nor the inclination to work for the common good. They think only of themselves and their next activity. The more you study the writing of J. Thomas Mattelin," Hayli said, "the better you will appreciate his brilliance. He says, 'Tell the people what you want them to believe. Tell it often enough, emphatically enough, and they will believe it! Give the masses some pleasure, don't tax them with too much truth. They cherish their comfort!' Are you willing to give them that comfort, Will?"

"More than anything," Will said, "I want to follow in your footsteps, Father." The word *father* leapt out, and Hayli did not chide him. Alone, they were father and son, more so now than ever before.

"Fortunately," said Hayli, "some of us have the vision and the energy to see the world not as it is, but as it can be. We, who are born to lead, have to keep the masses motivated. We have to know how to use both the stick and the carrot. It begins at the highest levels and must filter down to every district, state, section, and colony. Every moment of every day must bring a reminder that the individual is part of the whole, of a plan, The Goodness."

Will nodded, mesmerized by Hayli's words, his penetrating gaze.

"Do you see yourself as a compassionate person?" Hayli asked.

"I try to emulate you, Sir."

"Compassion is a strength," declared Hayli, "but only when tempered with resolve. Compassion for its own sake, without an ultimate plan, is sheer waste of energy. Do you understand me?"

"Yes, Sir," Will said, but he was beginning to feel uncomfortable.

"We need to accelerate our programs. I will order stepped-up quarantines of districts and dominions that hinder our progress. We'll expand our Compassionate Removals. Above all, Will, we must be practical. Your brother, Berk, understands this. No regime can function without money. Every policy must be judged in terms of cost. Money is power. Don't worry about having friends. With money you can buy loyalty. A leader doesn't need friends. He needs followers." Hayli stood back and coldly surveyed him. "Your brother," he said, "has more followers than you."

Will leapt to his feet, aroused. "I have enough!" he protested vehemently. "It's better to have a few faithful followers than to have hundreds, any of whom might betray you. I don't need masses of followers. The masses are like an animal that obeys instincts. They can, just as swiftly, turn to deceit."

His outburst stunned him. Never had he burst forth in that rebellious manner, and for a moment he was terrified. Then Will saw Hayli's radiant smile of approval, the smile repeated a hundred times in the mirrored walls. "Splendid! Now, I want you to go out and work on those reports. Find people you can trust. That girl could be a good supporter for you. She has the street smarts and the lower-status sensibility that you lack. Use her."

"Leora?"

"Leora. Because she is Status Two, she will do anything to retain your favor. That is a valuable commodity. She will overlook any weaknesses of yours. She will stand up for you to any opponents. And she will be your eyes and ears. A leader can't be everywhere at once. *Use her.*"

Leader. The word made him giddy. Was he being singled out? Or would Berk later be called into this place?

"Don't underestimate yourself, Will," his father said. "Don't let anyone surpass you."

Will's heart seemed to plunge. "Even Berk?" he asked.

"Especially Berk."

The Compassionate Director stood up. A robo-servant appeared with a decanter. It filled two goblets with a golden, fizzing liquid.

"Will," Hayli said, "it is your destiny to rule. Accept this destiny! Fight for it!" Hayli raised his glass. "To The Goodness!" he said. "Think of it, Will! In a few years' time, we will have cleansed our Dominion of all pollution. We will create a new, wholesome, and genetically fit population. Soon," Hayli said, his eyes shining, "we will have the ability to prolong life far beyond our furthest expectation, even to immortality. There is no reason humans have to die."

"That is Hayli's Creed," Will said softly. "I have memorized all of it. I repeat it every night, before I sleep."

"And so you should. Ours will be a Dominion like no other, a Dominion of sheer Goodness. It will last—"

"Forever," Will breathed.

"At least for a thousand years," said his father with a laugh. "That ought to be enough for us."

"A thousand years!" Will agreed.

Hayli held the goblet to his lips.

Looking back, Will realized that Hayli had set the goblet down again, full. Indeed, he had never seen his father eat or drink anything.

He had felt his father's hands on his shoulders. "Are you ready to change the world, my son?"

Will had nodded. "Yes."

And then the Compassionate Director put his hands on Will's head and pressed his lips to Will's forehead.

Now Will lay staring at the ceiling, watching the flickering shadows. He felt a hollow, dead ache in the center of his body. Since last night, since his visit to the laboratory, everything had changed. His mind had sharpened. He recognized that if one thing is false, then everything stemming from that premise must also be false. He was not Hayli's son. He was not destined for greatness. He was, in fact, doomed. It would take all his skill simply to survive.

Once again, from outside, he heard the singing. "I will give you honey . . ."

Painfully, Will rose from his bed and went to the window. He saw a large, tall tree, its branches outspread and filled with lavender blossoms. Beneath the tree sat Leora with the girl. She was perhaps eight or nine, with dark hair woven into a braid, and large eyes. And as she sang the expression on her face was peaceful and sweet.

Will opened the window and leaned out. The smells of greenery embraced him. "Hullo!" he called.

Leora, seeing him, leapt up, smiling and waving. "Can you come outside?" she called.

"I don't have any shoes," he called back.

"Come out anyway," Leora called, her tone lilting and teasing. "You don't need shoes. You can feel the earth under your feet—if you dare!"

Will hesitated, looking out over the field. It probably harbored nasty, stinging things. It would be hot out there, maybe stifling, the air impure. Hadn't he learned that the only pure place in the Dominion was Washolina? Washolina was the model for the future, for perfection.

Lies beget lies, he thought darkly. Will pulled on his robe and moved out into the hall. Sileus was gone, probably to some investigation of his own. Will walked slowly, painstakingly, to the door that led outside. Braced in the doorway, he stood for a moment gazing at the tree with the purple blossoms. He inhaled deeply of the freshness. Then he stepped outside. Leora ran up the path to meet him, her hands outstretched, calling, "Welcome to the world of the living! Welcome back."

Will smiled slightly, warily. Surely it was a different world than it was yesterday.

CHAPTER 13

EVERYTHING WAS STRANGE, the ground under his bare feet, bits of leaf and bark scraping at his skin, and the lavender petals with their faint fragrance sprinkled all about. His PAAR, alerted by his movement, clattered along behind him.

"What kind of a tree is that?" Will asked, as Leora came up beside him. He stepped carefully. Every pebble and depression surprised him. He was accustomed to flat, uniform surfaces of a single texture.

"Jacaranda," she said.

"Jacaranda," he repeated. He felt weak, out of breath. Leora stepped nearer.

"Are you all right? Hold on to my arm," she said.

He gave her a sidelong glance. "No, thank you," he said. "I can walk on my own."

She shrugged. "I guess if you fall down," she said tartly, "your PAAR will pick you up."

"He's not designed to do that," Will retorted. Maybe, he thought, he should not have come out here. He felt an edge of antagonism, heightened as they approached the girl, who stopped signing abruptly and gave him a strange stare. "This is my sister," Leora said. "Stand up and say hello, Kiera!"

"Hello," Will said.

The girl remained silent, staring up at him with a blank expression. She pushed her index finger up into her nose. Roughly, Leora pulled her hand away, repeating loudly, "Stand up, Kiera."

The girl remained silent, sullen.

"What's that on her wrist?" Will pointed to a blackish bracelet, a series of carved loops.

"Probably something she and Antone found," Leora said. "He takes her out to look for salvage. They go all the time."

"Does she sing all the time, too?" Will asked rather sharply. "That bizarre song about honey?"

"It's not bizarre," Leora retorted. "It's an old song."

"I've never heard it. What does it mean?"

"I'm sure I don't know."

The girl got up slowly, reluctantly, and stood with her hands clasped in front of her, still looking down.

"What's the matter with her?" Will said. "Is she afraid of me?"

"Nothing's the matter!" Leora exclaimed. "Why should she be afraid? She's just shy. A little girl should be shy with strangers. You never know—"

"All right!" Will reached out and touched the tree trunk, smelling the bark, feeling the rough surface. There was something powerful and alive in it. He imagined putting his arms around the trunk, pressing his body tight against it, but he put away the notion. It would seem odd. And he needed to appear confident, strong.

Leora stood beside him. Her arm grazed his. He wanted to look into her eyes, but he could not bring himself to turn. Everything was strange, the feeling of being nobody left him bereft but also free. If he was not the son of the Compassionate Director, then his life belonged to nobody but himself; he had choices. But that meant he would have to make his own decisions. So far every detail of his life had been planned, from the first blue drink in the morning, to the final reading of Mattelin and the whispered Creed that put him to sleep.

"Do you want to see the forest?" Leora asked.

He pulled in a deep breath of air. It felt good, almost exhilarating. "Why not?" he said, realizing that he was beginning to adopt Leora's way of answering a question with a question. It made him smile.

"I haven't seen you smile before," Leora exclaimed.

"That's not true," he argued, frowning.

She laughed. "It is too. Don't smile. I dare you not to smile!"

"I won't," he said, pulling his lips tight. It seemed wrong to tease, to play, to pretend that life was normal. He was a clone! He was condemned. And yet, he was here outdoors, walking, talking, even smiling. It was incredible.

"Are you all right?" Leora asked. "Can you walk?"

"Yes." Will bent down and picked up a stout walking stick. With it he felt stronger.

Behind them lay the vast, multitiered compound that was the center of the colony, modern and sleek, similar to the structures in Washolina. But out here, some ancient force seemed to be returning, reclaiming its position, allowing green things to start up and grow, and birds to fly about, insects to buzz and whisper with their wings. They walked past the houses and the silos, past rows of crops where workers stooped, placing, gathering, moving in slow, steady rhythms.

"What are they doing?" Will asked.

"Planting," Leora said. "Reclaiming the soil. It is not forbidden," she added hastily.

"It is a waste of energy. We can get wholesome food from the yellow trucks, with no waste, no effort." He had learned it early on, *Synthetic is better, more wholesome, less waste.* He liked the food from the silos and the canteens, the neat yellow-and-black packages, and it was infinitely healthier than the foods people used to eat—or was that, too, a lie?

Leora remained silent. Kiera sang softly to herself. Will looked out over the field, to the larger trees with thick trunks and all manner of pods and seeds and dry leaves dropping down onto the ground. "I thought all the trees were gone," Will said.

"Many disappeared altogether," Leora told him. "Some were stunted, or they lay dormant. They have come back now because of the work of the Tree People."

Will stopped to rest for a moment, leaning on the stick. Leona said, "They found seeds under rocks and in crevasses. There is a certain tree beetle that burrows into the soil and purifies it. Reese and some other people bred those beetles. Now they are reclaiming the soil. The bees have come back, too, because of the flowers."

"In Washolina," Will said, "we have our own synthetic ecosystem. It is much more efficient."

"Do you have roses?"

"Of course not—those things with thorns! I've seen some in the Vi-Exes."

He told her about the visit from the schoolchildren. "The teacher invited me to a Release. What is that?"

Leora looked at him in astonishment. "It's a ceremony at the end of school, when people are fifteen. They start their work life, and they are given their allotment of food and pleasure stamps. The Released get all excited and wild, you know, rushing to use up their pleasure stamps."

"I see. Did you have a Release?"

"No! I was sent to the Academy instead. Those Released are going into their permanent occupations. Mine isn't decided yet."

"I see. How are the occupations decided?"

"You really don't know?" She shook her head. "It is all according to tests. And I suppose according to what is needed."

"What if someone doesn't like their assignment?"

"I only heard of one person who ever objected," Leora said. She glanced around fearfully. "Enforcers came. She's gone now."

"Where?"

Leora shrugged. "It happens. How come you don't know?"

"I know enough!" Will exclaimed. "A leader doesn't have to know everything." He was aggravated that once again Leora challenged him. How dare she?

"Yes, he does! He should!" She took a deep breath, then she said, "Do you believe in accidents?"

"Of course. I just had an accident, a burst appendix."

"Maybe things happen for a reason. Reese says there is no such thing as coincidence. He says there is a larger plan in the world."

"Who is Reese?"

"He's a cousin of ours. Of Antone's."

"He sounds *dissy*," Will said.

Leora stiffened. "Look, just because you haven't heard about something before doesn't mean it's *dissy.*"

"Oh, don't think I haven't heard about those ideas, and they are *dissy,*" Will said. "All that talk about plans and higher forces. This Reese sounds like one of those mystics, sowing confusion, fomenting discontent."

"You're making a whole damn speech!" Leora cried.

"That's what I do!" Will retorted. "Soon I'll be Minister of Information!"

"And what do you tell the people?"

"The truth. What they need to know." He stopped. "Look, let's not fight. Do you know Hayli's Creed?"

"Yes, of course."

"It states very clearly," Will said, "there is no omnipotent force. That is a myth designed to keep people subservient."

"How do you know?" Leora asked.

"Just as I know I am alive," Will said. "Just as know anything, the history of The Goodness, the Collapse, everyday reality . . ."

"Which now," she said pointedly, "has suddenly changed for you. Hasn't it?" She stepped carefully around a thick root.

"I don't want to talk about it!" Will shouted. She had a way of stabbing him with her comments. He looked skyward, seeking refuge. Several butterflies twirled round and round. Inadvertently, he ducked.

"You've never seen a butterfly?"

"Of course I have! In the Vi-Ex and in games—"

"I mean, really. Games are just for fun," Leora said.

His legs felt weak. He leaned against a tree, suddenly weary. "Well, we used to play this game when I was small. It was terrible."

"A game about wild beasts?"

"Yes, how did you know?" He did not want to talk about it. But the memory was too strong, the words rushing out now. "It was a sort of maze game. We'd start off together, my brother and I and some other children. First one to the tower was the winner. There were obstacles, water and barbed wire, and then the animals were let loose upon us . . ."

"Real animals?"

"They seemed real at the time. I supposed they were virtual animals, images, but I was only four years old, and I didn't realize . . . I fell into a hole. It was dark and cold." He looked at Kiera. She was listening, her eyes wide, hands clasped beneath her chin. Will took a step and stumbled, nearly fell.

Leora stopped him, reaching out, quickly withdrawing her hand as the PAAR advanced toward them. "Back, PAAR!" Will commanded, and the thing retreated.

"What a cruel game," Leora exclaimed. "What have they done to you?" Her eyes suddenly filled with tears.

"Look, I don't want to pursue this," Will said brusquely. "I'm not feeling that well. Maybe we'd better go . . ." But Kiera took his hand, as if to comfort him. Her hand felt soft and very warm. The PAAR started toward the child. Will motioned it away.

"Tree!" Kiera cried. "Come! The nest." She pulled at him, and they walked together, her small hand in his. He could never remember having walked like this, connected to another person. When he and Berk were very young, they used to walk with their arms around each other's waist, trying match their steps exactly, but it never lasted more than a few moments because Berk would start to kick up his feet, stepping high, higher, until he pulled Will down.

Kiera slowed her steps, instinctively aware of his fatigue. Will murmured to Leora. "Why doesn't she go to school? She is surely older than five."

"She doesn't have to go," said Leora. "We teach her at home."

Will looked down at the child. Education was rigorously monitored, but he did not want to argue. With Kiera's hand in his, he felt protective, strong. She looked up at him, beaming, and he smiled back and tightened his grasp on her hand.

Kiera stopped near a tree and she pointed. "There! There!"

"What are we looking for?" Will asked Leora.

"Wait. You'll see." A small brown bird darted from a distant shrub to the tree.

With a scream, Will dropped to the ground, shielding his head with his arms.

"What is it? What's wrong?" Kiera and Leora crouched beside him.

Will grasped the stick. "The birds . . . peck out people's . . . eyes," he said, struggling to breathe.

"No!" Kiera cried.

"Listen!" Leora exclaimed, her hand on his back. "Look up. You can see the nest. Inside it were the little eggs." She stopped to listen. Will heard small peeping sounds. He saw the underside of the mother bird, her tail feathers straight out, body bobbing up and down. He still felt the pressure of Leora's hand on his back, though she had drawn it away.

"Bird," said Kiera.

"What's it doing?" he whispered. The three of them lay close together, looking up.

"Feeding the baby," said Leora. "It finds worms and softens them up and puts them into the baby's mouth."

Will sat up with his back against the tree, feeling his heartbeat settle down to normal. He tried to imagine it, the bird feeding its young, mouth to mouth. He glanced at Leora, saw her parted lips, full and soft, pink and moist. His own throat felt parched.

He watched as the bird flew away. Nothing had happened, no harm had come to him. He grasped the stick and, with difficulty, stood up.

With a slight gasp, Kiera leapt up and darted away, her feet making small, rustling sounds amid the leaves. She ran to a hollowed-out log, peering into it.

"What's she doing?"

"Some feral cats live here," Leora said. Her voice was low, and she did not look at him. "Nobody can get near them. But Kiera has her ways. They trust her. Look!"

Keira sat down on the log. In her arms was a large gray cat with a very round head and sharp, piercing yellow eyes. The creature lay against Kiera's shoulder, claws resting on the child's back.

Will recoiled. "How can you let her do that?"

"She's fine," Leora whispered. "She loves animals, and they love her. There are kittens, too. One of them is white. Come. I'll show you."

"No!"

"What is it, Will? You look so pale."

"I'm going back. I need to lie down." He was feeling weak, his legs buckling under him as he walked. He leaned on the walking stick, also using it to whisk away flies and insects, too proud to indicate his weakness.

As they approached the clinic, a man stood there, all but blocking the door. He had a long, melancholy face, accentuated by a pair of old-fashioned spectacles with dark green rims. He wore the yellow-and-white-striped shirt of a silo employee, with the foreman's black cap.

"Antone!" Kiera screamed as she ran toward him.

The man stood straight in front of Will, gave him a long, appraising look, and spoke to Leora, his eyes still fixed upon Will. "Where have you been?"

"Just showing Will around," Leora said defensively. "He wanted to see the colony. He has to send reports," she added.

"Well, Senna needs you. She wants you to help her."

"With what? Senna isn't even home yet. It's only five."

"Don't argue with me, Leora!" he said sharply. To Will he said stiffly, "I'm Antone. Responsible for the wheat and grain section. You want to see the colony? Come to my silo. I'll show you around."

"Thank you," Will said. "I'd like to see it." He felt awkward beside this man with the sad, long face and the pouches under his eyes. He felt as if his status were stenciled on his forehead. And indeed, Will noticed that the top of his tunic was open, and that his implant with the gold stud was prominently displayed.

"Well, I hear you will be leaving us soon," said Antone in his dour voice. "Back to Washolina, is it?"

"We have to wait," Leora said, "until Will is stronger."

"We'll see," murmured Antone, still staring at Will, whose discomfort held him paralyzed, then prodded him to anger. And yet, at the edge of reason he understood the man's concern at having his girls escorted by a clone.

"I need to rest now," Will said, glad to be the one who ended the interview, retaining some small sense of control.

Later that evening Berk padded him, and Will felt inordinately glad to see his brother's image. "Berk! How are you?"

"Everything's fine," Berk said. "Lost my pulse pad for a while, couldn't call you."

"How can you have lost it? Isn't it always on your wrist?"

"I don't know. Why are you so critical?" Berk said, sounding irritable.

"I'm not critical. You sound strange. Are you all right?"

"I'm fine!" Berk shouted. "Think I need lenses, though. Sometimes the Screen seems to wobble."

"I've had that sensation, too," Will realized. "Not often, though."

"What's it like out there in the west?" Berk asked.

Will took a deep breath. He wanted to tell his brother about the purple jacaranda and the open sky, the way the ground felt under his feet, and the smells of vegetation. But all at once he felt disloyal, sucked in by the common, the ordinary, when his entire life was geared for superiority. So he murmured something about "the masses," and said scornfully, "They actually eat food that they grow themselves. In the dirt."

"Well, be careful of contamination," Berk said. "I make Cullah taste everything before I eat. In our position, we have to suspect everything and everyone."

"I haven't eaten any of their food," Will said defensively.

"I didn't say you had," Berk argued. "I wouldn't trust that girl, if I were you."

"I don't," Will said, too readily. Berk's image faded, and Will was left to wonder what was true. If he trusted Leora, did that mean everything she said was right, and everything he had been taught was wrong? True, Hayli had lied to him. But one had also to see the bigger picture. Hayli had brought order. His methods might have been harsh, but then, the masses could only be controlled with strict rules and firm measures. This he knew in every fiber of his being.

That night Will had the first of a series of strange and wonderful dreams. He was standing on a platform. He was speaking to a crowd. A thousand people cheered and screamed out his name, "Hail, Will!"

He woke up full of energy and purpose. Perhaps this was a premonition. Perhaps he was truly ready to replace Hayli.

CHAPTER 14

ON HIS PULSE PAD Will received word from the information minister: "Report received." Hayli commented, "Excellent! Insightful! Continue."

When Leora came to see him the next morning, Will was dressed, standing by the window. "I want to see the main departments," he told her. "I need to continue sending in reports. Hayli expects it."

"Are you well enough?" she protested. "And do you think it is safe?"

"Safe? I am still known as the son of the C.D.," he said. "Besides, I'll have my PAAR with me."

"It's too far for you to walk," Leora said. "Wait here while I get the Photoval."

Will stood outside. The clinic was a long, low building joined to innumerable others. Contained within the sprawling complex were the schools, the local ministries, the silos, and other production companies necessary to sustain the people. It was obvious that the complex had grown sporadically, without much concern for aesthetics. The building materials were inferior, the design awkward.

Will recalled the pristine Academy, with its controlled climate and atmosphere, its sleek interior streets and gleaming walls. Somehow, he missed the constant bustle and the stimulation, the comforts and information provided by the Screen.

He felt awkward standing here, a stranger. A clone. Maybe Hayli meant to tell him. Soon. Maybe there was a good explanation. Maybe he was allowing his worst fears to lead him to false conclusions. He must find a way to speak to Hayli and get at the truth.

Will heard the strange wheezing sound of a horn. Leora sat behind the wheel of a small, squat Photoval. Will had heard of the old solar-battery powered vehicles, but he had never seen one outside a museum.

"Do you mind if Kiera comes along?" Leora asked.

"Of course not," Will said, though he felt a stab of annoyance. Kiera was already seated in back of the Photoval. She gave him a smile; he felt disarmed. *Trust nobody!* The admonition rang in his mind—did that include children?

Will motioned for the PAAR to get into the back seat. Kiera laughed slightly and patted its metal front. Will climbed into the front seat, holding on as the Photoval began to move, skimming just inches above the ground. No friction, he observed, no fumes. "Maybe," he said reluctantly, "some of the old things weren't so bad."

"This is an antique. Senna and Antone were lucky to get it."

Kiera began to sing. Today the sound of it was irritating. "Why isn't she in school?" Will asked. "I don't see any other children running loose."

"She's been . . . sick. Right now she's recovering. She'll go back in a few weeks."

"What about you?" he persisted. "Don't you have friends?"

"Not many," Leora said with an abrupt turn of the wheel. "Do you?"

"Enough."

They rode through a gate into a holding area. Several uniformed officials stood guard. As they approached the electronic beam, Leora opened her tunic at the throat. Her implant was plain, without studs or gems. Will did likewise. Leora started the Photoval. The barrier remained in place. The guard strode toward their vehicle. "The child," he said. "Where is her I.D.?"

"She is under age," Leora said. "She doesn't have to show it."

"How old is she?"

"Seven."

"We need to see the implant."

Leora's breath came in swift bursts. She glanced at Will, her eyes pleading.

"I don't believe you checked my I.D. thoroughly," Will said commandingly. He pulled open his tunic at the throat, showing the full splendor of his implant, complete with the bright golden stud and its diamond in the center. "My number is 0103. And this child does not have to show her implant. It is the law!"

The man's eyes widened. He took a step back. "I . . . I don't know . . . we weren't told . . . I'm sorry, but I have my orders. We will have to detain this vehicle." The man stepped to the side of the Photoval, reaching for Will's arm.

Instantly the PAAR swung one leg over the side of the Photoval. The man backed away. "What . . . what's that thing? I've heard about them, but I never—"

"I will issue a report as soon as I return to Washolina," Will said coldly. "You are either *dissy* or blind, that you do not recognize the son of the Compassionate Director!"

The man paled and leapt aside, pressing the lever to override the electronic eye. Instantly the barrier retracted. "Sorry, forgive me, Your Excellent Grace, I didn't know you were in the area . . ." The man continued to babble as the Photoval sped past.

Leora gave a deep sigh. "Thank you," she said. And then, "It must be gratifying to have rank."

"What was all that about?" Will asked rather sharply.

"I'm sorry," Leora said. "I'm grateful to you," she added. "Kiera doesn't like to show her implant."

"Why not? What's wrong with her?"

"Nothing!" Leora snapped. "I told you, she's shy."

"She has to learn about authority!" Will exclaimed. "You spoil her."

Kiera rocked back and forth, singing in a barely audible voice: "I will give you honey. Honey, honey, honey from the rock."

"Why is she always singing about honey?" Will asked irritably.

"Stop it, Kiera," Leora commanded.

Kiera fell silent.

They drove through the long winding corridors of the compound. Signs advertised the Dance Dome, the Vi-Ex, and the Serotonin Bar. "I have to get back to Washolina," he said with sudden urgency.

"You miss it," Leora remarked. Her tone was strained.

"Yes. In a way." Here were the bustle and the brightness he was used to. Maybe The Goodness wasn't perfect, but it fulfilled people's needs. He saw the familiar green and silver hologram, with its promise of pleasure. A stream of light-words advertised: WELCOME TO THE SYMSEX; ONLY SIX PLEASURE STAMPS. People entered in a steady procession, emerging contented, smiling.

"Do you come here often?" Will asked. His heart pounded strangely as he waited for her answer.

"We don't usually have extra stamps," Leora said. "Besides, I'm not that fond of the Symsex."

Will's heart leapt. "Why not?"

Leora shrugged. "I don't know. It feels . . . odd."

"But before the Symsex," he said, "people used to be promiscuous." He said the last word softly; it sounded obscene.

"I've read the releases, Will," Leora said dryly.

Will's face felt flushed, as if he had been racing. "I saw you at the Academy, just leaving. You and that girl. I heard you talking."

"Do *you* like it?" Leora asked.

"Yes," he said stubbornly. "It's wonderful."

"Then you must go often."

"As often as possible," he said grandly. "It's the first thing I'll do when I get back home!"

"Why not go here, then?" she asked.

"Why do you keep bothering me?" he shouted. He stopped, as Leora's hand swiftly flicked across her eyes. Was she crying? He felt abashed, alarmed. "What's wrong?"

"Nothing," she said. "Some dust in my eyes."

He sighed. "I'm sorry. I get these—I'm sorry."

"Moods," she said. "Well, you've been sick. It must be terrible for you, not knowing . . . I mean . . . And then, you've had bad news."

"You might say so," he said, smiling slightly at the understatement.

"Awful news," she amended. "Look, I'm sorry, too. I shouldn't have brought Kiera without asking you."

"No, no, it's your Photoval, after all. Besides, she's no trouble. I like Kiera," he said, turning to look at her. She smiled and waved, as if she had not seen him in a while. He waved back, feeling guilty. "Actually," he said in a low voice, "I lied. I'm not all that thrilled with the Sym." He avoided looking at her. It was an awkward moment, relieved by their arrival at the entrance to the silo, where a series of upper and lower motion paths converged. Leora parked the Photoval in a narrow slot and stepped out.

Several passersby stopped to stare at the conveyance. A man noticed Will, pointed, rushed up, and waited as they got out.

"Son of the Compassionate Director!" he enthused. "I recognized you at once! Welcome to our colony. We heard you were here in Fresmofield. What an honor! Perhaps you will visit the silos? Our team won the top production contest for the last two years in the row." The man pointed to his companion. "My coworker, here, received eight pleasure stamps for first place!"

"Congratulations," said Will. "We must all keep working tirelessly and continually for The Goodness." The slogans sprang so easily to his lips! Confusion held him, as in a trap, the arguments raging in his mind—*Lies beget lies. Or maybe some lies are necessary.*

"If you would put in a good word," gushed the man, "we would be most grateful. We always keep the plant moving at top efficiency, never ceasing, never ceasing at all."

"I will try to visit your plant," said Will. "We are proud of you. The Supreme Compassionate Director is proud of you."

The men watched and waved as Will took his leave. He saw their amazement and heard their murmuring. It was an event in their lives, actually seeing, in person, the son of the Compassionate Director! They would rush to tell their friends, marking the occasion with still more stories and embellishments. Will knew how people reacted to Hayli. This time, it was for him. *If they only knew*, he thought. Would they want to kill him as a clone?

He had to steady himself as they went onto the conveyor belt, grabbing the railing.

"Are you all right?" Leora asked.

"A little dizzy," Will admitted. "I suppose it was the surgery."

"Probably," she agreed.

"Does Antone know we're coming?" he asked.

"I told him," she said.

"I don't think he likes me much," Will said.

Leora pushed back her hair. "He's just nervous," she said.

They passed the yellow building, where food and pleasure stamps were dispensed. Reassuringly, a line of yellow trucks moved to and from the huge loading zone, delivering the same synthetic foods out here as in Washolina. Of course, here people had to pay with food stamps, but at least there was food enough for everyone. Before The Goodness, hunger and even starvation were widespread.

"Everything seems calm and orderly," Will remarked. He'd seen news tapes of dissidents breaking into customs houses to steal stamps and sell them on the black market. He made a note in his pulse pad. *All's in order.*

Leora said, "This is the silo where Antone works." Leora laid her hand flat against the impression. A beam scanned her implant.

"Others," intoned a gravely voice.

"Child of worker 5709. And guest. Number 0103."

The heavy shield was raised up, exposing an immense factory. They stepped inside, the PAAR following, as usual. Will was overcome with the sounds and smells, the humming, grinding, buzzing tone that resounded throughout the enormous plant. Odors of chemicals converged, bringing a sour taste to his mouth.

"Are you all right?" Leora asked. She held Kiera tightly by the hand.

Will nodded.

Antone approached, his long strides and worried look reflecting the concerns of a busy man forced to take time out to placate a visiting celebrity. Yet today he greeted Will with a smile and an outstretched hand. "Welcome to Nuts and Grains," he said. "Here we manufacture seventeen different products. Nutri-cones and SNABS are our most popular."

"SNABS are my favorite," Will said. Antone's eyes, through the large lenses, looked small and round and worried. *He wishes I were dead*, Will thought, while aloud he said in a bureaucratic manner, "I suppose these are the processors. And what is that, on the electrical board?" Will eyed the flashing words and numbers, stroking his upper lip as Hayli did. This visit, Antone's responses were a clear symbol of how the two of them stood in the scheme of things. Will pressed his advantage, as recognized son of the C.D. He stood with his head cocked, his posture oozing superiority.

"These are current recipes for each product," replied Anton.

"Aren't the recipes constant?" Will asked. "My SNABS never seem to change."

"The taste is always the same," said Antone. "The supplements are tasteless."

"So, the recipes are for the desired supplements?"

"Exactly. Sent along from the Fourth Pillar, Nutrition/Sanitation Center."

They walked over to a series of gleaming aluminum canisters that reached from floor to ceiling.

"These vats," Antone explained, "contain the synthetic fibers and proteins that make up the fruits and nuts variety. After they are mixed and processed, just before they are crisped, we add the stimulants or depressants in the proportion shown here. During times of national crisis, we also add tranquilizers and mood markers."

"I suppose the chemicals affect the color," Will said. He was feeling that odd disorientation again, as though he might fall. He leaned against one of the vats.

Antone said, "Uppers and antianxiety supplements are usually green."

"Of course," Will said, coughing slightly, concealing his ignorance and his growing apprehension. He had not known that the regime tampered with food production to this extent. It was one thing to introduce vitamins, another to regulate the national mood.

"Who approves the finished product?" he asked. The momentary lapse had passed. He took a deep, grateful breath.

"Supervisors check the mix twice a day. We're right on target here," Antone boasted. "We've never had a punitive closure, like some of the silos in the northern section. On the whole, our workers are diligent. They rarely lose their stamp allotment. In fact, most months we earn bonus stamps. That's how I was able to get the Photoval." He smiled for the first time and reached for Kiera's hand.

All this time Leora stood silently by, looking from Will to Antone as if she might discern a subtext to their conversation.

A sharp tone sounded, a blast, a summons: "Zabarre, Zabarre, come to Silo Eighteen."

A stocky, dark-haired man hurried into a small cart and sped down the moving corridor. Seeing Antone, he slowed down and called, "Don't worry, boss! It's that same regulator—I'll fix it up in a minute!"

"That's Zabarre," Antone said. "Our top mechanic. This is Will," he called, "son of the Compassionate Director!"

The man got out, rushed over, and gave Will a congratulatory sign, both arms raised. "Welcome! Welcome!" he called. "We're honored to have you visit our plant. Hail, Hayli!"

"Hail, Hayli," Will said, and Antone and Leora echoed the response.

"How are we doing here?" Zebarre gave a penetrating look at the production line of SNABS. "Perfect, perfect," he said with an expansive nod at Will, another wave, and a quick apology as once again came the urgent summons, "Zebarre! Zebarre!"

"A wonderful worker," Antone said. "Keeps everything moving." He snatched up one of the containers and gave it to Will. "A sample for you," he said. "Our special batch for workers and performers. It contains high-dose, time-release energy. You don't want to eat them late in the day; they'll keep you up all night."

Will took the box of SNABS and opened it. "Thanks. These might help get my strength back." The SNABS were shaped like small horns, crisp and flavorful.

Kiera held out both hands. "SNABS!" she said.

"Kiera, no!" Antone said sharply. "Too stimulating for youngsters," he told Will, as if he were confiding something important. "You will no doubt make a report," he added, "on the workings of our silo. Hopefully you found it in order."

Once again Will took advantage of his status. "I understand that you have a Screen. Leora said I might be able to use it."

"Of course! Anytime." Antone flashed Leora a reproachful look. She averted her eyes. Will pretended not to notice either of them.

"We should go and visit Senna," Leora said hastily. "She's in the next complex, Gestation Lab."

A wavering, pulsating sound coursed through the factory. Two squat robo-enforcers, painted regulation yellow, rushed past them and turned a corner. In a moment they returned, dragging a woman between them. "Please, what are you doing?" she screamed. "I've met my quota, I swear! What are you doing? Where are you taking me? The register is faulty. I have done my quota! Please, please listen."

The robo-enforcers rushed on through the doorway, until the woman's cries were shut out by the heavy metal doors.

"Does this happen often?" Will asked.

"Once in a while," replied Antone. He took off his glasses and rubbed them vigorously with the edge of his shirt, as if to erase the unpleasant scene.

"We should go," said Leora, "if you want to see the lab. You must be getting tired."

Workers gathered. They waved, calling out, "Son of the Compassionate Director! Thank you for coming!"

Will struggled against a surge of weakness. What could he say? "Go with The Goodness," he shouted out, drawing from his store of slogans. "Sublimate selfishness!"

Will turned to Leora. "I'm so tired. Please, let's go back."

"Just a quick stop at the lab," she urged. "I promised Senna." She exchanged a look with Antone, then said, "Kiera, you stay here. Antone will bring you back."

Outside, Leora swung the Photoval around to another set of corridors. Watching her, Will was impressed. "You have many accomplishments," he remarked.

"So do you," she said. "You are a marvelous orator."

His mind flashed on the dream, with thousands surrounding him, applauding him.

"Thank you," he said.

At the Gestation Lab, Leora showed her implant, then Will showed his. The door opened to a series of long narrow rooms set behind observation windows. Each laboratory contained glass cases from floor to ceiling, with a large round vat in the center.

Leora pointed. "There's Clorey, my mother's friend. She does from conception through the first six weeks."

A tall woman, her hair bound in a white cap, checked the petri dishes set under a thick magnifier. Computers monitored metabolism. Small round blobs of living tissue throbbed and pulsed. Clorey moved from one set of dishes to another, sorting, appraising. She looked up and waved briefly before returning to her duties.

Will approached. He could see, through the magnifier, bundles of tissue etched with faint veins. Some were slightly curled. A round appendage had formed at one end, the beginning of a head.

They moved on to the next lab, where Senna worked. She and a tall man bustled to and fro, checking glass incubators. Above each incubator, a screen showed the enlarged image of the fetus. Will peered through the window. One fetus, only the size of his index finger, was moving. An appendage that looked like an arm was clasped around its curved body. Will could see the indentation of an eye, sealed shut, as if the fetus were asleep. Small buds appeared to be the beginning of fingers on a miniature hand.

"How old are those?" he whispered, feeling embarrassed.

"These are six weeks to two months," said Senna from the other side of the glass. The assistant pointed to the fetus that Will had been watching. Senna pulled out the tray and with a swift motion she shook the fetus loose from the glass incubator into the vat. There was a churning noise. Senna dipped the empty tray in solution and returned it to its place on the wall. Immediately the assistant refilled it with another fetus, taken from a covered petri dish.

Will approached the glass. "Senna!" he called.

She came to stand opposite him, close to the window. "Yes?"

"What was wrong with that one?

"The donor wants a tall boy. This one would only be of medium height. We can project adult height at this point in development—amazing, isn't it?"

"Amazing," Will breathed. He turned to Leora. "I have seen enough," he said.

All the way back he sat silent with his eyes closed, feeling the air currents against his skin. Nothing made sense anymore. He was tormented with conflicting thoughts: *Some things are beyond your understanding. You must leave them to the experts, the leaders. Do not try to tread where you cannot stand. The Powers have their reasons.*

But the vision of that small, throbbing bit of life kept coming back all through the night, and Will felt shattered, as if he himself had destroyed it.

CHAPTER 15

WHEN SENNA SUGGESTED that Will move into the back room of the house, he realized it was not from pure kindness and not without debate. Leora's mood, her oblique comments and sudden silences spoke volumes. They didn't really want him, didn't trust him, thought it best to keep a sharp eye on him. He could imagine the arguments. "Who knows what he's doing out there in the clinic? Snooping, sending back reports, getting into documents. Better to have him here, where we can keep an eye on him. We'll tell him it's because he wanted to use the Screen. He can sleep in the back room. Besides—he is still called the son of the C.D. We have to show hospitality."

Will readily agreed. He hated the clinic, the constant intrusions from the medic and Sileus. Sileus would still sleep at the clinic. By day, Sileus would continue to visit the silos and the labs, to write down production techniques and results, which he sent back to the Ministry, using his pulse pad.

Will was settled into the back room, a small chamber that housed all the flotsam from Antone's nightly salvaging excursions. Shelves were packed with all the hardware of a lost civilization, relics whose importance had long since faded, along with trinkets that had, in the interim, become valuable. There were rusty pearls and copper coins, doorknobs, seashells, books gnawed and wormy, a length of red velvet cloth pitted with holes, glassware of all sorts—bottles large and small, stoppers, cups, mugs, vials. Rolled up and tossed into corners were miles of cable, recording tape, and parts of sundry appliances. The main feature was an old bathtub with claw feet and disconnected pipes hanging from its underside. Every morning when Will awakened from his troubled sleep on the narrow cot, he first saw that tub and had a flashing recollection of the Sani-tube in his pod in Washolina, where within twenty seconds one's entire body was cleansed and invigorated by wave action that left no residue, no mess.

In the entire colony of Fresmofield, Will had not seen a single Sani-tube. He was embarrassed to ask how people bathed. He used the Sani-tube at the clinic.

Leora's was a strange, archaic living arrangement, Will thought. They all slept in the same house; they ate together, and while they ate they talked. People came and went. They visited. They looked at Will and tried to make conversation. Nobody seemed to understand what he was really doing here. Their eyes expressed skepticism; was he here to spy on them?

Will tried his best to meet them, but he was not accustomed to small talk or to camaraderie. Senna made excuses for him. "He is still recuperating," or "He is out of his element, here, as you can understand."

Leora and Kiera were nearly always together. Seeing them, Will was seized with loneliness for his childhood, when he and Berk lived in the youth compound together. But maybe memories lied, because after the first flash of regret and longing, Will had to admit that he and Berk had never really been close. Berk's scathing sarcasm and perpetual suspiciousness pushed Will away. If ever Will weakened and expressed a strong feeling, a doubt, or a dream, Berk would snarl a quick reprimand. "What a *dissy* you are! Keep your mind on business and you'll go a lot further." And once Will had asked, "Do you want me to go far, then?"

"Yes, indeed. Far away, you idiot!"

Late in the afternoon, Leora came to remind him that he must walk. "You're supposed to get exercise every day, to strengthen your muscles."

"At home I go the bionics lab. The machines do the work."

"Here, people walk," she said with a smirk.

"Come with me, then," Will said.

"I intended to," she replied. "What about the PAAR?"

"It's staying here," Will said, closing the door firmly behind him. Somehow he needed to be free, even from his own robot.

They walked slowly, the path now familiar. No longer was Will troubled by the birds or the small, scurrying creatures. He was used to Kiera, to her song and the feel of her hand in his. She would skip alongside him, then run ahead, only to return and take his hand again.

They came to the large tree where the nest still straddled the branches, and Kiera ran to look for the cats. Will lay back, looking up into dappled leaves, with Leora sitting beside him. He breathed deeply, contentedly. Leora smiled down at him. "Why did you ever want to leave Fresmofield?" he asked.

Leora sighed. "It is seemed that I had the capability," she said. "I was singled out."

"By your teachers?"

She nodded. "They told Senna and Antone that I was—well, very bright and could possibly rise to leadership, Status One. All I need now is to complete the year at the Academy, to take some tests and get recommendations from my proctors."

"From your proctors?"

"Yes. Every candidate reports to three proctors, who after a year meet and make the final decision."

"I see." He swallowed, hard. Mara had told him otherwise. Was it a lie, or just a mistake?

Leora continued. "It would be a great triumph for the whole colony for me to make Status One. We'd all get free food stamps."

"I know. But most Status Ones live in Washolina."

"Yes. I realized that I would have to leave them."

"And now you don't want to leave," he stated, watching her face, her eyes.

"Sometimes people have to make sacrifices," Leora said. "You of all people should know that."

"Sublimate selfishness," Will quoted.

"It would be selfish of me to stay here," Leora said, smiling slightly. "After all, if I can get to Status One, I can help change the world."

"Oh, is that all?" Will said lightly, all the while recalling Hayli's kiss and his words, "Do you want to change the world, son?"

Kiera ran over with the white kitten in her arms. "Sweet and soft," she crooned. She held the kitten out to Will.

He drew back, then stopped, seeing the hurt in Kiera's face. "Love kitty," she pleaded. "Love Will."

He reached out tentatively with his fingertips. He touched the soft, slender hairs on the kitten's head, traced the line of the little pointed ear. He began to breathe again, slowly touching the tip of the ear, moving his finger down to the soft fur on the kitten's face.

Beside him, Leora seemed to have stopped breathing, too, but Will felt her nearness, as if the warmth of the kitten were enveloping both of them.

"Love kitty," Kiera said in her singsong way. "Sweet and soft." She put the kitten into Will's arms, and he held it, gingerly at first, then he pressed it against his chest. The softness and warmth of the little creature astounded Will. He looked at the paw with its pink pads and perfect little nails, curved downward. He put out his finger, and the small paw clasped his, like the delicate tendrils of a vine. The kitten opened its mouth, and Will saw the pink tongue and felt its rough swipe against his hand.

He turned to Leora and covered her hand with his.

Antone said he was welcome to use the Screen, and Will did, delving into its information banks far into the night, for he found it difficult to sleep. The Screen frustrated him. It was small and slow and certainly outmoded. Still, Will persisted, using various source codes to search for his own origins. He reviewed the history of clones and cloning; stem cell research; robotics; combinations of machines and living tissue; transplants, organic and synthetic. It was interesting, but a dead end.

One evening, as he explored further, a banner across the bottom of the Screen caught his attention: *African quarantine begins; relocation of citizens in former Tanzania complete; land undergoing decontamination procedures. Compassionate Removal expanded to include anyone who is below grade by two years. Tests by Education Minister to ascertain performance ability . . .*

"Hello—do you want to walk?" Leora strode over to the Screen. In a moment she had seen the banner. Her face reddened, then grew deathly pale. She took several steps back, as if to deny what she had seen.

Will took her arm, holding her tightly in his grip. "Tell me about Kiera," he said. "What is wrong with her?"

"I told you, nothing!" She twisted away from him, her eyes blazing.

"Why isn't she in school? Leora, how can I help you if you don't trust me?" The words sounded hollow even to his own ears. Why should she trust him?

"How can I trust you?" she cried. "You don't even know who you are!" She stopped, aghast, and sank down on the cot. "I told you," she said. "Kiera has been ill."

Will clenched his teeth. "Leora, that's not good enough! I want to help her. There are doctors in Washolina, modern clinics where they might be able to cure her."

Leora put her hand to her hair, clenched it at her cheek. She was breathing heavily. "She's a bit slow, that's all. It's nothing that time won't cure. She is so sweet! She sings beautifully . . ."

"Her singing doesn't change the fact that she is *different*. Sileus has spoken to me about her! He knows. Everyone knows. How long do you think you can keep hiding her?"

"We're not hiding her!"

"Of course you are. She's not in school. She's probably not even registered. Does she have an implant? *Does she?*"

Leora broke away, shouting, "Stop it! Kiera is normal. She is not an Ab. She is just . . ."

"Retarded," Will said, hating the word, hating himself for saying it.

Leora's body seemed to crumple.

"Leora, listen! They are going to test people like Kiera. You saw the edict yourself. Then they will send her to Compassionate Removal. You know what that means." He wanted to show her his report about the Removal, but it seemed too cruel to spell it out. Besides, she knew. Deep down, she knew, for she began to weep.

"Kiera isn't like those others! Maybe she can't do puzzles or use computers, but she knows the words to a dozen songs, she remembers them all, and she sings like an angel!"

Will's head throbbed. What could he possibly do to keep Kiera safe? Nothing! Unless he himself were the Supreme Director, or could somehow get a dispensation from Hayli. But how?

"They can't take her!" Leora cried. "I won't let her go!" Tears spilled out, a torrent of grief.

Will went to her. He sat down beside her. Hesitantly, carefully, he laid his arm around her. Her closeness was electrifying. He drew his face down to her neck and felt the silk of her hair against his cheek. He inhaled the smell of her hair, her skin, a fragrance like no other. He dared not move, for he was terrified of the feelings and of the thought that she would push him away.

Tentatively he spoke. "Leora, you must have known this would happen." He thought of his report, his lying praise of the Removal. Had that influenced Hayli to announce the new edict? No! He forced the thought aside.

"How did this happen to Kiera?" he asked.

Leora wiped her face with her hands. She shook her head.

"Senna works in the Gestation Lab. She would have known from the beginning that things weren't right," Will said.

Leora looked up, her tearstained face accosting him. "You don't understand!" she said. "There was no petri dish. Kiera was not turned out in a lab. She was . . . she was born. *Born!*" With that she broke away and dashed out into the night.

Will followed, screaming to his PAAR to *stay.* He stumbled, stubbed his foot on a rock, nearly fell. He staggered on to the jacaranda tree. Leora sat on the ground beneath the shelter of branches. He sank down beside her.

"Go away," she said, muffled, unconvincing.

"I wish we could go away," Will said. "Someplace where there aren't any edicts or enforcers."

Leora nodded. "Me, too," she whispered, wiping her eyes, her cheeks. Hesitantly, tenderly, he reached for her hand. It would be enough, he thought, looking up into the starlit sky, just to sit like this all night.

"I don't know what my parents were thinking," Leora finally said, her voice low and halting. "Maybe they thought things would get better. We always imagined that if I got to Status One, I could protect Kiera somehow. I'd have power." She gave a harsh laugh. "I guess nobody really has power except for Hayli."

"I still have some power," he said staunchly. "I have to think. Maybe I can help."

Leora said, "They were probably planning, eventually, to send Kiera to Reese's place."

"Does Reese live beyond the reach of the enforcers?" Will asked, frowning.

"He has a small farm at an outpost. The enforcers don't usually go there. If they do . . ." she hesitated. "Reese and Nadia like to keep to themselves." Leora gave him a swift glance. "They are trying to restore balance."

"Balance," Will echoed. He could hardly think, with Leora's body so close to his. He almost stopped breathing. "Why did Senna and Antone . . ." He did not know what words to use. "Why did they do it? Make a child?" His voice broke. "Didn't they understand the risks?"

Leora stared out into the night. "Senna said she checked herself and Antone. They are both healthy. She was sure they'd have healthy children. They felt it was a personal, private thing, making a child. Senna said nobody, not even The Goodness, has the right to take that away from people."

"But—that is so selfish, Leora! We have to suppress our urges for the good of society."

Leora pressed his hand tightly, so tight that it hurt. "Open your eyes, Will! Innocent people are being killed, just because they're not perfect. Who is perfect?"

"We are. You and I." It felt good to tease a little; he was always so sober, and now, suddenly, he wanted more than anything to make Leora smile, even laugh.

"Hush! That's not true. Listen, Will, you don't understand what it's like for Senna to have to go to that lab every day. She hates it! At first it was only the most deformed, terrible cases. She thought she was sparing them misery. Then, later, things changed. The decrees were harsher. Now thousands of fetuses are destroyed, and for stupid reasons: wrong body type, the wrong sex."

"But the fact that Kiera is defective only proves the point, don't you see?" Will exclaimed. "I hate to say it, Leora, but if she'd been created in a lab, they would never have let her come to term. Natural is too risky. It's selfish, polluting the gene pool . . ." The words spilled from his mouth, the same words he had rehearsed and repeated, as if they now had a life of their own.

"Really!" Leora shot back. "Do you think I am polluting the gene pool? Did I turn out so badly?"

"No! Of course not. You are bright and ambitious."

"And a natural born." She pulled away, stood up in front of him, hands clenched on her hips.

He stared at her. "You are not." He rose to face her fully. "You can't be."

"Yes, I am," she cried. "I am the child of Senna and Antone, just like Kiera. Will, I am a natural born."

He stepped back "No, you are not," he insisted. "I saw your I.D. on the Screen, it said you were turned out . . ."

"They falsified it," Leora said. "I was born from Senna's womb, born naturally. Because they made love! They wanted me. They hated those petri dishes and random killings!"

The word *womb* struck Will like a thunderbolt. Nobody used that word. It was the butt of jokes, obscenities. Natural? Natural born? Maybe he had suspected it. Maybe he should have known. But how could he? He had never known anyone who was a natural born. The very idea had always been repulsive.

He turned away, and he began to walk so swiftly that his side ached and his breathing was labored. He wanted only to fire up the transport and take off for Washolina, escape, pretend none of this had happened.

But Leora came running after him. "Wait!" she screamed. "How dare you run away and judge me? You think I'm so repulsive!"

"I never said that!" he cried.

"Your expression—your face. How dare you? You are a clone!"

They faced each other like two warriors, breathless, furious. At last Will said, "I'm the same person I always was."

Leora stood there, panting, irate. "So am I," she finally said. "*So am I.*"

They stood there in the darkness, and Will felt limp, defeated. At last he looked up and saw the half moon, like a broken thing in the sky. It was how he felt. Broken.

"Leora," he said, "please, let's not fight. I'm sorry. It was a shock, but it doesn't matter. You and I are so alike! Both of us were born outside the system."

"I hate pretending all the time!" she burst out.

"I hate the lies," Will breathed. "I just want to be with you. Maybe we can help each other. I want to try."

She nodded. "I want that, too."

They sat together under the jacaranda tree. They sat without touching, talking until the darkness reached its zenith and slowly the dawn came. And Leora explained how Senna had hidden her pregnancy, how she had given birth both times at Reese's farm, with Nadia to help her.

"They made my implant," Leora said, "just three days after I was born. And so I was registered. But with Kiera it was different. Senna and Antone knew from the start that she was frail. She has a heart condition. They did not think she could withstand the implant surgery. Later they realized something else was wrong. She didn't respond like other babies. They thought she would outgrow it. When she didn't, what could they do? They loved her. Do you understand? Have you ever loved anyone, Will?"

"Yes," he whispered.

Will got up and walked back to the house. Until he knew who he was, he would not be free to say more.

CHAPTER 16

L EORA SAT ON THE COT, twirling her hair around her fingers, watching as Will worked the Screen. Using his personal code, he could access special history tapes and Vi-Exes and even the secure files.

He typed in file numbers; this machine was so inferior that it was not even voice activated. "The age doesn't fit," he said. "The person whose DNA was used to make me was fifty-six years old. I keep thinking, Who would Hayli want to be the father of his cloned child? And why wouldn't he clone himself?"

"I don't know," Leora said. "Maybe you don't look like him, but often you sound like him. And your gestures are like his—look, you're stroking your upper lip just the way he does." She laughed lightly. "Hayli would want someone with traits like his," she went on. "Someone spectacular. Charismatic. Very intelligent, organized. We know he was an orphan, abandoned. All his life he had to struggle."

"Struggle is the father of all things," Will said. "I once used that line in a speech. Hayli loved it."

"He would," Leora said. "Let's think. Who did Hayli admire most?"

"Mattelin," Will said.

"What does Mattelin say about clones?"

They scanned through the voluminous Writings on the Screen. Leora read them aloud: "*There is only one source of control, and that is the human brain. Now, this cherished human brain, powerful and unique though it is among living creatures, this brain can and is being augmented by modern technology. There is no reason humans have to die."*

"That's Hayli's Creed," Will said. "Hayli took it directly from Mattelin."

Leora mused, "I guess, in a way, a person could gain immortality through cloning. Hayli revered Mattelin. So, why not clone him?"

Her voice rose. "It makes perfect sense. Hayli adored him. Mattelin shaped the entire concept of The Goodness. Things went wrong. Some people corrupted it. Will, maybe Hayli decided to speed up the Time of Perfection, and he decided to raise all these perfect people, using Mattelin's DNA. So maybe you and Berk are the beginning of a whole new race!"

Will gave a laugh, a gasp. "Berk and I? A new race?"

"Thousands, millions, why not?" Leora exclaimed. "All they have to do is take a cell from your body, and it will multiply."

"Except for one thing," Will said grimly. "My cells are already seventy-two years old."

"Maybe they are finding a way to correct that," Leora argued. "Science is constantly expanding and improving. What if they can reverse the aging process? What if a new J. Thomas Mattelin, age zero at birth, can be cloned indefinitely?"

"A whole universe consisting only of men?" Will asked with a slight smile.

"Maybe somewhere a woman is being cloned," Leora said. "A perfect partner. A new Adam and Eve."

"Who are they?" Will asked.

"Have you never read the Bible?"

"No. I've heard of it. But I've never been interested in legends."

"According to the Bible, they were the first humans. Some people believe it, literally."

"Mattelin, biography," Will typed in.

It responded quickly. J. Thomas Mattelin: Born 2216. Died 2270.

Will quickly calculated. "Mattelin was fifty-four when he died. My donor was fifty-six. But DNA could be saved—why didn't Hayli use Mattelin's cells?"

He typed rapidly, seeking the answer. At last he got it. "Aha!" he exclaimed. "Look. That's him. J. Thomas Mattelin. He's not so perfect, is he? I've never seen his picture before."

Leora gasped. "He's so *ugly*. Almost . . ." She put her hand to her mouth.

"Deformed," said Will.

"Hayli would want a good-looking son," Leora said.

"Yes. Hayli surrounds himself with attractive people."

Leora said, "Then why didn't he clone himself?"

"Maybe looks aren't enough. Maybe he wanted a certain personality. We're going around in circles, Leora."

"Wait!" Leora said excitedly, pushing her way in front of the Screen. "Let me try something."

"What are you going to do?"

Leora brushed him aside, squinting at the Screen as she typed out instructions. "I'm going to put in your features, your traits, everything about you—bright, great orator, moody, temperamental—"

"Hey!" he interrupted. "What about charming?"

"That, too," she said, laughing. "And I'll go back into the history banks. Far back as I can. I'm going to put in some of the lines you always say. Your obsession with weakness and perfection, and Hayli's Creed." She worked busily, muttering phrases to herself. "Straight brown hair, brown eyes, leadership qualities . . ."

"I can't do this anymore," Will said at last. "I'm exhausted." He lay back on the cot and finished the SNABS Antone had given him. They provided a swift burst of energy, but it was quickly gone.

"What are you doing now?" he asked languidly.

"Hush!" Leora said "This is great. I've never been able to get so deep . . . with your source codes I can . . ." She was intent on the Screen, her fingers tapping rapidly over the keys.

He must have fallen asleep, for he became aware of Leora standing over him.

"I think I've got it," she said.

"What?"

"Your donor," she said, her voice trembling with excitement. "Hayli did get the DNA of a dead man."

"No!" Will cried. "Leora, that's absurd."

She spoke rapidly, breathless. "He lived a long time ago. I don't know how it is possible, but I feel certain that he is the one."

"Who is it?"

"His name is Hitler. First name, Adolf."

"Who is that?"

"Look." She led him to the Screen.

Trembling, he read: "Adolf Hitler, twentieth-century German ruler, conqueror of much of Europe, World War II ally of the Empire of Japan." He glanced over the rest of the page. "How did you get this?" he demanded.

"Look. I'll show you. I put in strings of words—some quotes about racial superiority and the masses and conquest. Then I put in terms like removal and relocation. I came up with a list of world leaders." She screened back. "And look, here's a picture of him. It rather looks like you. Look at the eyes, and the way his hair goes straight down over his forehead, like yours."

Unwittingly Will pushed back his hair as he read the list aloud: "Attila the Hun. Genghis Khan. Alexander the Great. Cyrus of Persia. Napoleon Bonaparte, Joseph Stalin, Adolf Hitler, Saddam Hussein." He stopped. "I've never heard of any of them," Will said dismissively. He read on. "Most of them," he said slowly, "started out in their teens, making war." He thought of Hayli, a leader at sixteen, now ruler of the entire Dominion of the Americas and soon, probably, of the entire world.

Leora looked over his shoulder. "They all had certain traits in common," she said. "They were all intelligent, highly energetic, charismatic, great orators, and—" She stopped and turned away.

"It says they were all ruthless," Will said, "Tyrants. Maniacs! Look, it says Hitler might have been insane." He faced Leora, furious. "Are you telling me that I'm a tyrant? That I'm like those men who . . . look what it says. This Hitler was responsible for the death of millions of innocent people! How did you get this? Hayli wouldn't clone a person like that! What gave you the idea . . . ?" he sputtered.

"I didn't create this!" Leora cried. "Look, I just put in certain phrases that I've heard you quote over and over again. 'Struggle is the father of all things.' 'The masses are like an animal that obeys instincts.' Hitler made those statements. You said them, too. You were taught to say them! From the moment you were turned out, you were taught to become like him, don't you see? Those awful games, to make you tough and ruthless, taking you away from Berk, always criticizing you, putting you into competition—"

"Stop it!" He wanted to shake her, slap her, make her stop. "What about Mara? She loved me! She doesn't think I'm mean and ruthless!"

"Look. Here's his biography. Hitler's mother adored him and spoiled him. His father was the tyrant; he beat him and humiliated him. Look at what Hitler said! 'What luck for rulers that men do not think.' Isn't that what Hayli taught you, too? And this man Hitler talked constantly about weakness. He was obsessed with weakness."

Will stood stock-still, frozen to the spot. His eyes ached; he felt as if he would faint. "You are saying I am like him," he said. "I *am* him. That's what you're telling me isn't it?"

"No! Nobody is an exact duplicate—"

"What are you doing, you two?" Antone's voice rang out harshly. "What have you done?"

Senna was with him. "You should be resting, Will," she said in a low, shaking voice. "Come, Leora. It's late."

Leora spoke out. "I researched it. I think I found Will's donor." She led them to the Screen.

Antone peered at the Screen, squinting. His skin looked gray. His eyes were puffy. He turned to Senna, wordless.

"Hitler," Senna whispered.

"You've heard of him?" Leora asked.

"Oh, yes," said Senna. "Yes, we have heard of him." She manipulated the keys, and next there appeared a biography. Everyone moved nearer to the Screen, intent on the words:

"Hitler, Adolf, born to Maria and Alois Hitler, formerly Alois Schickelgruber, 1889. Twentieth-century dictator—head of the Nazi Party, proponent of the theory of racial superiority. State-sponsored glorification of the dictator, persecution of Jews and other minorities, and fanatical worship of the regime led to systematic deportation and mass killings. Hitler was responsible for the deaths of millions and the destruction of most of Europe."

Will could hear the thud of his heartbeat in his ears. Surely now they would kill him. Son of a tyrant, murderer, why wouldn't they kill him? Anyone would be afraid to let him live.

The biography ended: "Death by suicide, 1945."

"That means he was"—Will made the swift calculation—"fifty-six years old when he died."

"And someone got his DNA?" Antone gasped. "How is it possible?"

"I thought the body was burned," Senna said.

"Somebody marked the grave," Antone said. "Came back later and collected bones or tissue or hair. For souvenirs. People do those things."

"Or to sell," said Senna. "Even then some people were already working on gene mapping. No doubt they thought a time might come when they could find the source of life—DNA—and use it to duplicate the donor."

"But who would want to duplicate a tyrant?" Leora exclaimed.

Senna and Antone only looked at her.

"Another tyrant," Will said.

Will sat alone in front of the Screen. He had to see it again, yet again. He had cried out to them, his hands clutching his hair, his entire body feeling aflame, "No! Listen, it could be a mistake. A coincidence, that's all. So, maybe I have the same hair and eye color. I make speeches. I was taught some of his phrases, but that doesn't prove anything!"

They only stared at him. Passionately he had argued. "How do we know DNA can live that long? It's been over three hundred and fifty years!

Tissue, bones, everything decomposes. It's insane to link this man with Hayli, with me. What does Leora know? She's not a trained researcher . . ."

But in the end, watching the history tape, seeing the stance, hearing the voice, following the gestures, understanding the nature of this man, Will fell silent. Senna, Antone, and Leora left him to watch the tape again and again.

It began with Adolf Hitler's birth, the mother a servant girl, the father a customs official—ordinary, boring people. The father was stern and forbidding; he beat young Adolf for the slightest infraction, humiliated him in front of other people, called him a failure. Young Adolf wanted to be an artist. He showed little talent. Disappointed, he became a street thug, starting fights.

And Will thought of Berk: Berk's drawings, Berk's fists and feet, his belligerent nature from the age of three.

The tape continued, showing young Adolf Hitler walking the streets of a large city with his renegade supporters, tossing bottles, setting fires, shouting slogans. And Will saw the firm mouth, the straight dark hair, the fiery eyes, so like his own—and Berk's.

Arrested for fistfights and disturbances, Adolf Hitler was thrown in jail. There he began to write his theories. Some races of men, he said, are inherently superior. Inferior types must be rooted out and destroyed, like a cancer. Resources must be protected and allocated to the most worthy. The race can be purified, if inferior types are prevented from breeding. If not, they must be eliminated, exterminated. It is necessary, for the greater good, to take firm measures, to show no mercy. There are those who are destined for greatness, destined to rule; unlike other men, they have the privilege and the responsibility to make decisions for the masses.

Will thought of Berk, and how easy it was for his brother to hurt people. He was never sorry for anything. How he laughed when he was the victor in a war game, or when he drew blood! Will recalled their last conversation, how blandly Berk spoke of annihilating the people in Africa. *It's not only me*, Will thought, *but both of us. We both have Hitler's genes, his nature, his mind.*

Will felt as if the walls and the ceiling of the room were about to fall in upon him. Stunned, he went to the window, thought of escape. Where could he go? He was imprisoned in this body, the body of a killer, a tyrant, without conscience.

The Screen now exploded into images of flames, backdrop for a long battalion of soldiers wearing high black boots, wide leather belts, stepping in unison with their arms raised high in salute. Bands played martial music. In a huge amphitheater Adolf Hitler stood on a dais, surrounded by soldiers with rifles and sidearms and truncheons. Flags waved everywhere, huge flags with strange, bold symbols. People shouted, cheered. Those who opposed the speaker were ruthlessly dragged away.

A parade of armaments rolled along the city streets—huge tanks, planes, cannon. Hitler spoke. His voice rose to a frantic pitch, along with his fist, raised high. His hands and arms slashed the air. His face was distorted into a paroxysm of hate and scorn, and though Will could not understand the words, the message was clear, *Kill. Annihilate. Rule. Supreme.* And the crowd shouted in frenzied unison, "Heil, Hitler! Heil, Hitler!"

And Will trembled, imagining himself standing on that dais, the center of attention, the object of adoration, everyone shouting his name.

Images continued—people being rounded up, carrying bundles on their backs, carrying babies and old ones. People were pushed into trucks, loaded into railroad cars. Terror and disbelief etched their faces. Little children screamed or stood mute with fear. Soldiers with rifles and dogs pushed and prodded the people. The enormous wheels of the train ground and shrieked against the steel rails. Doors were slammed shut and bolted. Hands waved out in silent supplication from between the slats. Nobody cared. Nobody saw. At last the train began to move, slowly, then faster, and from within came the cries and the groans. Then the people were flung out onto the platform. Piles of discarded clothes and shoes lay beside the railroad tracks. The people were naked, shivering. Barracks. Smokestacks and thick, constant streams of dark smoke rose skyward from the ovens.

Will blinked. There were bones. Skulls. Piles of bones, so many that one could hardly imagine they had once been human beings.

The light came on, full, flooding the small room. Antone stood in the doorway.

Dazed, Will rubbed his eyes. He felt empty, filthy.

Antone said quietly, distinctly, "Hitler wanted to produce a master race. He wanted to create a perfect world. In his own image, of course. He planned to rule for a thousand years."

When Antone was gone, Will went to the small mirror. His face was stern, the eyes blazing. *Who am I?* he whispered to himself. He clasped his arms tightly over his chest, felt his muscles, skin, the slight stubble on his cheeks. He was nearly a man. And as a man, he was destined to rule. Hayli had spoken of this destiny. Created and bred for it, there was no reason he should not fulfill it.

But now Will moved beyond the question of who would follow Hayli. What was the ultimate goal of the regime? Hayli said it was perfection, but what, exactly, did that mean? What was the price? Who was expected to pay?

Will shuddered at the recollection of those bones and bodies. Never would he be able to erase that horror from his mind. He was created—yes, he had to see it all clearly now—he was created to carry out the plan of a monster who had died before it could be completed. He and Berk together were the embodiment of evil. But what if he were really different from Berk? Different from Hitler? Was it possible?

He wanted to tell Berk, wishing that his brother would recoil, deny it, disown it. But if Berk knew their heritage, he would probably revel in it. He would seize the opportunity to take up Hitler's role. And if Will were to object, what then? Berk would surely kill him without hesitation. Will was certain of it.

CHAPTER 17

SOME NIGHTS WILL FELT as if the walls themselves were speaking. He had trouble falling asleep, always, but lately when he did sleep it was deep and drugged, and then the argument seemed to be seeping out from the walls.

"It's different now there won't be any more elections he is a dictator like Hitler like Hitler someone should stop him who you're crazy if you think I'm going to let Leora go you have no choice she's been accepted I won't allow it she has a right to try you were the one who encouraged her that was before when there was a chance being with a clone is dangerous she could get caught in a crossfire she's only a girl they will kill him wait and see you'll hear about it why did he ever have to come here in the first place?"

They were right, of course. There was no point in bringing Leora back to Washolina. Her very association with him would put her in danger. But how could he leave her?

"I need to get back to Washolina," Will told everyone. They sat at the table eating together. Sileus was hunched over his food, looking awkward, like a gigantic robot. He ate straight from the yellow containers that Antone set before them.

"Tomorrow," Will told Sileus, "contact the Ministry and tell them we're heading home."

Sileus nodded. "It will be good to get back."

"It hasn't been two weeks," Senna objected, shooting a glance at Antone.

"I'm fine," Will insisted. "I'll send my report in the morning, and I'm certain we can get the transporter programmed."

"So, you are leaving tomorrow," Antone said with a sober expression, but an unmistakable glint in his eyes. He covered his mouth with a napkin, giving a slight cough. "Maybe Leora can follow later."

"I'm going with Will," Leora said firmly.

"We'll discuss it privately," Senna said.

Sileus spoke through a mouthful of stringy brown food. "Anyone lucky enough to be accepted to the Academy," he said, "should not waste a moment outside of Washolina."

"I agree," said Leora.

"We could send the transport back for her later," Will suggested. The tension was almost audible, defining the space between Senna and Antone. Will felt Leora's defiance, he heard Sileus's hostility. He wanted, at this moment, only to be gone. Alone, at least, he did not have to measure people's moods and try to sidestep their tempers. He hated Sileus, had hated him from the first moment, the large head, beady eyes, enormous hands. Senna was like a bird, fluttering and pecking. Antone irritated him with his constant anxiety. Being with these people put him on edge. Their emotions pulled at him. Will recalled for a fleeting moment the few times he had been alone with Hayli, that feeling of grand confidence, being singled out, being smiled upon as if by a beaming sun. Nobody, nobody in the world could make Will feel that way. He resented the memory as much as he longed for the feeling.

"Try some of these natural foods," Antone said, pushing a plate toward Will almost challengingly.

Will stared at the bowl of greens. They broadcast a pungent smell. "No thanks," he said with a glance at Sileus. He needed the man, needed him as a follower, conspirator.

Leora flamboyantly ladled the greens onto Kiera's plate. "Peas," she said in her lilting way. "From the garden." And Will hungered for those peas; she made them sound piquant and exotic. But he only muttered, "I saw no garden."

Kiera piped up, "Reese has the garden."

"Hush, Kiera," said Senna. She lifted her hand, as if to slap away an insect.

"I always say, nothing can compare to a SNAB," Antone said briskly. "Nothing like it in the world!"

Will broke open another of the yellow packages, a mass of gelatinous noodles, disgustingly bland. He eyed the greens and the soft mound of potatoes, his mouth turning sour with desire.

"Who is this person called Reese?" Sileus suddenly asked. "I would like to meet him before we leave."

"He lives at an outpost," said Antone. "On a small farm."

Senna, tight-lipped, told Sileus, "Private farms are not forbidden."

"Nor encouraged," Sileus said.

Antone and Senna would not meet Will's eyes. He might be a time bomb, about to go off. They knew that destruction was in his genes, his nature. All night Will had recalled his own outbursts of temper, fury, the desire to dominate. He recalled the gestures he often practiced, sweeping arm movements, hands chopping the air, the grimace, the outspread arms, the raging voice.

"A very good evening to you!" someone called, and three people entered. The speaker was a tall, very thin man with an extravagant halo of frizzy blond hair. With him came Zebarre, the mechanic from the silo, large and commanding, swinging his arms. The third was a robust, full-bodied woman, who breathed heavily as she walked. She was dressed in a red turbo-suit, which bulged around her like a tent.

Antone rose to greet them. "Good evening, Clarissa!" he exuded, leaping up to greet the woman. "Daran, Zabarre! Glad to see you. Have a seat. Would you like something to eat? This is Will, the son of the Supreme Compassionate Director. He is our guest, following an accident. And his mentor, Sileus, from the Fifth Pillar."

In the next moment everyone's eyes were busy flickering, assessing the situation. Zebarre directed his gaze to Sileus. The woman, Clarissa, appraised Will, eyes squinting. "Of course, we recognize you," she said flirtatiously. "You are more handsome, even, in person. I am a great admirer of our Supreme Compassionate Director." She gave the proper salute. "To The Goodness," she declared.

"The Goodness," echoed Will.

Daran bowed toward Will, his frizzy hair standing on end. "Delighted, honored, Compassionate One. I am head of the local Enforcement Committee, at your service."

Zabarre paced the length of the room, eyes down, as if he were searching for a lost item. He looked too large for the room, muscular and energetic. Thick brows and pronounced stubble on his face gave him a dark, brooding appearance. It was strange to see someone with facial hair. Of course it was not prohibited, but neither was it encouraged. Most people thought it *dissy*.

Sileus stood up and faced the men. "Enforcer?" he reiterated, shaking Daran's hand. "Then you know about the new edict."

"Indeed, I have come personally to be sure that everyone is informed." He gazed at Kiera, who sat in her place eating mashed potatoes with a spoon.

Daran faced Antone fully. "The new edict," he said, "requires anyone two years below grade to assemble at the State Commons two weeks from now. Clarissa was kind enough to urge this visit. Everyone should be properly, personally informed."

"We do our best to serve The Goodness," said Clarissa, drawing herself up to full height.

Sileus stood up, clapping his fist into the palm of his hand.

Daran continued, facing Sileus as he spoke. "A pity, of course, that they weren't nipped in the bud, so to speak," he said with a swift glance at Will. "All anyone had to do was rinse out the petri dish, and we would all be spared the trouble. But then, there are compensations, and one mustn't complain, must one? The Powers know what they are doing. It's not for us to say."

Senna's features looked frozen, immobile. "Yes, well, thank you very much, Daran, Clarissa."

Clarissa enunciated with enthusiasm. "The Compassionate Removals will take place every month now. Anyone bringing an Ab will, of course, receive the usual compensation—food stamps and pleasure stamps."

"And the punishment for noncompliance?" Sileus prodded.

"Reduction of stamps, as always," said Daran. "But," he said with a slight chuckle, "that never happens here in Fresmofield. Our committee always obtains total cooperation." He turned to give Will another full look, bobbed his head obsequiously.

When the three had left, Sileus walked over to Kiera. "This child must be tested," he said. He turned to Will. "Do you want to arrange it, or shall I?"

Will drew himself up, facing Sileus. "I was planning to send a report about the matter," he said sternly. "I'll take care of it."

"Very well," said Sileus. "I will be happy to review your report, as usual."

Kiera looked from Will to Sileus. Wordless, she went to a shelf and picked up a strange instrument, a rounded disc with a long shaft, intersected by wires. She sat down on the floor, cross-legged, and began to strum softly, while she sang:

> "I will give you honey
> Honey, honey, honey from the rock . . .
> I tell you do not worry,
> Beloved of my flock."

"What is that thing?" Sileus asked skeptically.

"An ancient instrument called a lute," Antone replied. His voice sounded distant, husky. "I made it myself, copied from a museum photo."

"The Compassionate Director frowns on people who make their own music." Sileus placed his large hand on Will's shoulder.

"Stop!" Will instructed his PAAR, though he shuddered at the touch and the familiarity.

"I'm going to turn in now," Sileus said. "I'll make my daily report in the morning, and I will also ask for transport." He bowed stiffly to Senna. "Thank you. Good night," he said, hurrying out.

They sat in silence, and Will felt like an intruder as the others obviously struggled to pretend things were normal. Leora focused on eating peas. Antone had picked up the lute, and he sat with it in his lap, stroking the wood with his fingertips. Senna's nostrils flared slightly; otherwise, she might have been made of stone.

"Everything will be fine," Senna said at last. "Nothing will happen to Kiera." Her gaze landed on Will, as if to solicit his assurance.

"But Senna, you heard them!" Leora cried.

"It is a special case," said Antone. "She has special talents."

"Look, everybody," said Will, "maybe there is something I can do."

Senna exclaimed, "Yes, yes, if you could help us!" She prevaricated. "I'm sure The Goodness provides for exceptions. Kiera has certain talents. She taught herself to play that lute!"

"It doesn't matter," Leora cried. "Didn't you hear? Anyone who can't pass the tests . . ."

Will looked from one to the other, caught up in their helplessness. What could he possibly do? And yet, there was this urge to solve it. Was it that leadership impulse? The unswerving desire to be in charge, to be applauded, appreciated, revered?

"They'll come for Kiera," Leora whispered, her tone nearly hysterical. Her eyes were wide, pupils large. "We'll have to send her. We will have to let her go. If we don't, they will take all our stamps. The enforcers will come!" Leora ran to her sister, pulling her close, stroking her hair, while tears spilled from her eyes. "Kiera, Kiera! Oh, Kiera, don't you mind. Don't you cry! You'll be with other children; you'll make music. There will be kittens and birds and lovely things."

"Stop it, Leora!" exclaimed Will. "*Stop it*." He knelt down and took Kiera's hand in his. "I will think of something. After all, I'm the son of the Compassionate Director!" He rose to his feet, hot with rage and frustration. "Listen to me! I have friends and supporters. I have power!" He clenched his fist. He heard the echo of his voice, a tyrant's tone.

Later that night, when he could not sleep, Will remembered how they had all stared at him, stupefied and frightened, until at last Antone asked the question, "What can you possibly do?"

"I don't know yet," Will had answered, mollified. "I have to get back, figure things out. I have to know what's really in store for me, and how to accomplish it. Maybe I can take Kiera to Washolina."

Take her to Washolina—with Sileus around? Take her to Washolina and keep her . . . where? Use his power? What power?

He had no power, unless . . . unless he were the only survivor of this dynasty. If something were to happen to Berk, if he alone was in charge of Security and Future Planning—he could make changes. He was immediately horrified at his own thought, the implication that he would get rid of Berk. But perhaps it took drastic steps to gain power. Now, he must concentrate on attaining power.

He slept fitfully, awakening to a sense of danger. It was deep night. From the window Will could see the moon shining brightly, its halo like a lantern. He sat bolt upright. There had been no sound of alarm, no wind. But something had startled him, or the lack of something, like negative space. Will looked around, and realized what it was. The PAAR was gone. Incredible. It stuck to him like a shadow, always, so that Will never consciously thought about it. But, yes, there were vague sounds and movements as when the PAAR reconstituted itself with periodic repairs and lubrication, and the whirr of the small fan that was its own cooling system. Will had become accustomed to this, and the slight clatter when the PAAR settled itself down.

The PAAR was gone.

Will got up silently, glancing about. Light flickered into the room, touching the clutter, accentuating the white porcelain bathtub. Will pulled on his clothes and went out. A slight breeze fanned his face, cooling his feverish body. Something seemed to summon him.

Will followed the path he often took with Leora and Kiera to the trees. Beyond was a rather steep declivity, and he had not been strong enough to attempt it. Now, however, he was urged on by other sights and sounds, flickering light, and an occasional voice, low and indistinct.

As Will approached the ridge, he saw people standing at the bottom of the hill in a meadow. They stood in a circle around a small fire. Some carried torches or candles. It looked like a scene from a primitive Vi-Ex, when men used spears for weapons and wore animals skins round their waists. But these people were properly clothed, and Will recognized some of the voices.

Will drew closer, moving down the hill which became ever steeper, so that he had to sit back and slide, for fear of losing control. Nearly at the bottom, Will stopped his descent, scraping his hands along the rough ground, feeling the prickly sticks and pebbles bruising his flesh.

He heard the voices of Senna and Antone and Leora. He saw a tall blonde woman and realized it was Clorey, Senna's friend from the lab. And there was his PAAR, lying in a heap near the fire, as if it had been disabled. There were half a dozen other people he did not know, talking heatedly, voices rising with emotion. He was astounded. A secret society, it seemed, existed in the shadows, underlying the daytime world of regulations and labor and sacrifice. Who were these people? Now he also recognized the mechanic, Zebarre, who stood with his arms folded across his chest, as if he were in restraint.

"I say we kill the clone," shouted one man. "We have nothing to lose by it. Since he is not even supposed to be alive, technically, we commit no crime. At least, nobody can accuse us of anything."

"Very clever, Mr. Locunda," said Zebarre. "Then how do we explain the fact that the son of the Compassionate Director has disappeared?"

"And we risk an attack by the enforcers," put in Clorey.

"But how can we allow this tyrant to live?"

"He is still young," said Clorey. "How do we know that he will become a tyrant, like Hitler?"

"Age has nothing to do with it. Tyrants start young." That came from Zebarre.

Will's entire body tensed, his heart beating madly, hands clenched. Everyone knew! He had been betrayed—betrayed by Senna and Antone and Leora. How could he have been so stupid as to trust them?

"I say we destroy it!" a woman shouted shrilly, and several others rallied around shouting, "Yes! Yes!"

"How can you talk like that?" Leora cried. "He is a person."

"Shut up! She is too young to speak."

"She is not! She is the only one in a position of real influence. Let her talk!"

"No! We need action." It was the gravelly voice of the man they called Locunda, a small man who carried a torch that sparked and flickered above him. "What if someone had caught Adolf Hitler when he was just a young thug and put an end to him? I say we take him down."

"I don't know," said Zebarre. "What about a trial? He hasn't done anything. What do we charge him with?"

"We don't need a trial! We can already predict what the child of Hitler will do!"

"The point is," said another, "nobody would clone a Hitler except for a nefarious purpose. No good can come of it, none whatsoever."

It went on and on, and Will clung to the hillside, mesmerized, as if he were watching his own funeral.

A woman said, "Maybe there are already hundreds like him. Ready to take over. I say exterminate them before they overrun us. That is the first law of life—survival."

Voices rose in agreement. "Hear! Hear! Gladys is right—our survival is at stake."

"Wait! This isn't a lynching party!" The speaker was of moderate height, with a muscular body, the kind developed by heavy work. He wore a trim, dark beard and held a lantern in his right hand. He raised the lantern, illuminating the crowd.

"We have to remember our mission," he said in a firm, calm voice. "We're not killers. We're only looking to bring some sanity back into the world. Now, a crazy person has cloned a tyrant. It is only one in a string of insanities that bombard us. We have to get to the source and transform the government, but not by killing. Our whole purpose was to infiltrate the system."

"Reese, how do you expect to do that?" someone jeered.

"We've a good start. We've got supporters all over the Dominion. These things take time. With luck, maybe this clone, this boy, can be used to our advantage."

"He is already disillusioned with The Goodness," said Leora.

Antone said, "He is planning to leave tomorrow. Once he's gone, we can return to normal." He hesitated, then added, "He offered to help us with Kiera."

The lantern shook in Reese's hand, casting shadows all about. "Maybe he will help us all," he said. "Wouldn't it be ironic and wonderful?"

The mood was altered now.

"Reese, you always say there are no accidents," someone said.

"Well, think how this young man came to us. Was it just an accident that his appendix burst? That he landed here? Or might there have been some divine intervention? Think of it! This boy has the DNA of Hitler. But his soul—his soul is separate and unique. It's his own."

There was silence, and Will heard his own heart pounding, felt it against his ribs. Soul? He had heard of such a thing as a myth, a superstition long outmoded. And here he sat, covered in dirt and brambles, concealed in darkness, with this stranger defending him on the basis of his *soul!*

Now everyone spoke at once.

"A clone can't have a soul."

"Of course it does! Every living being has a soul!"

"We don't know how tendencies are passed from generation to generation . . ."

"Evil has to be destroyed; that's all there is to it."

One voice broke through, loud and determined. "We simply do not know the outcome." It was Senna. "Maybe there is a gene that overrides violence, that instills compassion. A goodness gene."

Now the clamor escalated. "What? Are you serious?"

"What a bizarre idea!"

"Nobody ever isolated a gene for goodness, not in all the years . . ."

They nearly drowned out her voice, but she continued talking. "Experiments prove that good children can come from evil parents. Genetics isn't everything. Neither is environment. It's a blend, and into the blend you have to mix mutation, accident, and something else we can't isolate. Reese calls it soul. I call it free choice."

Will clung to the hillside, scarcely daring to breathe. The lanterns and the torches together with the movement of people created a kaleidoscope of light and shadow, and at the edge of it came a commotion, a flashing light and a powerful blast.

"What is going on here!" The man came running down the hill, pointing a micro-laser threateningly. "In the name of The Goodness, I forbid you to—"

Now Will could make out the large head, the doddering body. Alarm seized the entire group, as if lightning had struck. "Stop!" Sileus shouted. "You are breaking the law! Any meeting of five or more persons is prohibited!" He lunged toward Zebarre, hand lifted menacingly.

Will saw a flash. He heard the crash of metal, saw the streaking form of his PAAR as it struck Sileus a single blow to the neck. Sileus fell backward, his body crumpling.

Everything seemed to freeze; only the flames from the candles and the bonfire still moved.

Antone was the first to speak, walking toward the crumpled form. "Is he dead? Reese, is he dead?"

Reese knelt down, put his hand to Sileus's throat, and nodded.

Will moved swiftly, silently up the incline, moving on all fours. Sileus—dead? How could he possibly explain it to the Ministry and to Hayli? It was impossible—the PAAR was not designed to kill. It was only a defensive weapon. Will would be blamed. He could not even fathom the consequences.

CHAPTER 18

AFTERWARD, Will had been unable to fall asleep. Each part of the night scene replayed in his mind: the flickering lanterns, the shrill cries for his death, the sudden attack of the PAAR. He struggled for many hours. At last he awakened, having dreamed of standing on a platform, immersed in oratory with thousands of people listening, shouting "Hail, Will! Hail, Will!" In the dream he was lifted up, so powerful that he actually began to fly above the crowd, seeing everything below with an omnipotent eye: the bleak past, and the brilliant future. He saw his own mouth, spewing forth words, and on his upper lip, the stiff, dark Hitler moustache.

Sitting bolt upright, Will discovered that his hand was on his upper lip. He leapt out of bed, ran to the small bath chamber, where he found a razor in the cabinet; and swiftly, with a trembling hand, he shaved.

Back in his room, Will looked into the corner, and there it was, the PAAR, as if it had never left. Immediately Will's mind was filled with problems. He had made promises he could not keep—what was to become of Kiera? He had witnessed a debate over whether or not he ought to be killed. And he had seen Sileus murdered with one stroke of the PAAR's iron hand. Sileus's death would have to be explained. It could very well be blamed on him. It was his PAAR, after all, and the thing did not kill without instructions.

Will went out to the large room and sat down at the plank table. PAAR followed. It was early yet. Nobody else was awake. Will opened a yellow-

and-black package of SNABS, ate one or two, then sat back, eyeing the food. It seemed tasteless.

Will went to the shelf and found a container of the crinkly food that Antone had prepared from his harvest. He took a bowl of heavy pottery, such as he had never before held in his hand. Its turquoise color captivated him for a long moment. Will poured some of the cereal into the bowl, added milk, took it to the table, and dipped in the spoon, bringing it slowly to his mouth. Cool and crunchy, sweet and wet and wholesome, all these adjectives were conjoined in Will's mind, and then he forgot about words and proceeded to devour every last flake.

Having eaten, he began to organize his thoughts. Who wanted Sileus dead? Probably everyone who knew him. Whom had he offended in Fresmofield? Probably countless officials in whose offices and workshops he had been snooping, taking notes in his pulse pad, conferring with enforcers. Surely Sileus's reports contained daily criticisms and suggestions, designed to win him praise and prestige. But who had both the reason and the ability to commit murder, especially murder by PAAR?

"Up already!" Senna greeted him cheerfully She busied herself with utensils, her head turned away, movements awkward, as if she had something to hide.

"Good morning, Senna. Did you sleep well?" he asked pointedly.

"Quite well, thanks. And you?" She eyed the empty bowl and the spoon, said nothing, while a slight smile played about her lips.

"I was disturbed," Will said, testing the waters, "by my PAAR. He sometimes gets restless at night. Oils himself, you know, and clatters about making small repairs."

"Is that so?" Senna said faintly. "How long has that PAAR been with you?"

"Since I started middle Academy. Before then, I had to fight my own battles. But when I grew older, they gave me this PAAR for protection. He will kill upon command."

Everything in his past seemed skewed now, his world turned upside down. The vicious games and fierce competitions had been his training.

Like the PAAR, he was designed to be a killer. Was this really his destiny? And was he, like a machine, incapable of changing it?

He forced himself to be calm. He made his tone casual, with effort. "By the way, where is Sileus?" he asked.

Senna busied herself slicing fruit. "Would you like some of these?"

Will glanced at the purple fruit. "I forgot what you call those."

"Figs," she said.

He nodded and took the fruit, bit into its soft flesh. He marveled at the color, the texture, the taste.

All night, amid the turmoil of his thoughts, he had remembered Senna's assertion about a goodness gene. Now he said, "Senna, tell me, how is it that twins, two people almost identical, born from the same egg and having the same DNA—"

"Like you? Leora told me you have a twin brother. Kirk?"

"Berk," he supplied. "We look the same. We have some of the same habits. But we are actually very different."

"How so?" Senna asked.

"Berk loves physical combat. He's a man of action. He never gets close to anyone."

"Would you say cold?" Senna asked.

"Ruthless," Will blurted out.

"Ah," said Senna with a slight smile. "Obviously, you aren't like your brother. You care about Kiera. You are concerned for Leora. I have seen you with her."

Will felt flushed. In fairness, he wanted to tell her about his dreams of glory, standing there in front of the crowd, loving their adulation, "Hail, Will!"

"Whatever it was in Hitler that directed him toward evil, it might be different in you," Senna said. "Maybe there's a counterforce in you that overcame the aggressive instinct." She drew her fingers through her hair, shook her head. "I don't know about your case specifically. But genes do change, mutate. A gene for aggression can be altered—one gene rides piggyback upon the other, so to speak. And, voila!" she said with a flourish, "you have a goodness gene. Amazing, isn't it?"

Will felt breathless, almost dizzy. "Has anyone proved this?" he asked.

Senna shrugged. "People have been investigating for centuries. Is there a gene for love? For spirituality? We have no proof. We've never had the funds to study it. Apparently questions of good and evil aren't a high priority here."

"I think it's important," Will said, his tone husky.

"I must tell you," Senna continued, "Sileus met with an accident last night."

"What do you mean?" Will exclaimed, pretending astonishment.

The PAAR unfolded itself and proceeded to walk outside, where it leaned against the window, looking in.

"It knows," she said in a strange voice. "How is that thing programmed, that it knows?"

"Knows what?"

"It killed Sileus. I don't know exactly how it happened. We were having a . . . a meeting in the Grove—"

"My PAAR killed Sileus? How? Why?"

Senna bit her lip, flung back her hair. "I don't know! I can't honestly say that anyone liked the man, but to be murdered . . . and by that *thing*."

"The PAAR is supposed to be perfect. I was told it would strike only if I were threatened."

"Nothing is perfect," said Antone, his steps slow and weary. His face bore the effects of a sleepless night. "A machine can go wrong. Just like a human."

Will shook his head. "Very rarely. Almost unheard of."

"But possible," said Senna, hands on her hips. "You must admit to the possibility, in theory, at least."

"I admit it," said Will. "But this PAAR has never made the slightest error. He never left my side, unless I ordered him to go away."

"What are his instructions?" Antone asked. He blinked rapidly behind the large glasses, as if to clear his vision.

"To keep me safe. It wouldn't just kill, unless . . ."

"Will, I was there." It was Leora, her hair tousled, eyes sleepy. "We all saw it kill Sileus. It was horrible."

"There was nothing we could do," said Senna, wringing her hands.

"We were all in shock," said Antone. "Nobody knows quite how it happened."

"Except for the killer," Will said, gazing out at the PAAR.

"Are you saying someone caused this to happen?" Antone exclaimed. "Are you accusing . . . ?"

Hand uplifted, Will interrupted. "Where is the body? Hayli might want him back in Washolina for proper disposal."

"We buried him near the silo," said Antone. "It seemed best, under the circumstances. We were holding a meeting, after all." He took off his glasses and rubbed his eyes. "We didn't have a permit," he said. "We were afraid of trouble."

"I'm aware of that," Will said dryly. "But now, how will we explain his disappearance?" Will realized with a start that the word "we" implied he was already a confirmed accomplice.

"That certainly is a problem," Senna said, glancing at Antone. "There could be repercussions. Serious repercussions." She tied her kerchief around her head, tucking in stray locks of her hair. "Maybe Locunda can help us. He works for Daran on the Enforcement Committee."

"Daran!" Will exclaimed. He remembered the man with the frizzy hair and the fawning manner. But Locunda had been in the Grove along with those others who opposed The Goodness, and so was Zebarre, the mechanic. Now, for the first time, Will came to grips with the fact that there was a resistance movement.

Resistance. The word sounded archaic, both exciting and frightening. People were already organized against The Goodness, despite Hayli's edicts and enforcers. He could join them, *join the resistance*. The idea was captivating. Now, he stood between two worlds, a stranger to both. Here, some people still wanted to kill him. They hated him for being attached to Hayli. But some, like Leora and Senna, seemed to want him alive. Why? Was he to be their guinea pig? Their negotiator? He was a symbol, had always been a symbol. Nobody had ever seen him as an individual, except for Leora.

Now she sat opposite him at the table, and he wanted to spill out all his thoughts and fears. But he saw her disconsolate gesture as she swirled the spoon round and round in her bowl. She was in pain.

"Leora," he said, "I'll take care of it. Don't worry."

The thought mocked him—take care of it, how? He could not do much alone, but as a member of the resistance almost anything was possible. He knew what Hayli could do to rebels. It was a dangerous choice.

"That's what Kiera always says." She smiled sadly. "But there is so much to worry about."

"Yes. For me."

"Kiera isn't your responsibility."

"Did your parents think they could hide her forever?" Will asked gently.

"Senna tried to get help, at first," Leora said. "She took Kiera to a clinic and found out that Kiera has a damaged heart. That was the word they used. Heart surgery would have cost more money and stamps than half the people in this colony possess. Kiera was just a baby then. The technicians suggested that Senna stop feeding Kiera and let her die."

Will shuddered. Most damaged people were left to die, or, if they were too long about dying, there was always the Compassionate Removal. It was coming together now. His thoughts flashed onto the Hitler tape: the speeches, blind adoration, and—death.

"That was one reason I wanted to get into the Academy," Leora said. "To make Status One and send Kiera to surgery in Washolina. If I was Status One, I'd have power. I could take care of her."

"Maybe," Will said. "Maybe not. I never knew of a Status One who wasn't . . ." He hesitated.

"Perfect?" Leora supplied, giving him an ironic look.

"Nobody is perfect," Will said lightly. "You taught me that." He paused, then said, "I need to go back to the silo where Antone works. Will you take me?"

"Of course, but why?"

"Someone I have to talk to," he said vaguely.

Back in his room, Will examined the PAAR. He opened the vent in back, looked inside, and saw nothing except the usual circuit board and the small fan that cooled down the mechanism. He had his suspicions about who had tampered with the PAAR. For now, he had to act.

Will pressed his pulse pad, sending his message to the Associate Director of the Fifth Pillar, with a copy to Hayli. He focused on the words he had heard in the Vi-Ex of Adolf Hitler. One quote reverberated in his mind. "Close your hearts to pity. Act brutally. The strongest man is right."

He thought, *So this is what I was meant to be. Hayli wants someone ruthless. I will tell him what he wants to hear.*

He fed the information into his pulse pad.

"Urgent message, this is to report the death of Sileus, official of Fifth Pillar. Place: Fresmofield, District Seven. Reason: punishment for disobedience, insolence, and possible treachery. The punishment was meted out by Will, son of Supreme Compassionate Director. Method: assault by PAAR. Note to the Supreme Compassionate Director: Sir, I took it upon myself to solve this problem immediately and with firmness. I am certain you will agree that pity and sentimentality are not luxuries that a true leader can enjoy. Your devoted son, Will.

He had intended to leave today. Now it seemed better to wait. He must find out more about the resistance movement before he returned to Washolina.

Will wondered what Berk would do if he were here. He would suppress the resistance, that was certain. He would immediately contact Hayli, activate the enforcers, find out who had programmed the PAAR, for surely the robot could not have taken the initiative. It was designed to destruct in case of a malfunction. No, someone was responsible. Berk had always criticized him for being too soft. But then, Will thought, Berk had never been to Fresmofield, never ate a real fig, never held the hand of a small girl and heard her singing.

Will took a deep breath to steady himself. Unwittingly, he hummed, his mind thinking the words:

> *I will give you honey,*
> *Honey, honey, honey from the rock.*

Will found Leora in the field, examining a row of plants. Dark green leaves nearly hid a small red fruit that came to a point. "Can we go now to the silo?" he asked.

She pulled the fruit off its stem and said, "Open your mouth."

He complied, and she popped it into his mouth. For a moment her finger remained on his lips. The taste of the fruit was sweet and tart. "What is that?" he exclaimed.

"Strawberry."

"Oh, we have that flavor in a drink, but it isn't anything like this!"

They walked together toward the Photoval. Her steps were slow, measured, as if they needed this time together, and Will matched his stride to hers.

Leora said, "Senna doesn't want me to go back to Academy. She thinks it's dangerous now."

"Because of me," he stated. "I'm also worried about going back."

"I have to go back," Leora said, "or everything I've worked for will be wasted."

"And we want to take Kiera," Will said.

"I'm going to help to . . . well, to change things."

"How will you do that?" he asked.

"By rising, getting into the Information Ministry, telling some truths instead of lies," she said vehemently, "The Vi-Exes only show what Hayli wants us to see. You know how the Ministry changes history. They say before the Collapse everyone lived in misery. It's not true. Senna told me how it was. People chose their own work. They chose their partners when they were young, and," she glanced away, "they made love. Not just sex, like the Sym, but making a child, someone new, like them but also different. Everyone is different. Everyone has—"

"A soul. Choices," Will supplied, catching Leora's arm as she whirled around, stunned. "I was there on the hillside," he said. "I heard all of you. How you defended me. And Reese and Senna, talking about destiny and soul. They said I have a soul. And that I can choose—"

"You were there!" she exclaimed. "Then you also saw the PAAR kill Sileus."

"Yes. But I didn't cause it!"

"I never said you did, Will." They had reached the Photoval. The PAAR climbed into the back, as before. "Sometimes," she said, "people have to kill, if it's in self-defense. Or to keep something terrible from happening."

Will turned on his pulse pad. "I want to show you something." He flicked on his previous reports, and the words flowed across the pulse screen. "This is the report I wrote about the Compassionate Removal." He watched Leora's face as she read, biting her lip, intent on the words. "And this morning, about Sileus's death."

She read the report, looked at him wonderingly. "You made all this up?"

"I wrote it the way Hitler would. Hitler said 'Close your hearts to pity. Act brutally.' I figured I'd borrow his words, convince Hayli that I am his loyal son."

"I see." Leora nodded. "In my essay, too, I wrote what they wanted to hear, so that I could get into the Academy. All that tripe about the masses, withholding information, telling lies to the people *for their own good!*" she said vehemently. "I guess we're a lot alike." She gazed at him, a look filled with admiration, devoid of any pretense.

Will touched her hand, fighting the desire that arose in him so powerfully that at this moment he never wanted to leave her side.

She drove the Photoval along the compound, through the gate.

"How come they sent you?" Will asked. "What about all the adults?"

Leora shrugged. "I told you. I was selected and tested and chosen. Everyone saw the potential of me going to Washolina."

"You're only fifteen years old!"

"Too young to help?" she challenged him, as she parked the Photoval. "What about you? What about Hayli and The Five?"

They made their way past the I.D. scanner, and once again Will stood with Antone at the processing machines. He told Antone the reason for his visit. "I need to talk to Zabarre."

Antone paged him, the sound ringing out over the factory. "Zabarre, Zabarre, report to Unit Three immediately."

He came at a trot, panting, eyes darting. When he saw Will and Leora, Zebarre stopped short, whipped his head around in both directions, as if he might flee. But there was no escape.

"What do you want?" he asked, confronting Will, arms folded across his chest.

"I want to know why you killed Sileus," Will said.

From the wavering look of fear in Zebarre's eyes, Will knew he had found the right man.

CHAPTER 19

ZEBARRE STOOD STOCK-STILL. Only Antone moved, putting his hand on Zebarre's shoulder. "You?" he breathed. "You?"

Zebarre seemed to slump. "Yes, me."

"But why?" Antone exclaimed.

"So many years," Zebarre said dully, "I have carried this with me. So many times I've wanted to tell you, Antone! I was afraid." He looked up at Will. "What are you going to do?"

"Nothing. Nothing that will affect you. I have taken responsibility for Sileus's death," Will said. "Now, I want to know why you killed Sileus, and how you did it."

The clatter of machines and the stifling air seemed to close over all of them. Antone said, "Let's go out into the courtyard."

Fearfully Zebarre glanced about. "What about the production schedule?"

"We can stay late tonight," Antone said, "and make up the time."

Zebarre's eyes flickered from one to the other. "Good thing there are only four of us," he said nervously. "More than four need a permit to hold a meeting."

"Come, my friend," said Antone. "You need a break."

They passed through the long passageway to a small courtyard where air chairs and a circular Serotonin Bar offered brief retreat. The drinks bubbled in dispensers, pale green, creamy yellow, and caramel color.

Behind the bar was a small-version Screen, with its continual band of messages streaming across the surface.

"Do you want something?" Antone asked.

"No," said Will and Zebarre together.

Zebarre remained standing, arms folded over his chest. "I was with Hayli at the beginning," he said. "We were just kids. I was eighteen, going to one of the few remaining technical schools."

"This was right after the Collapse," Antone said grimly.

"It was mass confusion," Zebarre went on. "Most people were just surviving day to day. They lived in holes or in alleys, in the burned-out forests and in caved-in houses. They assaulted people for whatever valuables they might have—a coat, a pair of shoes. A few of us still had some hope left. We wanted a future. So we studied science and mathematics, mechanics, history. There were still professors around. We lived at the college, made it our fortress. We even built some crude robo-guards, to keep the rabble out. And so we stayed for three years. The best three years of my life."

Zebarre's dark eyes shone as he was transported by his memories. "A few of us immediately found each other. We stuck together. Our parents were all gone, victims of missile attacks or nuclear accident or virus diseases. Only the fittest survived."

"And the lucky," Antone put in. "I was lucky, born a bit later, and in the Heartland."

"So you were relocated," said Zebarre, "while my new friends and I started rebuilding the world. There was Hayli, immediately our leader. You should have seen him! He held us in the palm of his hand, made us laugh, made us cry, made us angry, made us a team. We were more than a team. We were an army, Hayli and Mara, Felix and Farleen. And me."

"You were one of The Five?" Will gasped. "I thought the man who was killed was called Taroo."

Zebarre pointed to his chest. "That's me. I had to change my name."

Antone rose to his feet, placed his hands on Zebarre's shoulders, looking him in the eyes. "I have known you all these years, and you never said a word. If we'd known you were one of The Five—"

"You probably would have killed me!" Zebarre cried. "Look, just last night they wanted to kill this boy!" He pointed a trembling finger at Will. "I know him. I understand him. Because once I was in his place."

"How did you get here?" Will asked. "How did you manage to hide?" His mind raced over the possibilities. Now, with an ally, perhaps he could stay here, too.

"I escaped," Zebarre said. He sat down on a stone seat. "Word went out that I died in an accident. It was something I had arranged, a simple matter of fusing some wires together, so that a tank I was supposed to be working on exploded and melted down with me inside, they assumed. It was announced everywhere. Later, as the Compassionate Director, Hayli took the credit for it, said I had betrayed The Goodness. People remembered that so-called accident. It struck fear into many a potential betrayer, let me tell you."

"We heard about those early betrayals," Antone said. "We never knew the particulars."

"You only know what the leaders want you to know," said Zabarre. "It's always the same." He motioned for them to gather closer. "Three things drive a man," Zebarre declared, "and when they get hold of him completely, it is disastrous. Power is one. Sex is another. Money is the third. Hayli was going to create a world where none of those mattered. But of course, he ended up wanting all three of them. He desired them more than any human being I've ever known. That is what, ultimately, made him ruthless. That is what finally made me leave."

"Didn't you want those things, too?" Will asked.

"Of course I did!" Zebarre cried. "Everyone does! But I wasn't going to let them rule me. I loved Hayli. And I loved Mara. I loved what we were going to do, bring back order and hope, destroy war and famine and disease. It was going to be a Utopia, don't you see? Our research was leading us to new realms, to the very possibility of immortality."

"A pipe dream," Antone said.

"No! Once Hayli came into power, that was his dominant quest. All the best scientists were put to the task. But there were dissenters, too. Hayli became increasingly frustrated and furious when anyone tried to argue with him. At first he still listened to our opinions. He asked for advice. But then, as soon as he reorganized and renamed the districts and sections and colonies, and his enforcers were in place, something snapped."

"Why did they change the names of places?" Leora asked.

"To signify that the world was different," said Zebarre. "Also to erase tradition and remembrance. Hayli is very particular about what people are allowed to remember. *He* wants to be thought of as eternal, as if he were a god."

"A god," Leora repeated.

Zabarre rubbed his fingers through his beard. "Yes, Hayli and Mattelin, with their philosophies and their theories, were convinced that people can mold their own destinies, and the destiny of the human race. But in order to do that, they had to wipe out the opposition, don't you see? They had to persuade the people that it was *for their own good!* They seized all the resources. They relocated people so they could control them better. They censored all the news and information. When they took control over reproduction, the last private and personal experience, their power was absolute."

"But you," Will said, "you refused to stay with them. You might have been in a position of supreme power yourself."

"Power? To do what? To kill and maim and deceive? That wasn't what I had bargained for. I was a fool." Zebarre laughed sorrowfully. "I believed everything Hayli said. I even believed that it was wrong to love a woman in the normal way, that love was only a word people used so they could satisfy their sexual urges, or to have children. Once Hayli removed those imperatives, he said there was no reason for partners or families or traditions. There was no need for God. Because *we* were creating new things, don't you see? We were creating life and dealing out death in those same laboratories, and controlling everything in between."

"Why did you leave?" Antone persisted.

"Because I—in spite of everything, I had these feelings in me that I could not deny. I loved Mara, as a woman, not only as a friend. And I loved the traditions, the things my parents had taught me, all the good things that they said came only from God."

"And so you left because of that?" Will asked.

Zebarre gave a self-deprecating laugh. "No. I would like to tell you that I was so noble, but it was much more vulgar than that. After all his talk of denial and the Symsex and everything, I found out that Hayli and Mara had . . . they had . . ."

"They were lovers," Leora said, her voice wistful, eyes misty.

Zebarre nodded. "Yes. They had a child. But it was worse than that. Hayli disowned the child. Said it was mine. Mine! I had never even touched Mara, though I loved her so!"

"What happened to the child?" Will asked. His voice was barely audible. A child? Hayli and Mara made a child? Everything he had learned up until now was only prelude to this agony. *I should have been that child! How dare you, all these years, to distort everything that is good and pure? You took away love and replaced it with machines! You made me believe you, want to be like you, and you are nothing but evil!*

Zebarre's beard trembled; his lips were moist. "I don't know. The child is probably dead. Hayli would rather kill his own child than let it be known that he had fathered him naturally, going against his own edicts."

"How did you manage to escape?" Antone asked, staring at Zebarre in disbelief.

"I made my way to the Heartland," Zebarre said. "I caught one of the last trains to the outpost. It wasn't hard to do. I dressed in rags, grew a beard, and carried a weapon, making myself look like one of the street thugs."

"You could have been killed by the vigilantes," Leora exclaimed.

"At that point, I didn't care, Leora. Anything was better than being part of The Goodness." He spat the word. "Besides, the vigilantes could be bought off. There were no courts anymore, no justice system. Just gangs of criminals and gangs of vigilantes. So I came here to Fresmofield. It was a desolate outpost, all of us poor beggars. I helped build the colony. Fortunately, I had a desirable trade. I could build and repair and—"

"Repair and reprogram machines," Will said. "Like my PAAR." He focused on Zebarre, on his eyes, his beard, his muscular frame. Only Zebarre seemed real. Everything in the past was a terrible delusion. And somehow he had to replace it with something better.

Zebarre laughed. "Oh, that PAAR! I figured it out the day you brought him here to the silo. I thought it might be useful to learn something about that robot. So I dropped by with Daran, and that busybody Clarissa, to get another look at the thing. It was obviously programmed to your implant, some radio-magnetic connection. I was surprised that I had no problem getting it to come with me."

"How did you manage that?" Antone asked.

"Just gave it a slight kick from behind, like you'd do to a donkey or a dog," Zebarre said with a grin. "It followed me, all right. And then I opened that trapdoor and worked on the mechanism to make it also react to a target beam from a hand switch." He reached into his belt and produced the switch, handed it to Will. "Here. This is rightfully yours. It worked beautifully when Sileus appeared. First, of course, I had to lure Sileus down to the Grove, which I managed to do by giving him plenty of uppers with his supper." Again he laughed. "Sileus was restless. Couldn't sleep. And then there was the matter of planting an urgent message on his pulse pad, suggesting subversive activities."

"So you lured him to you," said Will, "to kill him. But why?"

"He recognized me," Zebarre said simply. "I saw it in his eyes. The minute he saw me at Antone's house, he knew me. He was with Hayli at the beginning, you know. Always nervous, always the underdog, wanting more than he was capable of handling." He glanced about, lowered his voice. "If I know Sileus—so slow and deliberate—he was going to sleep on it. By today, he would have done something to me, I'm sure of it.

"I think he also killed Chip, that young lab assistant. I was out early that morning. I saw him coming from the silo. He didn't see me. He was carrying this thing, a tool for cutting pipes. I wondered at the time what he was doing with it."

"You mean, he killed Chip with it?" Antone said with a shudder.

"Why would he?" Will asked.

Zebarre said, "I would suppose that he followed Chip to the lab and either Chip told him what he'd discovered, or Sileus saw it on the printout. Either way, Sileus would have been terrified." Zebarre looked at Will and went on, "I figured if he knew you were a clone, it was his job to protect that secret. He'd kill anyone who might reveal it. After all, Sileus was in a very difficult position."

"But what if he hadn't known about Will?" Leora asked.

"Well, I figured Sileus might have thought Chip was lying about this cloning. In any case, news about making a clone would certainly discredit the Compassionate Director. Sileus couldn't allow that to happen either. Sileus was supposed to protect Hayli's image, and that included everything involved with The Goodness."

"So you think Sileus didn't realize that Leora and Senna already knew."

"I suppose not," said Zebarre, with a fearful look at Leora. "They would have been in mortal danger, too. That man was without conscience."

"He was all set to send Kiera to Removal," Will said dully. "He told me so."

"What are you going to do about her?" Zebarre asked Antone. "Such a sweet child."

"Will might help," Antone said. "He even offered to take her to Washolina."

"No!" exclaimed Zebarre. "That would be a terrible mistake. A sacrifice, a kindness, surely, but you cannot take her there."

Zebarre gazed at Will for a long moment. He put out his hand, placed it on Will's shoulder. "I am ashamed of it, but I must tell you, I wanted to kill you, along with Sileus. The others dissuaded me. They said that you were different. And now I see it."

Zebarre's touch conveyed a fatherly concern. Was it true that he was different? Will wanted to believe it. He wanted more than anything to be like Zebarre, courageous and strong. "How can we save Kiera?" Will asked.

Antone replied, "We can't hide her. Too many people here know about her. We have to buy time." Antone pointed to Leora. "Tomorrow, take Kiera in the Photoval to Reese's place. I can't go. It would arouse suspicion if I didn't appear at the silo. Maybe Reese has an idea."

"I'd like to go with Leora," Will said.

Antone hesitated. "All right. Take the PAAR."

Will nodded. "Of course."

Zebarre rose. He unbuttoned his collar, exposing amid the dark hair on his chest a large gold medal, surrounded by diamonds, with the Roman numeral V in the center. He slipped the medal over his head and held it out to Will.

"When you return to Washolina," he said, "you will need to talk to Mara about these many things. Mara was one of the founders of The Goodness, but I suspect she has had enough of it by now."

Will looked up at Zebarre, and he saw the tiredness and the pain in the man's face. "Why did Hayli make me?" he asked. "If you know, tell me!"

Zebarre shook his head. "I don't know. That's what you'll have to find out."

Will ducked his head, feeling the onset of tears. "Yes," he said. "I'm going to investigate."

"Tell Mara that you saw me. Taroo. And if she asks for proof, show her this."

Will took the medal. It felt heavy and warm in his hand. "How can I thank you?" Will breathed.

"Expose the truth," Zebarre said. "Help the people regain what they lost. As I know Hayli," said Zebarre, "it won't be easy."

Will felt as if he were standing on a precipice from which he must, inevitably, climb down or fall. Whatever lay in front of him, he was certain that he would have to meet Hayli head-on.

CHAPTER 20

IT TOOK TWO HOURS to reach the compound. Leora, Kiera, and Will settled in the Photoval, along with the PAAR. The landscape changed quickly from colony to arid land, dotted with bits of sage and scrub, a lone lizard scuttling about now and then.

"Not exactly Washolina, is it?" Leora said to Will. He mentally compared this wilderness to Washolina's sleek streets and motion paths, the huge Screens and hundreds of people gathering in the pavilions.

"What will you do when you get back?" Leora asked.

"Find answers," he said brusquely. "I have to talk to everyone, do some research, find out what Hayli has in store for me. I have to see Berk most of all, and Mara. Hayli said Berk and I are to be his right and left hands. That means he's planning to give us high positions. From there, I maybe can begin to make changes. It will be slow, dangerous work."

"You'll be careful, won't you?"

"Yes," he said quietly "I don't exactly have an army behind me." He glanced about at his PAAR. "We have no weapons."

"What will you tell Berk?" Leora asked. "About being a . . ."

"I don't know yet," Will said heavily. Some decisions would have to be made on the spot.

They rode in silence, then Will asked, "What does Reese do?"

"He has a small farm. He doesn't have a regular job. Reese was a brilliant researcher. He still is. But he refuses to work for The Goodness." She turned around again to check on Kiera. She was nodding, almost asleep.

"How can he manage without food stamps?" Will asked.

"They grow all their food. It's hard. He and Nadia refuse to eat synthetic food."

"But you and your family eat it," Will argued.

"We're not as idealistic as Reese. We're just survivors," Leora said.

"I see." Will stretched. His back and neck ached. He realized that the ache had been spreading for days, and also that the irritation above his elbow and on his hip had spread. Patches of prickly red skin itched and stung whenever he moved.

"What's wrong?" Leora asked.

"I have this rash," he said, scratching.

"Maybe Reese will have some ointment for it."

"Is he a doctor?"

"He was trained in medicine, I think. He knows about many things."

After a time Leora pointed to a narrow trail that bent its way around a thin grove of slender trees, their pale green leaves like long fingers. "Look. That's the beginning of The Farm." She pointed to the damaged land. "They have cut down the sagebrush. They use it for fuel. Not many trees yet, so they can't spare the lumber. They get some coal; I don't know where or how."

"They struggle for everything!" he exclaimed.

"They want to be independent."

They rode past several small huts and storage barns, until at last they reached one patched together from sheets of wood, metal, stone, and old bricks. Outside the dwellings were small gardens in neat rows. A large fenced-in field contained bundles of straw and stacks of debris—plastic and aluminum, rope and hides and machine parts.

From the barn came Reese, smiling broadly. "Leora!" he called happily. As they approached, Will saw that he was built like a gnarled tree limb, his jaw and cheekbones sharp and prominent. His gray eyes fastened on Will. "Welcome, welcome!" he said.

"Thank you," Will said, greatly relieved by Reese's warmth.

Kiera jumped out of the Photoval and ran into his arms, calling, "Reese! Reese!"

He caught Kiera up and held her, then set her down again, and she began to run about the field, as if she had been imprisoned until now.

"You can park the Photoval in the barn," Reese said. He looked questioningly at the PAAR. "Do you want it with you?"

"No," Will said. "I think I'm safe here. We'll leave it in the Photoval."

Reese called out, "Nadia! They're here!" He turned to Will. "We have heard so much about you. I know what you did for Zebarre, how you took blame for that . . . incident. And that you wanted to take Kiera to safety. We can keep her with us for a while. There aren't many places to send a child like her."

"But there are places?" Will asked eagerly. "Where?"

Reese touched him lightly on the shoulder. "We'll talk later. Come in. You must be hungry. We have some apples, believe it or not, a wonderful crop this year! We use them for everything—cider, sauce, pie, and just plain eating."

"I have never had a real apple," Will said.

At that moment Nadia appeared, her dark hair gleaming, her full mouth soft with feeling. "You shall have one right now, Will," she said, smiling, and she took his arm to lead him into the house.

They ate the apples. Will was astonished at the tart taste, the way the ripe skin clung to his teeth and the sweetness lasted on his tongue. They ate in an enormous room, long and narrow, its main feature a table that could seat some twenty people, set in front of a window which gave a full view of the surrounding countryside. Along the wall were two black stoves and numerous storage bins filled with fruit, nuts, grain, and potatoes. The entire room exuded the fragrance of fresh fruits and vegetables. Will savored it all.

Reese had a way of bending toward him to listen, nodding encouragement.

"You know who I am," Will said. "Clone of Adolf Hitler." He said the name with a shudder of revulsion. "My father."

"Your father in physical terms only," Nadia said gently. "Many great men and women have had terrible parents."

"History is of full of examples," Reese agreed. "We're all born with a

---
190

certain code, that's true. But you are your own person. Come, let's go and give you a look around the place." Reese rose and led them to the door. "Nadia, will you take Kiera to the children?"

Kiera clapped. "Yes! Yes!" she exclaimed, and Nadia took her hand.

"Where are the children?" Will asked.

"You'll see them later," said Reese. "Now I want to show you The Farm and the Remembrance Place."

Will walked between Reese and Leora. "What did you mean about a place for Kiera?"

Reese shook his head, avoiding the question. "Kiera remembers melodies and the words to many songs. If you give her a drum or a flute or a stringed instrument, she can play it immediately. But she can't follow the simplest instructions on the Screen or on any electronic device. This cuts her out of the workforce. And those who don't work," he paused, "perish."

Reese stopped at a wooden gate attached to rail fence. Within, various creatures stopped grazing and looked up with curiosity.

"We kept hoping something would change in time to help Kiera. But now with the new edict, I just don't know."

Will felt ashamed and responsible. He sighed deeply.

"Come," said Reese, smiling, "let's go into the barnyard, Will. I hear you haven't known many animals."

"Only a bird," Will said, "and a white kitten."

"This is one of our small herd of goats," Reese said. He held out his hands, and a brown-and-white goat walked stiff-legged toward him, its horns thrust forward.

Frightened, Will recoiled. He watched breathlessly as the creature gently butted Reese's legs, shifting from side to side as Reese rubbed the stubby protrusions. Reese laughed. "He likes to be petted. Do you want to try?" Reese's dark eyes were upon him, filled with expectation.

Will nodded and tentatively reached out. He laid his hand on the knobby head, felt the coarse hair and warm body of the goat, a communication that left him breathless.

"Isn't he lovely?" Leora said in her lilting voice.

"Yes," Will agreed, laughing as the animal gave a snort and raised its lip, showing large, grinning teeth. He looked around, breathed deeply of the fresh, free air. It felt good to be without his PAAR, to have found a sanctuary.

Several chickens flapped and screeched. Geese swayed and twisted their heads and spread their wings, more entertaining than the dancers at the Dance Dome.

Leora said, "See why I like to come here?" To Reese she said, "Let's show Will the Remembrance Place."

"Definitely." Reese led the way across the field into a barn, weathered and leaning to the side, so that it seemed ancient and dilapidated. But inside, to Will's surprise, was a large, high-ceilinged room with dark, insulated windows.

"With the help of Zebarre and a few other talented mechanics," Reese said proudly, "we have created this space. We can project images onto all these surfaces simultaneously, drawing from Vi-Exes and ancient films that we have managed to gather from the deleted or destroyed files and films."

"How can you regain destroyed data?"

"That's the secret," said Reese with a grin. "Nothing is really ever destroyed. It changes form. We can restore anything that was electronically recorded, whether on film or by satellite, on the Web, even music." He patted an innocent-looking box, quite plain, with only a few dials and switches. "We call this the Truth Machine," he said, "because it will show us a real look at the past. Some people are trying to revise the past," he said with a long look at Will. "Maybe that will change."

He led Leora and Will to a couch. "Sit down. Relax. I'll show you." Will sat between them, aware of Leora's warmth, Reese's strength.

"This was Fresmofield in past generations, before the Collapse," said Reese, "when the forests still stood and the rivers flowed. You'll see."

Immediately Will experienced open fields and low houses with large porches surrounded by flowers of every color. Lush green fields, hills, and crags showed shadows of lavender, green, and blue. Orchards fanned into the distance, and long harvest tables for drying and preparing fruits and nuts. Granaries and factories emitted a faint frosty mist that soon merged into the blue sky. No pall shrouded the atmosphere. An olfactory simulator sent out a rich, leafy smell. Rows of leafy vegetables gave off their rich fragrance. Insects of every variety hopped and buzzed, chirped and sawed their legs together in endless refrain. Water rushed from a stream, fish flipped and arched underneath the water, pebbles shone. Children played at the edge of the water, healthy children of all ages, laughing and splashing. In the distance horses grazed. Will could smell the special scent of horse, and now of dog as a playful, shaggy creature raced by, its curly fur wet from the creek. Somewhere a band was playing thrilling music, with a host of wonderful instruments.

"Oh," murmured Will, affected beyond words. "Oh."

The scene shifted to a building filled with spots of color from stained-glass windows, and music from a strange instrument filling every space. The music was familiar. The words rang in Will's mind.

> *"Fear no evil,*
> *Shed no tear.*
> *I am with you,*
> *Always near."*

Mara's song! Will thought, startled. He was about to speak, but from above came the droning, unmistakable sound of a Bumblecop. Reese sprang up.

"Oh, no!" he cried. "Stay here, out of sight!" He ran out, and Will and Leora peered from the window to see the black-and-yellow Bumblecop make its landing. It settled for a moment, the door panel slid open, and a pair of long thin legs touched the ground. Then the tall, bent shape of Daran, the enforcer, unfolded itself and stood before them. Another man crawled out from the copter, and Reese ran to meet them.

"Locunda! Daran!" Reese exclaimed distractedly.

"What are they doing here?" Will whispered to Leora. Sweat coated his forehead. The accusation "betrayer" clattered in his mind. Could Reese have betrayed him?

"Probably responding to the new edict," Leora said in a low voice. "They're searching for children. Abs." Her voice broke.

"What are you saying! I thought this place was secure, a secret!"

"Nothing is really secret," Leora said fiercely. "You know The Goodness has spies and enforcers everywhere! They know everything, and they take full advantage."

"What are you taking about?"

"We pay them off in pleasure stamps. That's why we never have any left over."

"But . . . Locunda, I saw him in the Grove that night at the meeting. He's in the resistance."

"Locunda is a double agent," whispered Leora. "He gets paid by Daran for helping, and we pay him for giving Daran misinformation. Lovely, isn't it," she mocked. "I hate them both!"

"But . . . does Daran know about me? Being a . . . a clone?"

"We paid Locunda not to tell him."

"How can we be sure he kept his word?"

"Locunda knows that if he betrays us, the game is over. And Locunda doesn't want to quit."

The men stood together, talking and gesturing. Then they turned in accord toward a thick hedge.

"Where are they going?" Will asked.

"To the children's meadow," Leora replied. All color was drained from her face. She switched on a monitor. "Shh. Don't say a word. This is a two-way system."

On the Screen Will now saw a scene both idyllic and horrifying—thick grass and clover, yellow daisies and a pale green pond, several large horses and their colts, a few bleating sheep with their innocent faces and curling manes—and then the children. Some were beautiful, with sweet features and glossy hair. And then there were those with a limb lacking, a protrusion from neck or spine, an opening that refused to close and from which oozed strange liquid. One boy was utterly white, his skin scaly; another was blackened, as with soot, and several girls of different ages tapped their way about with sticks, their eyes sealed shut and blind. Kiera was walking with one of them, talking earnestly, and the blind girl nodded and smiled.

"How many do you need?" Reese asked.

"Five," said Daran.

"No. Impossible," said Reese. He fumbled in a pouch at his waist and drew out a handful of pleasure stamps. "I can give you two. The boy with the pale skin; he is in constant pain. Deliverance will come to him, at least. And the girl with the fissure in her back hasn't long to live. You see, she cannot stand anymore."

Daran stared at the offering. He bent down to consult with Locunda. He straightened himself, shaking his head. "One more. And not only the worst cases. I have to make a report, you know. If I offer only the worst, the Powers will know I have been negotiating."

"Everyone negotiates," said Reese brusquely.

"We need a good one, not so deformed looking," agreed Locunda, "or they will think we are ignoring the new edict."

"We'll take Kiera now," Daran said. "We've let her go far too long."

"No!" Reese stood before them, a stolid figure, and fierce. "The son of the Compassionate Director is planning to take her to the Dance Dome in Washolina. We dare not cross him."

"Then why is she here?" Daran asked suspiciously.

"They only brought her to say good-bye," Reese said. He gestured. "The two of them are in the house. Tomorrow they'll take Kiera with them to Washolina. I don't think you should cross him," Reese repeated. "The son of the Compassionate One has a temper, like his father."

Locunda gave a laugh. "The Dance Dome, is it? Well, that is exactly the right place for her."

"But we need at least three Abs," came Daran's high-pitched voice. "Otherwise the Powers will become suspicious."

Will could see only Daran's back as he walked toward a tree, where a small bundle lay in a basket, wrapped in a blanket. "We'll take this one," Daran said. "What's wrong with it?"

"Missing fingers," Reese said. "Oh, please!"

Locunda snatched up the baby. The Screen went blank as the men were out of range. In the next moment Will heard the sputtering, roaring sounds of the Bumblecop as it lifted off. And then he heard Kiera's frantic screams.

CHAPTER 21

"BABY! BABY! BABY!" Kiera threw herself down on the ground where the grass lay flat from the heat of the Bumblecop. The craft was reduced to a small yellow disc in the sky, then it vanished from sight.

"Baby!" screamed Kiera, writhing and kicking. Her breathing was hoarse and shallow.

Will and Leora ran to her. The child's flailing arms and legs struck Leora in the face and chest. Will approached and was stunned by the violence of Kiera's screams, and the foaming wetness of her mouth. "Reese!" he called.

Reese came running, and Nadia, too, and together they knelt down beside Kiera as still she writhed in uncontrollable spasms. "We have to get her quiet. Quick, get some water."

Nadia said, "With her condition, Reese, such an outburst could be . . ."

"Kiera, Kiera." Will knelt down beside her. He stroked her damp forehead, took her small hand in his. "Shhh, listen," Will whispered into her ear. "I will give you honey. Honey, honey, honey from the rock." He hummed softly, feeling a terrible ache, as if he had been wounded. As Kiera's sobs diminished, Will gently lifted her and brought her into the house. He and Reese laid her on a narrow couch in the long room that was the kitchen and the dining place.

Nadia prepared tea and tried to feed Kiera with a spoon, but the liquid spilled from her mouth and made thin rivulets along her throat. They all surrounded the couch, and, as Will watched, he felt almost numb with fear. Kiera lay motionless, her closed eyelids looking waxen, her mouth pale. He heard Leora's deep breathing as she knelt beside him. It was Leora's sister, not his, who lay here dying. But it was not pity for Leora that he felt; it was his own sense of failure and loss and, inexplicably, love. Will felt the emptiness, the loss of family. Always in the past, that word had held a derogatory sound. Now it filled Will with regret and sorrow.

"I feel so helpless," Will whispered. He clenched his teeth. "You'd think transports would be available for times like this."

"Transports are only for Security people," she said. Her eyes glistened with tears.

"Let's take Kiera back in the Photoval," Will said, ready for action.

"We can't drive it in the dark," Leora said. "It has no lights, and there are too many hazards along the way."

"I'll pad Senna and Antone," Will said, "and let them know we'll be back with Kiera in the morning."

As they kept their vigil, the night air became cold. Nadia laid an afghan over Kiera, and Reese stoked up one of the old stoves so that soon the room was warm and pungent with the smell of wood smoke. Will's feelings vacillated between urgency and reluctance. If only time could stop now, while Kiera still breathed and Leora and he were safe here with Reese and Nadia.

"I knew that song," Will said into the silence, speaking softly, "from the Remembrance Place. I heard it many times when I was small."

"Who sang it?" Reese asked.

"Mara," he said. Everyone knew about Mara, one of The Five.

"That's strange," Nadia said. "The Goodness discourages prayer."

"Prayer?" Will asked. "What does that song have to do with prayer?"

Reese and Nadia looked at each other. Nadia said, "The song is really a prayer. 'At evening now we pray.'"

Will bolted up. "But that's not what the song says—I've heard it hundreds of times. 'At evening now we play. *Play.*'"

Nadia shook her head, smiling sardonically. "No. Somehow it got changed with time. It's a prayer for comfort and help."

"Hayli says that prayer is nonsense," said Will. "His Creed says there is no God."

"Of course," said Reese, folding his arms over his chest. "Hayli makes the rules, Hayli metes out punishment, and he even creates life. So, Hayli is God. Can he give you honey from a rock?"

It caught Will like a lightning bolt. Providing food from a stone, making something from nothing—not even Hayli could do that. He wondered whether Mara had ever thought about the song and its meaning.

Kiera's breathing changed to a harsher sound. "What's happening?" Leora asked, alarmed.

Reese rushed to Kiera's side. Gently he laid his head upon her chest. "Her heartbeat," he said at last, "is very irregular. Weak."

"She is going to die, isn't she," Leora cried. "Then they can't take her. They can't send her away from us." She was trembling.

Will went to her. "Shh, don't let Kiera hear you. Just hold her."

Darkness enveloped the house and lay over the fields. Reese motioned for Will to step outside with him. "I don't think she will survive the night," he said. "It is probably for the best."

"How can you say that?" Will exclaimed.

They stood on the wooden porch, gazing up at the stars. Will smelled the sagebrush, the wood smoke, the lumber, and all the mingled smells of plants and animals. It revived him, made him long for something more. He wished Leora were out here with him.

Reese seemed to know. "Leora will need you now more than ever."

Will only nodded.

Reese said, "As for Kiera, girls like her, with beautiful voices and learning disabilities are sometimes taken to Washolina to the Dance Dome and made to perform for ministers and directors."

"Perform?" Will echoed, his heart thumping. He remembered the delicate, sad-looking girl at the anniversary pageant. Hayli had called her "angel."

"They are pumped full of drugs, to give them energy. They sing and dance and provide pleasure for the men. Don't think for a moment that the top officials use the Symsex!" Reese said angrily. "The girls are used up, enslaved, then discarded. Disposable people." Reese looked away.

"They would do that to Kiera?"

Will could not take his eyes from the black sky, from the stars, cold and distant, and the tilted crescent moon, like a mouth that was smiling in disbelief at his naïveté.

"The girls live at the Dance Domes," Reese went on, his words crowding out all of Will's thoughts, suffocating him, it seemed. "There they are dosed with energizing drugs so that they can go on for hours without stopping. They become dehydrated, exhausted, and burn themselves out. This is what they call an angel," Reese said contemptuously. "That is why I refuse to eat their food or take their pleasure stamps or anything else. All their pleasures are bought with pain."

Will tried in vain to warm himself, his arms pressed close. "I never liked the Dance Dome," he said. His teeth clattered, as if he were freezing, as if his entire body had been seized by some alien force. "What happens to them, finally?"

"Most of them perish," Reese said simply. "Some manage to escape."

He asked, "How do you know all this?"

Reese hesitated. Then he said, "We have connections, operatives in Washolina. We haven't been completely stagnant these past twenty-five years."

"Spies," Will said.

"Yes."

"And Leora is supposed to join them."

Reese did not answer.

"If the girls can escape, where do they go? Where can they possibly go?"

"Some can get to the Great Desert. Nobody looks for them there," said Reese.

"I thought only criminals live in the Great Desert! It's a wasteland."

"Yes, they say it's a hideout for dissidents. I have never seen any criminals there. I do know about a remnant. Those left after the Relocation."

"How do you know?" Will asked. His breath made small white bursts in the night air.

"I've been there," Reese replied.

Will was shocked. This incredible man, Reese, traveled with impunity, knew the inner workings of both The Goodness and its enemies. And yet he lived so simply.

"How did you get there?" he asked.

"I have a cart and a horse," Reese said.

An idea formed in Will's mind. They stood quietly for a time, looking up at the night sky. Then Reese asked, "What will you do when you get back to Washolina?"

"Somehow I have to stop the Removals. And other edicts. Change things. First I have to find out who I am."

Reese smiled, his teeth showing white in the darkness. "You aren't Hitler, you know," he said. "DNA only defines a body. Your soul is your own."

Reese leaned back, gazing up at the stars. The moon was nearly hidden now behind stringy clouds. "Hayli managed to find a way to clone a person. But he can't control the outcome."

"What about that song," Will said, "about the shepherd, this invisible guardian, God. You believe in all that?"

"Yes. It's what keeps me going," said Reese.

Will shivered.

"Come inside," said Reese. "It's late."

Will felt an urgent vibration on his pulse pad. He stepped aside, pressed the Mode button, and in the next moment the message came through: "Return to Washolina at once. Hayli."

He spoke into the pulse pad, which glowed a luminous green. Hayli's face appeared. "Yes!"

"I received your message, Sir, that you want me back immediately," Will said, speaking softly, for the pulse pad's sensitive receptors could transmit the merest whisper. "Is something wrong?"

"I am concerned about your health," said Hayli. "I want you here, where my doctor can keep an eye on you. Your brother, too."

"Is something the matter with Berk?"

"He has been complaining of some muscle weakness and changes in vision. I want you both checked out at the clinic here in Washolina."

"Yes, Sir!" Will exclaimed. "I'll leave tomorrow. Shall I bring the girl? Leora?"

"As you wish," Hayli countered. "She is of no consequence. But what about the body of Sileus?"

Will thought swiftly. "Completely dissolved by chemicals, Sir. I saw to it. No sense leaving traces for some dissident group to use for indictments against us. They would say we abuse our functionaries."

"Quite right. Good job. You will leave tomorrow, then," Hayli ordered.

"Will you order my transport to be programmed, Sir?"

"No need. I will institute the override. Your transport will be voice activated."

"Thank you, Sir!" Will said. He had a plan. It held him in its grip. Will tensed, scratching at the rash on his hip.

"I will see you in my quarters after you have been to the clinic. You have an appointment three days from now," Hayli said. "Is that clear?"

"I will be there, Sir."

"By the way," Hayli said, "are you feeling any aftereffects of the surgery?"

"No, Sir."

"Then I suppose, physically, you are better than before?"

"I would hope so, Sir."

"Have you been taking your daily powders?" Hayli asked sharply.

"Yes, Sir."

"Good."

With that, the image was gone, and Will was left in darkness. He was exhilarated at his success. They would make a stop on the way. Nobody would question or censure him. Will felt elated. As son of the Compassionate One, everything stood at his disposal. Hayli obviously trusted him. That was vital. But Will was also perplexed. Hayli had never inquired about his health before. Of course, there were the paternal tapes, but those were only perfunctory. Was Hayli worried that his clone was self-destructing?

He had lied to Hayli. Actually, he had not taken the blue powder for several days, ever since Sileus was killed. It had been easy, without Sileus's remonstrance, to forget.

He spoke Berk's name into the pulse pad. Instantly Berk's face came onto the viewer. He looked startled, confused.

"Berk!" Will whispered. "How are you?"

"No problem. No problem," said Berk.

"Where are you?"

"Here."

"Are you sick?"

"I don't know. Ask the doctor. He keeps saying no problem. He stands over me rubbing his hands together. He's *dissy!*" Berk laughed a strange laugh.

"Dr. Varton," Will said.

"I don't know his name. I can't remember. Where are you, Will?"

"I'm coming to see you tomorrow," Will said.

"Good. Bring the maze game. I'll bet I can beat you!"

"Good night, Berk. Try to get some rest." Will closed the connection and lay back, a heaviness rising in his chest. Berk sounded so odd, disoriented. However distant they were, Will did not want to lose his brother. Tears stung his eyes. He supposed he loved Berk. After all, they had been conceived together, lain together in the nursery.

The thought burst in upon him: clones were known to fail, to self-destruct. Panic seized Will. He imaged Berk dying. Hayli's urgent call could be a prelude to his own illness and death. Or maybe there was an antidote, and that was why he was being summoned to the clinic.

He wondered about his own thought processes, his faculties. Berk had asked for the maze game. They hadn't played that game since they were little children.

CHAPTER 22

EESE, LEORA, AND WILL walked together along the fields, looking for a place to bury Kiera. Tears streamed steadily down Leora's cheeks. At last she stopped on a knoll where a single pepper tree grew. "Here," she said, and she wiped her eyes.

Will held Leora's hand in his. It felt cold. He wanted to wrap his arms around her and keep her warm. Instead, he took off his cloak and laid it around her shoulders.

Someone had taken the Photoval back to get Antone and Senna. They all gathered together under the pepper tree—Reese, Nadia, Will, and several of the older children. They sang Kiera's favorite song: "I will give you honey . . ." and Mara's song about the shepherd. Reese spoke about "Our Father in heaven." And Will felt a strange floating feeling, joy amid sorrow, brightness in the midst of fog. At last Senna and Leora tossed several flowers into the grave, and it was over.

"We need to get back," Reese told everyone. "Will has a schedule to keep." He gave Nadia a long look. "Do you have something for me to take?"

"Of course." Nadia went into the house, and after some time she returned with a large satchel and handed it to Reese. "It will keep fresh for several hours," she said.

"What is it?" Will asked.

"Food," Nadia said. "For the journey. You never know . . ."

Leora laughed slightly. "You are such a mother, Nadia!"

They made their way back to the colony in the Photoval, and this time the ride seemed short, for Will's mind was filled with plans. He had told Reese, just before the burial, "Hayli has sent for me. I have to leave for Washolina today. I'm planning to make a slight detour," he added.

Reese met Will's eyes. "And what is your destination?"

"I think you know," Will said.

"You want to see the Great Desert," Reese said.

"Yes. I need to see it."

"Let me come with you," Reese said.

"And afterward? You want to go Washolina with us?"

"Yes. I went to university in Washolina. Of course, then it was still called D.C. That was before the Collapse. I haven't been back in twenty years."

"What about I.D.?" Will said.

Reese opened his shirt collar. "I still have my implant. It will identify me as an alumnus and a medical researcher. Once you're in the files, you remain there for life."

"But that beard . . ." Will began. "Nobody in Washolina wears a beard. It's considered subversive."

Reese laughed. "I'll shave it off. You'll see—my face will be pink as a baby's! And I have a turbo-suit. Don't worry. I'll fit right in."

Now Will, Leora, and Reese stood at the transport, ready to leave Fresmofield.

"Leora, will you be all right?" Senna said, her hands fluttering. "Are you sure you want to go through with this?"

"Yes, I'm sure. I have to go back to the Academy." Leora stood with her hand on her hip, features firm, a copy of her mother.

"Leora, it is risky," Senna said. "Before, there were good reasons for you to go to the Academy. Now, I'm not sure."

"There are even better reasons," Leora argued. "Will might need me. And if it is possible to bring change, I want to be there to help. This is what you wanted for me, isn't it? To help bring back balance?"

Antone nodded, turning to Senna. "You see," he said, "how our children throw our own arguments back at us."

"Go," Senna said suddenly, giving Leora a slight push, but then she pulled her back into an embrace.

From far away came a rustling sound. It drew everyone's attention. Voices mingled with the metallic clink of robots and the pounding feet of a multitude, all surging toward the field where the transport stood.

"We have come," Clarissa called shrilly, "to bid farewell to the son of the Supreme Compassionate Director! Of course, we have obtained the necessary permits," she assured Will. Clarissa lurched forward on one knee in an unsteady curtsy.

"We could not let the occasion pass," she breathed, "without proper farewell. Your visit to our poor colony," she gasped, "has thrilled us. Let us hope that all who are gathered here are significantly aware of the magnitude of this moment." She turned to the crowd, which now had gathered close.

"To The Goodness!" shouted the people at Clarissa's signal. "Long life to Hayli! Long life to the son of the Compassionate One. Hail, Will! Hail, Will!"

Then, over the jubilant voices came music so loud that it drowned out every other sound. The beat seemed to shake Will's very bones, filling his senses completely. Everyone sang, repeating Will's own words: "One heart, one blood, one unity!"

Will found himself nodding and waving, gesturing in the same way he had seen on the ancient Vi-Ex, the movements feeling so natural, so uniquely his own.

"Friends," he shouted, head high, "your devotion fills my heart! I will never forget this moment." He encompassed them with his arms outspread, absorbing their homage, uplifted by the looks of awe and admiration on their faces. And now, all the voices chanted in unison: "Hail to The Goodness, and to the Supreme Compassionate Director, most true, most powerful, most benevolent. To him we vow our allegiance and our love. . . . We exist to please him. We long to serve him!"

Afterward, when Daran led them to the transport, Will stumbled, as if his legs had suddenly buckled. "Excellency!" Daran cried. "Are you all right?"

"Yes, yes," Will muttered, though he felt, for a moment, out of place, almost out of his own body. Sometimes when he woke up in the morning, he had difficulty standing up without wavering. His heart leapt with fear. There was so much still to do. Was time running out?

"Let's go," Will said. He nodded to Reese, and they all climbed into the transport, Will going last, with the PAAR following.

The door slid shut. Will sat at the front, with Reese and Leora just behind him. "Prepare for takeoff," Will ordered. The engines started. A slight vibration shook the craft. Will gave the coordinates. The transport lifted, leveled itself. The sun glinting on the surface below created a silvery carpet that touched the edge of the horizon.

Will felt shaken. His heart still pounded, and his hands were moist. How happily he had accepted the crowd's adulation! They had pledged their love and their obedience to him. To *him!* Yes, they were fickle and thoughtless, of low intellect and low status. And they had lifted him up and made him a king.

I am my father's child, he thought. *The tyrant lives in my blood, in my bones, in my heart.*

He turned to see Leora slumped in her seat, eyes closed. He pondered the fragility of fate. In a single moment everything had changed for both of them. But Leora had never wavered. Her mission was always the same, to help bring balance back into the Dominion. He watched her sleeping. How good she was, after burying her beloved sister, to come back with him, to work for a better world. *Sublimate selfishness:* the words rang back at him. Until now, he had never known anyone who truly lived them.

"That was a good show back there," Reese said over the sound of the engines. "You played along with them, so as not to reveal your true intentions. You did it brilliantly."

Will did not answer. He couldn't tell Reese the truth; he had loved being adored.

CHAPTER 23

A T LAST THE TRANSPORT SLOWED and dipped and seemed to flatten itself, and Will saw the swift approach of dry land. Several cavernous depressions resembled the surface of the moon. The transport shivered and rattled as it sank down and touched the ground, skidding to a stop.

The door slid open. They climbed out—Leora, Reese, Will, and the PAAR.

"You won't need that," Reese said.

"I thought there are marauders and dissidents hiding here."

"I've never seen any," said Reese.

Will motioned the PAAR back into the transport. He stood looking at the vast expanse of gray earth, overlaid with dust, pocked with pieces of shrapnel and broken stone. In the distance stood the stern, purple-black mountains, dusted with snow.

"It's so desolate," Will said, amazed. Leora, beside him, shaded her eyes against the glare.

"Before the Collapse and the Relocation," Reese said, "we did all kinds of crop experimentation and genetic research here. My laboratory was in a place called Kansas. Kansas," he repeated, letting the word bring back memories.

"My grandparents lived here," Leora said. "Senna says it used to be beautiful farmland. There were creeks and rivers. Where are the people?" She turned to Reese.

"They stay out of sight," he replied.

Will looked all around, until the monotony of the landscape seemed to adjust itself, various shapes and muted colors creating variety where at first one saw only a monotone.

Leora clutched Will's arm, pointing, and Will saw a man walking toward them. As he slowly approached, he waved. Now other people emerged from behind brush and boulders. Slowly they came, about a dozen of them, walking cautiously with heads bent, like people recovering after a long illness. As they drew nearer, Leora whispered, "They're so old!"

Their faces were framed with blue veins, etched with many lines. Their sparse hair was gray or snow white, and Will saw that all of them were thin, almost emaciated. In the forefront, like a general, strode a man with long gray hair tied back with a bit of string. He was wearing a filthy green coat and threadbare trousers, and in his right hand he held a rod of twisted steel.

A woman pushed ahead of the others. "Reese!" she cried. "Oh, Reese, it's been ages!" The woman's white hair was a tangled mass tucked atop her head. Her corded arms were stick thin, as was her body. She was dressed in a gray sack-like garment, tied with a thong.

"Greetings, Wanda," Reese said, and he went to them, calling, "Tyrone, my friend, I see you are still in charge of things."

The man chortled. "Nobody's in charge here," he said with a sly grin. "We've all got one foot in the grave." The man's face was covered with scabs, and his eyes were bright, as if with fever. "Oh, we have missed you, Reese! How are you? How is Nadia? I can't wait to show you the new system." He stopped, looking first at Will, then at Leora.

"These are my friends, Tyrone," Reese said with a reassuring smile. "This is Will, and the young lady is Leora. Senna's daughter."

"Senna's daughter!" the words were relayed from person to person. "Senna's girl!"

Wanda approached Leora and Will, looking closely into their faces. "Oh, they are *young*," she breathed. Her eyes glittered with tears. She asked Reese, "Are they going to stay here with us?"

"No, Wanda. They have other work to do." Reese held out the satchel. "I have brought you this."

"Not here," said Tyrone glancing about nervously. "Is he—the young fellow, isn't he . . ."

"He is one of us," Reese said. "You have my assurance."

And Will remembered the history tapes, how all who were able had been removed to the new colonies. Those who could not travel, the sick and the old, remained behind. These, then, were the remnant Reese had mentioned. Some had to be ninety years old or more, Will thought.

They began to walk, following Tyrone.

A goat bleated from a scrubby hillside.

"You have animals!" Leora exclaimed, and Will knew she was thinking of Kiera.

"Thanks to Reese," said one of the men, panting as he walked.

Reese took the man's arm. "Hey, Bert, you old devil! You've turned out to be quite a herdsman."

"Now we also have some horses. They were wild, but we managed to tame them. Quite a feat for old people like us, isn't it?" Bert laughed hoarsely and slapped his thigh, until he was overtaken by a raucous cough.

A woman, wearing a plaid blanket and bent nearly double, tottered up beside them. Her bare arms showed a network of thick blue veins. She had only three teeth in her mouth. "I will tell you everything," she said, "because you are young. The young need to know these things. After we are gone, who will tell it?"

"Tell it now, Emme," cackled another woman, her lips encrusted with sores. "Say it quick, before you keel over!" She laughed heartily.

"Three years after the Relocation, government transports came here," said Emme. "They didn't land. They sent down probes, to test the soil and the atmosphere. Then they sent robots to collect specimens. After that, they released their rivers of fire."

"Rivers of fire?" Leora cried. "Why?"

"They meant to destroy everything that remained," said Emme. "Including us. They didn't want any people left here. They wanted to sanitize the land."

Sanitize, quarantine, relocate—the words Will had heard all his life took on a new reality. Beside him Leora put her hand to her hair, as she had done the first night they met. The gesture, far from annoying Will, made him want to protect her.

"We fled to the dugouts we had made," the old woman continued, "and to the caves. As long as they think we're dead," she added, "they won't bother us."

Will searched the horizon and realized that there were no buildings, towers, or satellite stations. The occasional surveillance aircraft would not notice any evidence of habitation.

"Horses," said the woman with the mouth sores. "A few colts have been born. Apparently they are not all sterile. A miracle," she added. "We, on the other hand, are a drying breed."

"Don't say that, Reba," chided Bert. "We still have hope. Thanks to Reese."

They walked along a series of narrow paths, half concealed by boulders, dipping down into shallow vales, passing deep depressions that were charred and forbidding, with signs posted: DANGER! KEEP OFF!

"Here the missiles struck," said Tyrone. "Some spots are still radioactive."

Reba pointed to a distance. "There the plants have revived. Reese brought us seeds and the reclaiming beetles. Without him, we would all be dead."

"And Senna," put in Emme.

"Senna!" exclaimed Leora.

A cluster of small, wispy trees grew at the base of a low hill. They nearly concealed the path and the entrance to a sod house, its roof a mixture of crushed pebbles, glass, soil, and thatch. Tyrone stopped. He pushed aside a heavy door, ducked down through the low sod roof, and motioned for his guests to enter.

"We build our houses into the sod," Tyrone explained, "and we use caves and dugouts. That way we can't be spotted from the air."

Will bent his head, following Reese and Leora, and to his surprise saw that they were in a large room with a smooth mud floor encrusted with bits of glass, stone, and shining metal. The walls, made of mud bricks and washed over with white clay, were adorned with oil-burning sconces.

Tyrone, breathless from the walk, held out his hands to Reese. "Boy or girl?"

"Girl."

"Ah, a double blessing!"

Reese chuckled. "You always say that, my friend." He reached gently into the satchel and drew out a blanket. Will saw the small head, sparse hair, the round face of an infant, its eyes tightly closed and mouth puckered as it began to stir.

"Oh!" Leona cried, rushing to Reese, holding out her arms. "Oh, so sweet! Let me hold her!"

Reese laid the baby into Leora's arms. "We had to sedate her for the trip," Reese explained. "Now she will be hungry. I brought some goat's milk." He reached into the satchel once again and brought out a nursing bottle.

Leora took the bottle, moved to one of the chairs, and sat down with the baby. "Here, sweet one," she crooned as the infant began to suck the milk, making hungry gurgling sounds. Will watched, transfixed. He felt breathless and overcome with love for Leora. He had never seen such a young infant, nor a woman holding one. It left him feeling meek and at the same time, resolute. For Leora, for this, he would even defy Hayli!

The old people stood around, awed, hands clasped, eyes wide. They murmured and whispered their amazement, their gratitude. "Now," Emme said breathlessly, "we will live."

"That makes fourteen altogether," whispered Bert.

"What a joy!" exclaimed Reba. "Oh, what a day when a new one comes!"

"What is her name?" asked Tyrone.

"We haven't named her yet," said Reese. "Senna only turned her out a week ago. We have kept her hidden at the farm."

"What was the problem?"

"They wanted a boy."

"Ah." A sigh swept over the group.

"How did Senna do it this time?" asked Tyrone.

"She told them the baby died. Fortunately, Senna was alone in the lab and could manage it. When the other workers came back, she told them she had already disposed of the body."

"How many does that make for Senna?"

"Eight."

With the baby in her arms, Leora stood up and went to Reese. "Senna, my mother, saves babies? I had no idea," Leora said softly.

Reese nodded. "She didn't want you to know. It is dangerous work."

The baby began to squirm, and Leora held her up over her shoulder.

"What shall we call her?" Emme asked.

"Let Will name her," said Leora. She held out the baby to him. He took a step back. Leora followed, chuckling. "Come on, Will. Hold her."

Will stretched out his arms and Leora laid the baby close to his chest. He was astonished at how light she felt in his arms. He gazed at the pale skin, the soft tufts of dark hair. The baby opened her eyes. They were dark blue, large and clear. The tiny mouth looked like a bud, ready to open. Precious, Will thought. It was a word he had never used in his entire life. It simply flew into his head.

"Precious," he said. "That should be her name."

"Beautiful," murmured the women.

"Everyone agreed?" asked Tyrone.

"Aye," said the mingled voices. "Precious. Our new daughter."

"Well done," said Reese. To Tyrone he said, "Let's show them the garden."

Tyrone led the way through a dim passage lined with rocks. Will felt the moisture and he heard the hollow sounds of their footsteps, and he realized they were descending into a cave with many divergent paths. A large round chamber was filled with thriving plants and flooded with light from a series of overlapping panels. "Solar," Tyrone explained, pointing to the uneven space that had been chiseled out to admit the light. An intricate series of pipes were suspended over long planter boxes from which rose up green shoots and leaves. Beans hung down from vines. Tiny ears of corn were curled between long, slender leaves, clusters of vegetables that Will had never seen before. Tubers lay in great vats, a new harvest.

"For all this," said Tyrone, "we thank our friend, Reese. He brought us the beetles that revitalized the soil. Still, most of our plants are hydroponic. Eventually we hope to be able to plant above. But that may take decades."

Will stood apart with Leora. Her smoky blue eyes were filled with tears. "Until there are no more Bumblecops or enforcers," she said, "these people have to live under the ground, hidden away. It's not a good way for babies to grow."

Tyrone led them back to the chamber, where Reba and Emme and the others were waiting.

"Are there other colonies like this one?" Will asked.

Tyrone hesitated. "Probably. Yes. We have tried to make contact," he said guardedly. "But our equipment is very primitive."

"How many are you?" asked Will. Plans were raging in his mind, impossible plans, perhaps, but how could he simply turn away from these people?

"There were hundreds of us at first," Tyrone said sorrowfully. "So many have died since those days. Radiation, illness, or just plain old age."

"We lose a few every year," put in Reba. "Thirty-two of us are left. We try to hang on, until we can teach the children."

"What do you teach them?" Leora asked.

"Everything we know," replied Reba.

"Then you must have a school," said Will. He recalled his own school days, the fierce competitions, warnings, and threats: *You are failing this examination, please focus, your performance is six points below the median. You are in danger of losing status.*

Will remembered how the sweat used to pour down his sides, how his stomach felt twisted with fear, and the strain of maintaining status, at all costs.

"We have no school building, no special rooms for learning," said Tyrone. "It is a constant process. We have refurbished some old-fashioned computers. And some years ago we dug up a vault where books were stored. Fortunately, most of them were intact. Now, everyone reads." He paused, glancing at Reese. "Do you want to see the children?"

"Of course," said Reese, smiling.

They came, all ages, exclaiming over the new baby, laughing, rushing up to Will and Leora and Reese. "Oh, visitors! Let me read for you. Let me play for you!"

"They love to recite," said Emme, stroking the hair of one of the girls.

One by one the children stepped forward in an impromptu recital of songs, poems, anecdotes, facts, stories. After each recitation came praise, even applause. Will was fascinated, envious. He had never imagined that learning could happen without grief.

At last Will glanced at his pulse pad. "We have to leave," he said. He went once more to the baby lying in Emme's arms, fast asleep. Leora stood beside him, touching the pink cheek with her finger. "Good-bye, Precious," she whispered. "Maybe we'll come back someday."

"Oh, please come back," the children pleaded. "Don't forget us!"

Tyrone put his hand on Will's shoulder, drawing him aside as they stood in the shadow of the transport. "I trust there will be some changes made," he said softly.

"What do you mean?" Will asked, looking into Tyrone's eyes.

"I know who you are," replied the old man. "I knew the moment you arrived, but Reese vouched for you." He laid his hand gently on Will's head. "Come back to us, Will."

For a long time after he was in the transport, bound for Washolina, Will still felt that touch.

CHAPTER 24

THINGS WERE NOT QUITE AS WILL remembered them.

From the moment the transport landed in Washolina, Will felt queasy, unsettled, as if he was going to be sick. The city was too bright, too loud, assaulting Will's senses. Enforcers, PAARs, and robo-sanitizers filled the streets. The Screen flashed continual images. Colors and sounds forced their way into one's thoughts.

Leora, too, seemed affected by the drastic change from the pastoral settling of Fresmofield. She walked slowly, wonderingly, as if she were comparing the fields they had so recently left behind to this electronic, carefully managed environment.

Only Reese seemed refreshed, gazing up at the towers and pavilions, smiling as they stepped onto the moving pathway. "Very, very different," he exclaimed over and over again. "So different from my student days. Look—that's the street where I lived. There was a men's dormitory. We used to sit at a café in the summer. I remember how we stayed up all night at the first session—brilliant scientists came to lecture. We would work all day, meet at night to discuss our findings, our theories—oh, it was exhilarating! Then, of course, came the Collapse. I was already in the Heartland then, doing research. But I heard about the changes. They seemed good. Hayli the Wise, we called him. I remember thinking I would join Hayli's team of scientists. Then I got wind of some of the ed-its, the repression, and I went with the others to the Relocation. Look here! We used to have a lab there, electron microscopes, a fantastic observatory—where is it? Gone, I suppose, along with so many other things." Reese turned this way and that, a tourist, a native returning home, his expression moving from amazement to longing and then to resolve.

"We'll bring back the balance, yes," he said repeatedly. "We have to restore sanity."

For Will, the trip back had been a miasma of increasing anxiety. All that homecoming ought to be, especially after a near fatal illness, the anticipation and excitement, was marred by the fact that he had changed. He was different now, not only by knowledge of who he was, but by his experiences. Everything he saw would seem different, too. The fact that he kept thinking of the little cot in the crowded, untidy room, the jacaranda tree, the goat at Reese's Farm, and Kiera's sweet face—that was not troubling. But Will dreaded the first meeting with Mara and Berk and finding . . . what? It was the uncertainty that made him afraid.

But he tried not to show it as he strolled with Leora and Reese through the streets of Washolina, nodding and perhaps even swaggering when people recognized him and gave him that reverential look. "I have seen the son of the Compassionate Director!" they would exclaim to the first person they encountered, and then relate the experience, making it much more than it was, feeling burnished with the light of Will's fame.

And yet he was only a clone. Worse than trash. How could he put it to Hayli, to Mara, and to Berk—to question the thing that was by its very nature so degrading?

Deep in his mind, behind the worry and the pretense, was the lingering thought that there *must* be a reason. Perhaps in a moment and with a flourish, Hayli would explain it all. Then how they would laugh together, laugh at Will's mistaken ideas, wipe away all the misunderstandings that had turned Will's perceptions upside down, thinking goodness was evil and compassion was only convenience. It could all be cleared up in an instant!

Reese brought him back to the present. "Look, there's the old science building, restored. I want to go and see it. Some of my old colleagues must still be there. I'm sure there will be a conference going on, as always." He stepped down from the motion path, taking Will and Leora with him.

"But will they let you in?" Will asked.

Reese nodded, brushed aside Will's concern. "Of course. I'm an alumnus. They'll look me up by my I.D. implant. Most of us had them done at the very beginning of The Goodness. Turned out, it was a smart move," he gave a smile of great satisfaction; he had duped the Powers. "It makes me one of the faithful."

"I'll be visiting my brother at the medical center," Will said. "Hayli says he's sick. Some kind of a virus, I suppose. Maybe you can find out something about it and we can compare notes later."

"Do you know who's treating him?" Reese asked.

"Hayli's personal physician, I guess. Dr. Varton."

"Thad Varton!" Reese exclaimed. "We were classmates. He went into neuropathology. I haven't seen him in years. I'll do my best," he said, "to find out about your brother." Without the beard he looked younger, and his eyes were less intense, but still dominant. He paused, looking worried. "What will you tell Hayli about the Great Desert? He'll expect your report, won't he?"

"I'll say it's a desolate place. Empty. I'll tell him we saw piles of bleached bones and empty caverns, that the place is uninhabitable."

"Good," Reese said with a firm nod. "I'll meet you later, at your pod," he said, his gestures hurried, showing his impatience to be off.

He quickly blended into the crowd.

"When will I see you again?" Will asked Leora.

"Anytime you flip on your Screen," she said teasingly.

"No. I mean, really." Glancing about, he took her hand, held it tightly amid the folds of his tunic. He drew back as they passed several government buildings with their Screens and cameras. "I don't think I can stand it here for very long," he murmured, feeling stifled and tense. "I keep thinking about . . . everything. The Farm. The desert and those people."

"I think about Precious," Leora said softly. Her face took on a tender look. "You said we'll go back some day."

"Of course!" Will said stoutly. "Things can change. The desert can become productive. It's happened before. Just imagine, if crops grew there again, and Reese continued his experiments. Antone and Senna might go back there, too."

"They'd restore the old name," Leora said, breathless. "Heartland. Isn't it a beautiful name?"

"Beautiful," Will agreed. His vision turned inward to a different expectation, a different sort of life, with real food and real trees, people doing whatever work they chose, finding a partner, touching, being close.

"We would all be together," Leora murmured.

"Yes," Will whispered. "We would be together." The only dream he had ever had was to be Hayli's right hand, Hayli's duplicate. He marveled that he had spent his life on a dream so empty. "I have to go now to see Berk," he said. "But later, I'll pad you."

"I'll be waiting," Leora said, smiling. She stepped quickly onto the motion path. Even after she was gone, Will felt her presence beside him.

All the way back to his pod, Will imagined being back in Fresmofield with Leora, without the constant Screen admonitions, enforcers, Pop Pageants, and edicts.

His pod felt different, constricting, even though it contained not one superfluous item. It was the antithesis of the small, cluttered room in Antone's house, with the wide window and ridiculous porcelain bathtub. It made him smile to think of it. Will checked his canteen; it was fully stocked. He peered into the Sani-tube, inhaling the sterile, almost antiseptic cleanliness of it. He took off his clothes and allowed the Sani-tube elements to cleanse him thoroughly, spreading his fingers and toes, shaking out his hair, lifting his face to the decontamination rays. He felt purified, prepared. Then he walked over to the Screen and summoned Mara.

To his surprise, she responded immediately. "Let me see you. In person. You can tell me your adventures. Are you well? Are you recovered?"

"Yes, yes. I'll come right over," Will said, hurrying to collect himself. "Come on!" he called to the PAAR, as if it were a pet. The PAAR obliged, clattering after him onto the motion path with its music and banners and the constant, instructive whispering, to the causeway that led to the government compound where Mara lived.

Once inside, Will strode past I.D. monitors and into the opulence of Mara's home. Several PAARS and robo-servants stood guard outside her door. Mara came to greet him. She was radiant in a long robe of fuchsia with deep blue embroidery on the edges. She held out her arms and drew him inside.

"Mara! You look so beautiful," Will said.

She laughed, pointed to the low couch. "You have been away from civilization," she said, "so an old woman in decent clothes looks good to you!"

"You will always be beautiful," Will said. He sank down into the couch and looked around at the gleaming mirrored walls and crystal lights that seemed suspended in midair. His own image was repeated a hundred times, diminishing to infinity, an artifice. It was the kind of decor that Hayli loved. Across the domed ceiling and worked into the jeweled floor were gilded letters: HAIL, HAYLI! Everywhere there were likenesses of Hayli: as a boy, a youth, a man, and in his white uniform and golden cap, wearing the new gold and diamond medal of Supreme Compassionate Director. He looked magnificent. For a moment Will felt old sensations—awe and fear, longing and dread.

"Now tell me everything," Mara said. She settled herself down beside him, while with a wave of her hand she dismissed several robo-servants. They scurried away to the corners of the room along with Will's PAAR, commanded to *stay*. "Are you well? How did they treat you? I heard Hayli sent his own doctor, Varton, one of the best. We were terribly worried." Mara touched Will's cheek, a gentle, quick touch, and as briefly as possible he told her about the emergency landing in Fresmofield, how he had almost died.

"But I recovered quickly. And Leora showed me everything, the silos, labs, and the countryside." Will's mind raced over his experiences, editing, amending, so as not mention the aspects that could launch them into controversy, and he realized there were many, so many! He dared not tell Mara about Antone's work or Reese's farm, the hidden children, the Great Desert. What was left? He wished he could tell her everything.

"What about that girl?" Mara asked, leaning toward him. "Leora?"

"She's back at the Academy," Will said. In the transport from the Great Desert he and she had sat side by side. Their hands touched, and then he clasped her hand tightly. They were connected, a team.

Now he began slowly, watching Mara's face as he spoke. "In Fresmofield," Will said, "I heard a song you used to sing to me when I was a child."

"A song?" Mara said vaguely, without interest.

"Yes, you sang it to me whenever I was upset."

"I?" She waved her hands, as if to push away the very thought of it. "I never sang. You must have been dreaming." She laughed lightly, a bird-like sound.

Will took a deep breath and sang:

> *"See no evil,*
> *Shed no tear.*
> *I am with you,*
> *Always near . . ."*

As he sang, Will pictured Reese's Farm and the Remembrance place, Nadia, the pasture, the goats, and the other creatures.

> *"Like a shepherd in the vale,*
> *I will keep you, never fail.*
> *Lead us to the better way . . ."*

Mara's face was turned away. Will heard her sigh, saw her reluctance in the way she put her fingers to her lips as she said softly, "My grandfather Drew taught me that song. He was a good man. A wonderful man."

"What happened to him?"

"Why, he was killed in one of the first missile attacks." She shuddered, wrapped her arms around herself. "I don't want to think about it. Let's talk about pleasant things."

"Do you remember the last line of that song?" Will urged.

"At evening now we play."

"No," Will said. "That's not right. It is *pray*. At evening now we *pray*."

"Pray?" Mara's voice rose. "That is archaic. Nobody prays. It is subversive and *dissy!*"

"That was the original song. Your grandfather didn't think it was *dissy.*"

Mara's face stiffened. "We do not pray here," she said haughtily. "You know that we have done away with all that superstition. I hope you told the people of Fresmofield that it's all nonsense."

"I didn't," Will said. "They seemed to find comfort in it."

"I'm sorry for them!" Mara exclaimed.

"I also found out something about me," Will said. How to put it? What words could he use, except for the truth? He could think of no way to soften it.

"When I got sick," he began, "they took me to the clinic."

"Yes, yes, I know." Mara dipped her hand into a crystal bowl of chocovites, eating several of the small confections at once.

"At the clinic someone checked my DNA."

"Quite normal," Mara remarked, wiping her hand carefully on a napkin.

"No. Not normal," Will said. "They found out that my DNA is old. Do you know what that means?" He did not wait for her to answer. "I am a clone, Mara."

"A clone?" She laughed. "How outlandish. What makes you think . . . ?"

"It's true. I proved it for myself. I wouldn't make a mistake like that."

Mara rushed to the mirrored wall, and for a moment Will saw her image in bizarre repetition. She pressed a button and instantly a pale gray film closed over the mirrors, providing privacy from the electronic eyes that loomed continually behind the glass.

She sank down onto the sofa, her fingers pressed over her lips, eyes staring. "So, you found out," she said at last. "I always thought you might. You are so inquisitive, perceptive."

"You knew? You knew all along?" By her expression he saw in her face that she really had no idea of how it felt to discover such a thing, no empathy, no understanding. And he wondered whether she had ever been different, or whether he had superimposed his own longings upon her.

"Look, it doesn't really matter," Mara said. "You have to see this in perspective, Will."

"But Hayli himself outlawed cloning!" Will exclaimed.

Mara waved it aside, an annoying detail. "That was because everyone was getting into it! Hayli's researchers were doing it under strict guidelines. It was for the sake of the people, even the masses, don't you see? You have to understand the whole cloning concept was for the sake of humanity. It was to improve the human race. It was meant to expand the potential of life beyond anything we've ever imagined, almost to immortality!"

"You really believe it doesn't matter?" he said, aghast. "Hayli lied to me. How many others are there? Dozens? Hundreds?"

Mara shook her head. "I don't know. I think at the beginning there were quite a few. Now, it's only you and Berk. Just the two of you. Will, you sound so angry. What difference does it make? You are still Hayli's son. You are still his heir, and he loves you."

"Of course it matters!" he cried. "Do you know who the donor was?"

She stood up and went to him, reaching for his hands, but he brushed her away. "Will, you have to understand. Our lives were devoted to The Goodness. Times were different. We had all suffered too much. We had to look to the future, to see the bigger picture. If there were sacrifices along the way, so be it!"

"But it wasn't *your* sacrifice!" Will cried, appalled that she should be thinking only of herself. "I'm talking about me, *my* life, and what Hayli has done." How could she refuse to understand what he was really talking about? But now he understood. This had always been her way, smoothing things out, refusing to see evil.

"Hayli meant no harm!" Mara exclaimed. "He wanted a son. What's so wrong about that? And when he got you and Berk, he gave you everything. He prepared you to sit beside him, to help him lead The Goodness."

"Don't make excuses for him!" Will cried, furious. "Hayli already had a son!"

"That's a lie! Who told you such a thing?"

Will leapt up and pulled open the fastener at his throat. He reached for the medal Zebarre had given him, holding it out to Mara, tilting it so that the diamonds glittered.

"Where did you get this?" Mara gasped, backing away. "It's not possible! Only five of these were ever made, and only mine and Hayli's remain." She clutched her own matching medal.

"No," said Will. "You see with your own eyes. This belonged to Taroo. He has changed his name now. He's called Zebarre. He lives in District Seven. And he told me about your son. Yours and Hayli's."

He felt as if he had struck her a blow, for Mara recoiled. Then, slowly, she went and touched one of the gray panels that covered the mirrored walls. "These draperies are usually only used when Hayli comes here to see me," she said. "Otherwise, I am under continual surveillance. For my own good," she said with a harsh sound. "I am like a pet bird in a cage." She paused. "Taroo lives," she whispered. "I thought he was dead."

"That's what he wanted everyone to think," Will said. "He planned that accident. But he escaped to the Heartland, and finally to District Seven."

"What does he do there?" Mara asked softly. She sat back against the cushions. Her posture suggested retreat to another time, when she was one of the illustrious Five, planning, creating a new world, leading the people out of the Collapse. How strong she must have been! Now, her power came only from association with Hayli. Her life depended on him. It was apparent in the arrangement of her furniture, in the mirrors and the mosaics and portraits that crowded her personal living space.

Will sat down opposite Mara, avoiding her eyes. "Zebarre repairs machinery in one of the silos that manufactures artificial food. He said he loved you. He always loved you."

"That time is gone," Mara said, settling her robe around her. "We must live for the future." She leaned toward him, executing her famous smile. "Now that you are back," she said, "what are your plans?"

Will refused to play the game. "Tell me about the boy," he said. "Hayli's real son." The words all but caught in his throat. "You can't pretend he didn't exist, Mara."

Mara looked away. He saw tears glistening on her cheeks. She drew a deep breath, wiped her face, and said, "You might as well know the truth. Nobody else does, except for Hayli. When I'm gone, someday, maybe you'll need to know."

Will nodded silently and waited for the tale to unravel.

"Everyone thought he had been turned out in a lab. Hayli insisted on that. I went along with it. What did it matter? Hayli said it was important for The Goodness, to set an example for people who might otherwise be lax and transmit hereditary defects." She gave a harsh laugh. "Little did he imagine his own weakness would surface! He thought he was perfect. Except for one little thing, which he didn't bother to mention. Hayli's immune system is defective. He has a terrible allergy."

"And that would be passed on?" Will asked, while simultaneously he focused on the irony that Hayli was, himself, flawed.

"Yes. It could be. You see, he is highly allergic to nuts. As a child, several times he went into shock and nearly died. That's how Mattelin found him, lying on the pavement, gasping for breath."

"The biographies say Mattelin found him at the archives building."

"On the steps in front of the building," Mara corrected. "Mattelin picked him up and rushed him to a clinic. He saved Hayli's life. It was the second or third time it had happened. The doctor said he could never eat nuts again or even breathe in the residue. Of course, Hayli never told anyone. Superhumans don't have allergies or illnesses, do they?"

"But someone has to know," Will said, "to protect him."

"Oh, yes. That's where I come in. Rondo and I test all the food that Hayli eats. You may have noticed, he never eats or drinks anything when he is with others. Only alone."

And Will remembered the small sandwiches Hayli had offered him, and the golden fizzy drink, champagne, that Will had sipped alone.

"That was one of the reasons," Mara went on, "that Hayli created artificial foods, to make sure none of the ingredients could harm him. Later he realized that if he expanded the factories, if he could control the food production, he held the entire Dominion in his hands."

"All this is because he is allergic to nuts?" Will exclaimed. "How stupid! How trivial!"

"It's not trivial!" Mara exclaimed. She stood up and paced, as if some long-confined energy now needed release, and she would talk until she was done, no matter how long it took. "In the beginning, Hayli didn't tell me about the allergy. He hadn't planned to father any children. It just happened. A common mistake, I'm told," she said mockingly.

"But—"

"Don't say it! You're going to tell me all that nonsense they spread to the people, that sex is dirty, sex is dangerous, sex is ugly. Hayli never gave up sex. Hayli thought the Symsex was a joke, he and his cronies."

Mara paced, her steps swift and furious. "Drew inherited his father's allergy. The first time he ate nuts, he went into shock. Drew started to choke and gag. He couldn't breathe. He turned blue. I screamed for help. I pushed the pulse pad, ran out to Hayli's conference room. The doors were locked and guarded by robo-enforcers. I stood outside with the child in my arms. I screamed until someone finally heard me and got Hayli. But it was too late."

"The boy died," Will said.

"No." Mara stopped and faced Will as she sat down opposite him on the sofa. Her lips were pursed, tight, as if she wanted to remain silent. "How often I wish he *had* died! Then I go to see him, and feel so guilty. Because Drew doesn't know anything. He suffered brain damage. He lived, but mentally, he never grew."

Will thought of Kiera and of all the people going to Removal, of Senna in the lab, rinsing away tiny bits of life. At last he asked, "Where is he?"

Mara sighed. "Three floors down. In this complex."

"Right here?" It seemed incredible. "Can I see him?"

Mara shook her head, brushing away tears. "Don't ask me," she said.

"Why not?"

"I swore to Hayli that I would keep Drew hidden."

"And you are loyal to Hayli," Will stated. "In spite of everything."

"Yes! How dare you judge me?" Mara retorted. "Hayli and I built the entire Dominion. We have saved thousands, millions of lives! I can't go against him now. Hayli is all I have."

"You have me," Will said. "Me and Berk."

"Berk is dying," Mara said coldly. "And you never really belonged to me."

"But you loved me!" Will clasped her arm. "Don't you still?"

"Yes!"

Questions flashed through Will's mind. Was it true that she loved him? Did she know who his donor was?

"Let me see Drew. I want to see him."

"Why?"

"Because he is your child. So much has been hidden from me." And he saw by her expression that she wanted to show him, to share the secret and the pain.

"Once you have seen such a thing," Mara whispered, "you'll never be able to forget it."

"I don't want to forget," Will said. "Someone should know, Mara," he urged. "If anything ever happened to you, who would take care of Drew?"

She took a deep breath. "Come," she said. "I'll take you to him."

CHAPTER 25

M ARA TOOK HIM to the mirrored wall. At the touch of her finger, the panels slid open, revealing a hidden passage that led to a thickly carpeted ramp. It circled down and down into a great white hall. The walls were adorned with photographs of Mara when she was young, Mara and Hayli, Mara with each of The Five, and the entire group in various poses, all suggesting the lively camaraderie of people working for a cause and loving it.

Among the photographs were certificates of honor and education. Mara held degrees in civil engineering and architecture. Several photographs showed Mara in front of an entire complex of her own design. She was, surely, an important member of The Five. As they walked, Will stated at the photographs, amazed and shocked at what time had done, what Hayli had done to change Mara from a vibrant, energetic girl to the powerless woman beside him.

At the electronic monitor, Mara showed her implant. The door slid open.

"He won't even notice you," Mara whispered when they stood before a heavy steel door. "Take off your shoes."

Will did so, and he stepped over the portal into the room, walking on a soft, spongy surface. Like the Cuddle Corner from Will's childhood, this entire room was designed to satisfy the needs of a baby. Here was a self-contained environment that offered complete physical safety and continual stimulation for someone with a mental age of two. Soft surfaces glowed with pastel colors that changed continually, a moving collage. Pictures of simple objects streamed across the wall. Suspended from the ceiling were various shapes, cones, spirals, feathery wands, twirling and spinning, inviting touch. And crouched on the floor, reaching gleefully for the spinning objects, was a man.

"This is Drew," said Mara.

He was dressed in a puffy white turbo-suit, the sort that babies wear, but his shoulders were broad and his hands large. He turned slightly, and Will saw that his eyes were a brilliant blue, like Hayli's. His blond hair was a wavy mane, like Hayli's, and his neck was thick and powerful.

"Drew," Mara called, holding out her arms.

For a few moments Drew remained mesmerized by the bright objects, reaching, gurgling. Then he turned with a shriek of pleasure, calling, "Ma! Ma!"

Now a woman emerged from behind a shimmering curtain of light. Behind her Will saw a man-sized crib and a chair equipped with restraints.

The woman was tall and athletic-looking, with a flat cap of dark hair. Good day, Mara!" said the woman. She ignored Will entirely. "Our Drew is fine today," she said. "He had his supper already. He liked his supper."

"Thank you," said Mara. "Is there anything you need?"

"No," replied the woman. "Everything is in order."

Will stood gazing at the child-man, this being who was so needy, utterly dependent. His heart seemed to cramp in his chest. There were no words he could offer to Mara, no consolation, nor did he know how to respond to Drew. Should he speak? Touch? Hold the man's hand? Will stood, helpless against the revulsion and the pity that overwhelmed him. And this, he realized, was what Mara had to live with every day. In that instant he forgave her the deception, the denials and evasions she always gave him. Now he understood her need to carve out an unreal world for herself, a world where nothing mattered much, where Hayli took care of her and she was accorded a place of honor.

"Come," Mara said, leading Will away. To the caregiver she said, "I'll come back tomorrow." They stepped out into the hall. The door snapped shut, and Will heard the lock slip into place.

"Does she ever leave?" Will asked. He felt numb. His own words sounded muffled to his ears.

"No."

"Is she . . . ?"

"A robot. Clever, isn't it? What can be done?"

They went quickly back up the winding ramp, Will in the lead. He stumbled and clutched the railing as weakness overcame him.

"Are you all right?"

"Just shaken," Will said. Mara was right. It was a sight he would never forget.

"Now you know," said Mara when they were back in her apartment, the opaque shields still drawn. "Now you know why I can never leave Hayli's side. He has told me if I ever leave him, he will stop feeding Drew. He will take away his robo-nurse. He will let him starve to death. It is a painful death, I hear, starvation."

"He would do that to his own son?"

"Hayli doesn't acknowledge him. Years ago Hayli broadcast the rumor that Taroo had a child, and that the baby was born deformed. Taroo—Zebarre—was charged as a betrayer. Then it was said that the child died. As far as Hayli is concerned, Drew is already dead."

"But Hayli let him live."

"Hayli let him live. It was the only thing I ever asked of him. It is understood that I will never ask for anything else." Mara ducked her head, a gesture of submission. "I tried to get over it. I became obsessed. Hayli was frightened at my condition. I lost weight. I couldn't sleep."

"Did Hayli make Berk and me, then, to give you a child? Because of what happened to Drew?"

"No, no," Mara shook her head vehemently. "He had that planned all along. But after you were turned out, he did encourage me to go to the nursery. He let me hold you and be with you. Of course, I wanted to bond with Berk, too, but he didn't like to be held. Hayli said you needed the love of a mother, that it would be important for your development. And I took the gift—oh, I took it so gladly!"

Will stood up before Mara. He watched the changing expressions on her face: confusion, sorrow, weakness. He weighed his alternatives. Should he continue to press her for answers?

Gently he asked, "Do you know why Hayli created me?"

"To have sons to help him, to be his left hand and his right. You heard him, didn't you?"

"And you think that's the whole truth?"

"Every man wants a son," Mara replied. "It's his passport to immortality."

"But I'm not his," Will exclaimed. He took a deep breath, steadied himself, and said, "Do you know whose clone I am?"

"No," Mara said. "I asked Hayli once or twice. I was curious. Someone sold him DNA that had been frozen long ago. I remember that. Hayli said it was a special person, a hero. Someone with strong convictions who would help usher in the Time of Perfection."

Will moved nearer to Mara, until he was beside her. He knelt down and took her hand in his. "Adolf Hitler," he said, looking into her eyes. "Hayli cloned me from Adolf Hitler's DNA."

Mara turned her head, shook herself free. "No. That's impossible. That tyrant from centuries ago? Think what you are saying! It's impossible." She made that familiar gesture with her hands, as if to push him away, a gesture of denial.

"He did it, Mara. He wanted to duplicate Hitler. And he has tried to train Berk and me to be just as ruthless. He tried to cut out any softness we might have developed. Those brutal games, the competitions, everything was designed to make us tough and aggressive."

"That's nonsense!" Mara objected, eyes wide. "All boys love war games!"

"Hayli always kept me and Berk in fear. Hitler's father was that way, too, cruel and cold."

Mara got up, moved away from Will, shaking her head. "No. This is ridiculous, Will. You say it was Hitler!" she accused, pointing. "How do I know it's true? You come here with this fantastic story, and you want me to believe it?"

Will went to Mara's Screen and put in the access codes and the command. Instantly the biography of Hitler began. Mara moved like a dreamer, uncertain, hypnotized. She watched, open-mouthed, her breathing swift and shallow, but her expression never changed. None of it seemed to move her, to touch her.

Will stood beside Mara, watching the entire display; he felt once again the horror, the rage, the despair of knowing that such a man had once lived and, more, that he was of the same flesh.

They watched the old films of Hitler's youth, his conquests, the brazen speeches and the methodical murder of millions. He saw once again the rising smoke, the piles of bones, the open graves. The last remaining evidence: Hitler's face, larger than life, and now there was no denying the resemblance.

For a long while Mara neither moved nor spoke. Then she went slowly to the sofa and sat down, her head nodding, hands limp at her sides. "Well," she said, her features oddly composed. "Well."

"Tell me about how Hayli got the DNA," Will said. "The man who came to him. Do you know anything more about it?"

"The DNA was frozen. Hayli never told me the details. I don't know who sold it to him. It probably cost a lot. With it, Hayli said, he would create a perfect race."

"And you believed him, of course," said Will. "Hayli has a way of making people believe him."

"Of course I believed him!" Mara exclaimed. "Who was I to say that Hayli couldn't do it? Hayli had saved the Dominion, after all. He had restored confidence and hope after the Collapse. He brought the most brilliant scientists into his fold. If anyone could do it, perfect the race, even reach immortality, it was Hayli!"

He said, "But why would Hayli want to clone Hitler? Hitler wasn't physically strong or good-looking."

"Hitler had convictions. He was determined to rule for a thousand years. You saw it just now, on the Screen."

"Convictions?" Will echoed. "Does Hayli think convictions are inherited?"

"I don't know!" Mara wiped her hands over her brow. She looked tired.

"I suppose he does. I remember that Hayli was doing some research on things like that, attitudes and heredity."

"And Hayli wanted someone exactly like Hitler," Will said bitterly, "to help him rule this new world of his." He went to the door.

"What are you planning to do?" Mara asked fearfully.

"I'm not sure yet," Will said. "First, I need to see Berk."

"Have you told him—Berk—everything? That he is a clone?"

"No."

"Berk won't care," Mara said. "He isn't like you. You take everything so seriously. Berk would jump at the chance to rule an entire dominion. Think about it, Will," Mara said. "All your life you've been trained for leadership. You said so yourself. All you have to do now is reach out and take it."

"Continue with all the policies of The Goodness," Will stated.

"Yes. Continue, expand, let Hayli's researchers do their job, and you do yours. Work with Hayli in the Ministry. Accept the gift, Will. Accept it gracefully."

"And say nothing to Hayli?"

"Say nothing. Let it be."

Mara pulled herself up and went to him, arms outstretched as in the old days. But Will stood back, and he realized that he was as tall as she.

"Are you going to tell Hayli that we spoke?" Mara asked, her face creased now with concern. "Are you going to tell him you saw Drew?"

Will hesitated only for a moment. "No," he said. "I'll leave you out of it. And you can't tell him about this conversation either, Mara. Is it agreed?"

"Agreed," she said. "Where are you going now?"

"To see Berk."

"I'm coming with you," Mara said. "I've been meaning to visit him." She drew her cloak around her shoulders, looking resolute. And Will knew she had avoided visiting Berk until now to avoid distress.

Outside, Will took a deep breath, wishing for the fresh cool air of Fresmofield. He hurried with Mara to the motion path, still uncertain as to how he would confront his brother.

CHAPTER 26

WILL AND MARA and the PAAR crossed the wide plaza that marked the government buildings, opulent and spacious. Portraits of Hayli and slogans from his creed were emblazoned over every doorway. Even now workers were carefully installing a series of huge panels depicting scenes from Hayli's life—a foundling wrapped in a blanket, surrounded by a halo of light; a little boy sitting at a table in front of a complicated computer screen; a young man leading a small group of bright-eyed reformers through rubble-strewn streets.

"Hayli is everywhere," Will muttered.

"Why does he want to see you?"

"I'm supposed to have a health check," Will replied.

"Have you been ill?"

"No." He scratched the patch of irritated skin above his elbow. "Only this itch. It's chronic."

"An allergy?" Mara asked, alarm in her voice.

"I don't think so. At least, I'm certain I have no allergy to nuts. I ate them all the time in Fresmofield. They grow there." Leora had brought to Washolina a satchel full of dried fruit, nuts, and some of the crinkly cereal that Antone made. Will understood now how much she needed to have something from home.

Mara walked ahead through a long hallway, showing her implant as they moved from one secure area to another. Will followed, hearing his

PAAR's clattering gait. At last they stopped at one of the innumerable rooms, and once again Mara and Will showed their identification. Will heard the release of a latch. He pushed open the door. A nurse in a white gown stood beside the bed, taking Berk's vital signs with a probe.

"Hello, brother!" Will called, making his voice cheerful, while his heart sank at the sight of his brother's pale, drawn face.

Berk turned his head. "Will?"

"Yes! Mara and I came to visit you!"

Berk raised himself on one elbow with obvious effort. He stared for a long moment, then he fell back against the pillows. A muscle spasm jerked at his cheek. Berk's voice was truculent. "Who is that? What is she doing here? Don't let her in here!"

"It's Mara," Will exclaimed. "Why are you acting this way to Mara?"

The nurse motioned strongly, mouthing the words, "He doesn't realize. Don't upset him." She went to Berk and smoothed the blanket, saying, "Don't worry, I won't let anyone in that you don't want to see. Relax, Berk. I won't let anyone hurt you."

"I'll go," said Mara, quickly turning away. "Will, let's talk after you've seen Hayli."

Will drew near to his brother. Berk's eyes were closed now. His hands were clasped on his chest, the fingers twitching involuntarily.

"What is it?" Will asked the nurse. "What's wrong?"

"I'm not at liberty to discuss his illness," she said briskly. "You may stay for ten minutes, but you must not tire him or upset him."

"I'll be good," Will said with a smile that he hoped was ingratiating. He sat down beside the bed, placing his hands over Berk's restless fingers. "I'll just sit here with him."

The nurse returned to a series of monitors. The very atmosphere felt heavy as Will sat eying the monitors while Berk alternately thrashed about and slept.

A flash of light and a buzzing sound summoned the nurse. She leapt up and darted out into the hall. Swiftly Will bent over his brother. "Berk! When did this happen to you?"

"Nothing happened!" Berk exclaimed, suddenly sitting upright. "I'm going home. Let me go home!" His arms jerked as if from an electric shock. Then he began to cry.

Frightened, Will went to the small monitor above the bed, searching for information. He pressed a red tab. A graph appeared, and a stylized image of a brain, with small arrows pointing to shaded areas encroaching on the white, healthy tissue. Berk's brain. Will felt like an intruder looking at his brother's brain, while Berk lay on his back, sobbing.

Will glanced about guiltily as he pressed another button with a back arrow. "Patient History," came the report on the screen. Swiftly Will read the words: "Lack of coordination . . . visual disturbances . . . involuntary movements . . . weakness . . . dementia."

Footsteps warned him. He sat down again, holding Berk's hands. They were cold and damp. Will shivered. Dementia. That meant brain damage. "Shh, I'm here, Berk," he murmured. "It's going to be all right. You'll be fine."

Will thought of Drew, the horror of it. Whatever disease had struck Berk, it could be genetic. Maybe it was only a matter of time before it claimed him, too. He needed time to get his bearings, to sift through all that he had discovered. But Will felt as if he were on a speeding transport, rocket propelled.

"Time's up!" said the nurse.

"I'll be back, Berk," Will muttered as he made his way out to the streets, onto the motion path. He felt a heavy ache in his chest, the same way he had felt at Kiera's grave.

As he approached his quarters, Will saw Reese and Leora standing at the door, waiting for him.

"Leora!" he called. There was so much to tell. They looked into each other's eyes. She nodded slightly, communicating understanding. His sorrow was reflected in her gaze.

"I saw Thad Varton," Reese said, placing his hand on Will's shoulder. "We spent several hours together."

"Did you see Berk?" Will asked.

"Yes. Varton is treating Berk," Reese said. "Look, can't we go inside?"

"Of course." Inside everything was sleek and cool. The Screen was broadcasting a familiar anthem: *One heart, one blood, one unity.* Will switched it off. Leora stood looking about at the conveniences of Will's pod, nodding to herself. "You have everything," she murmured.

"It all adds up to nothing," he replied. They moved to the conversation cove. "Tell me," Will said to Reese. "What is it? What's wrong with Berk?" He watched Leora's face. She looked very tired and strained.

Reese flung himself down into an air chair. Will and Leora sat opposite him on a low body-form lounge. "It's not good," Reese said, rubbing his chin as if he missed the beard, needed it for comfort. "Your brother is very sick."

"How sick?"

"Very sick," Reese repeated, avoiding Will's eyes. "He has a rare disease that affects the brain." He paused, and Will tried to absorb Reese's words. "Didn't you find him changed?"

"Yes, he is confused and very upset. I saw the monitor, a picture of his brain." He shuddered. And he thought of all the missing years, the conversations he and Berk never had, the things they hadn't shared. "He was fine just a few weeks ago," Will said. "We were together at the anniversary pageant."

"And you didn't notice anything different?" Reese asked. "Any impairment?"

"He stumbled on the stage," Leora said. "Remember?" She did not look up, as if meeting Will's eyes would be too direct, too painful.

"He forgets things," Will said, recalling the odd conversations. "But everyone forgets things sometimes! How can someone get sick so quickly? Now he didn't even recognize Mara. He's like a different person."

"It only seems quick," Reese said, his tone reluctant. "Actually, it's probably been building for nearly a year. Lack of coordination, forgetfulness, changes in vision."

"Berk said he needed to get lenses," Will recalled. "He said things looked wobbly. What kind of a disease is it that makes a person decay that way?"

"It's a variant of CJD. Its official name is Creutzfeldt-Jakob disease," Reese said.

"CJD," Will repeated. "How in the world could Berk get something like that?" He stood up, paced, came back again, distracted.

Will heard only phrases, words that stood out and repeated themselves while he tried to get his bearings. "Degenerative . . . eats up the brain . . . progresses quickly, dementia . . . paralysis . . . death. Death. Death."

A hundred images swept through Will's mind, past and future mingled together, Berk as a toddler, pulling him along the playground, Berk challenging him, arguing with him, laughing with him. And now Berk was dying.

"How long?" Will asked tensely.

"A few months, maybe."

Will sat motionless, incapable of further thought, it seemed. Finally he asked, "Is it genetic?"

"Why would it be?" Leora said quickly.

"We are *clones*," Will said sharply. "We have the exact same genetic code. So I should also have this—CJD disease. Maybe it's just a little slower to develop." His breath felt heavy and choked.

"Hold on," Reese said. "You might be all right."

"Can one twin have the disease and the other be healthy?" Leora asked.

"Of course," said Reese. "It's possible. You need to be examined, your brain scanned."

"I'm supposed to go in tomorrow for a complete examination," Will said.

"Look," Reese said. "This is only a guess, but maybe Berk picked up some virus that activated this disease. He might have been prone to it all along."

"Then wouldn't I have the same virus?"

"Not necessarily. The two of you haven't had exactly the same environment, have you?"

"No," said Will. Still, he had that constricted feeling, as if he were trapped in a hole, and it was damp and dark.

"Will, I'm sorry," Reese said.

Will nodded. "Berk and I had health checks all the time. Why didn't anyone discover this sickness sooner? Maybe they could have done something."

"CJD is very rare," said Reese. "Originally doctors discovered that it was linked with HGH."

"Human growth hormone?" Leora said.

"Yes, exactly." Reese gave Leora a nod. "It's been used for centuries to improve stamina and build muscles, and as an antiaging drug."

"What's that got to do with Berk?" Will asked.

"Perhaps Berk had some flaw in his immune system," Reese said, "and along with his exposure to HGH, it created a reaction that resulted in this illness."

"You mean Berk was taking HGH?"

"Oh, yes. Thad Varton told me that both you and Berk have been taking supplements for quite a while. Hayli wanted to ensure your perfect health. Also, as it turns out, the supplements were supposed to suppress and even reverse aging. Most probably it included HGH or something similar."

"The blue powder," Will said. "I've been taking that for years!" he exclaimed.

"Hold on!" Reese stopped him with his hand uplifted. "Don't panic. It confirms what we already know. You were given antiaging drugs to retard not only aging but also the diseases that accompany it."

"What diseases?" Will asked sharply.

"Skin rash, for one thing. Not too serious. Joint pain. And sometimes worse things—arteriosclerosis, heart disease."

"Are you saying the supplements work, or that they don't?"

"They work, to a degree, I suppose," Reese said. "Apparently Dr. Varton and Hayli have been conducting a little experiment. Several possible antiaging drugs were proposed. All had some side effects. The two most promising were being tested, one on you and the other on Berk. I suppose the new enzyme is simply mixed into your powder supply."

Will took a deep breath, recalling Sileus's constant nagging. "That's why they made sure I took it every day."

Leora stared at Will, her blue eyes wide with disbelief. "You mean, Hayli was using Berk and Will as . . . as . . ."

"Human guinea pigs," Will said, his voice shaking. "Giving one enzyme to me and another to Berk. Not caring that one of us might die."

"That's why I stopped doing research," Reese said grimly. "The regime would have pushed me to the limit to get what they want. Thad Varton made that very clear to me today." Reese shook himself, as if he were shaking off some obnoxious substance. "He and his colleagues have been working for years on brain transplants and antiaging, Hayli's primary interest." He gave Will a long look, then he said, "Dr. Varton used a word that struck me as being most unscientific. But he used it several times, and he seemed very smug about it."

"What was the word?" Will asked.

"Immortality," said Reese.

"That shouldn't surprise us," said Leora. "Hayli has been talking about it from the start. His creed says it: there is no reason humans have to die."

Reese stood up and put his hand on Will's shoulder. "Varton hinted that they have found a way to defy death."

"But first they kill my brother!" Will cried.

Reese said, "One of our former colleagues has been working on transplanting human tissue into Synthetic Individuals. S.I.s."

"Robots," said Will.

"Have they made any S.I.s?" asked Leora.

Reese shook his head. "Apparently it hasn't worked out. They haven't been able to coordinate body and brain. There always seems to be a missing element. Of course, I didn't say this to Varton, but it's true; you can fill a robot with knowledge, but you can't give it wisdom or judgment. Or feelings, for that matter; you can't give it a soul."

From the Screen came the sleep signal: whispers, fragrances, dimming of lights.

"I'd better hurry," Leora said. She looked exhausted. "The proctors check our pods at eleven."

"Shall I walk with you?"

She hesitated, glanced at Reese. "If you would," she said softly.

Outside there was no darkness to shelter them, no silence. Bright lights and messages invaded Will's senses. "I need," he began, "I need to . . ."

"I know," Leora murmured. "If only we could go someplace quiet."

"I'll find a place," Will said ardently. "Someplace we can talk and . . . I just want to look at you." A strange combination of joy and longing seized him. All he could think about was to be with Leora, alone in a room, close to her, without anyone or anything else to distract him.

"I have to go," she said, stepping away. "Good night, Will."

More than the words, her tone clung to him as he made his way back to his own pod. Her tone said, *Yes, I know how you feel, I feel the same way. I want you with me. Always.*

It was later, in the night, with Reese asleep on the guest cot and Leora back in her own pod, that Will maneuvered his way through the long discourse, the possibilities, the endless questions.

He slept, but even then his mind was working, trying to piece it all together. Berk was dying. The brain disease might also affect him. And one word rang continually though his thoughts: *immortality.* He felt certain that the S.I.s were somehow connected to Hayli's plan for him. But how?

Hitler the conqueror also moved through his dream-thoughts. Some people said Hitler was insane, demented. At the end, they said, he stumbled when he walked. Was it possible, Will had asked Reese, that Hitler suffered from CJD, and that it was transmitted to him and Berk by Hitler's brain tissue?

"It's possible," Reese had said, "that the tissue used for cloning *was* brain tissue. If it was infected, then the bacteria would have been frozen, too, and it could be transmitted to . . . a clone."

Leora had objected. "But Hitler's body was burned."

"The head," said Reese, "would be the most difficult to burn. Some tissue, especially that encased in the skull, could have been saved."

All night the questions revolved in Will's mind. In the morning, the moment Will awakened, the idea was fully formed. He called out, and Reese leapt up from the cot.

"What is it?"

"I need you to do something for me."

"Of course. Anything!"

"Can you see Dr. Varton again?"

"Yes. As a matter of fact, he asked me to have lunch with him today."

"Then find out, if you can, about Hayli's medical history. Find out about his general health. Can you do that?" Will said urgently.

"I'll try. I can't promise anything. But I'll try," Reese said, looking perplexed. "Why do you want to know?"

"I have an idea," Will said. "It's pretty extreme, and I have to make some more inquiries. Let me work on it, and then I'll tell you. Now, I have to go out."

"It's barely daybreak!" Reese objected.

"Mara hardly sleeps," Will replied. "I have to see her before I see Dr. Varton. It's a matter of life or death."

"Whose?"

"Mine."

CHAPTER 27

ARA'S HAIR WAS WOUND UP in a silk turban. As she reached out and touched her cheek to his, Will smelled the fragrant oil on her skin. She glowed. Without makeup Mara looked even more beautiful, her eyes large and expressive.

"I need to talk to you," Will began.

"That would be obvious," Mara said with a slight smile. She motioned him to the couch. She seemed fully in control, entirely different from yesterday, when she took him to see Drew. The incident, it seemed, was entirely forgotten, put aside.

Will sat down. He took a deep breath, composing himself. "I need your help, Mara. I don't know exactly what Hayli is planning to do next, but I'm afraid. He's been giving us all kinds of supplements. Some of the stuff might have caused Berk's illness. The same thing could happen to me."

"That's preposterous!" Mara cried. "Will, Hayli has nurtured you, he needs you, he had you created!"

Will faced Mara fully, feeling strangely calm now, as if he stood at the edge of a precipice ready to leap into the sea. He must make the leap if he wanted a chance at life. And he wanted so much to live!

"Mara, tell me about the S.I. program," he said.

Mara looked around. The silvery curtains were still closed over the mirrored walls. "I don't know what you are talking about," she said.

"Yes, you do."

"Look, Will, I'm not involved in scientific research. I never was."

"Human engineering," Will said. "That's what they're doing in the S.I. program, isn't it?"

"I don't know," Mara insisted. "It's obviously an abbreviation for something."

"Synthetic Individuals," Will said. He focused his gaze upon her, unrelenting. "Taroo was working in that program, wasn't he?"

She turned her face away. "I don't know what Taroo was working on."

"But you said you were all connected! You were together all the time. I saw all those photographs of the five of you. You must have talked about your projects, your work for The Goodness. What else was there?"

Mara squirmed back on the sofa. She dipped her hand into the dish of confections, but it was empty now. "If you think Taroo knew something important, why didn't you ask him?"

Will waved her aside. "I didn't know about the S.I. project until now. Is that why Taroo left? Because he didn't agree with Hayli?"

"They used to argue all the time," Mara said. "About everything. You said it yourself, Taroo was in love with me. It created a lot of tension."

"About the S.I.s," Will said, breathing heavily. "What gave the S.I.s their intelligence? It wasn't circuitry, was it? They tried that, and it didn't work."

"I don't know anything about that," Mara insisted. She got up, went to the drapery, pulled it tight together. "This is ridiculous. It all happened years ago. What's the difference now?"

"They are still doing it," Will said. "The project isn't dead at all. They are still working on the S.I.s, trying to resolve the problem of intelligence. Because synthetic people don't have a feel for what it is to be human. They don't change with the circumstances. They can't exercise judgment. So they are sterile and they do things that are foolish or even dangerous."

"If you know all this, why are you asking me?" Mara objected, turning toward Will, her chin thrust out.

"Because you were there. You heard the arguments. You know what it was that made Taroo so outraged that he had to leave, even though he loved you. What happened?"

"He became disillusioned, I suppose."

"Why? My guess is that they were putting some human parts into those Synthetic Individuals, to try to make them more real. Isn't that it?"

"I don't know!" Mara cried. "You have no right to question me like this!"

"What part, Mara? Did they have an entire clone bank to provide body parts? Hearts? Lungs? Brains? Because you have to know it, Mara, they *are* going to use Berk and me. I've figured it out. Why did Hayli clone us? Why has he been pumping us full of antiaging drugs? Why does he keep talking about immortality?"

"I don't know! I don't know!"

"I think he's been planning to use us for replacements, somehow, to make a new thing, something that can last forever."

"A thing!" Mara cried, aghast. "You are not a thing. You are my boy, and I love you!"

"What about Berk? Berk is dying because of Hayli's experiments!"

"No!" Mara cried. "Berk got sick. It's a virus or something he picked up in Africa. Hayli would never harm you or Berk," Mara insisted, twisting to and fro.

"Really? Look how he treats Drew."

"Stop it!" Mara cried, covering her face with her hands. "Stop it; you don't know anything. They did try. For years they cloned for different body parts. The idea was to put together a perfect person, arms from one, organs from another, and so on. It never worked. There was always the problem of rejection and incompatible aging. And the most difficult problem was the brain. They tried artificial brains, but that was too impractical, and the result was flawed, as you said."

"So they have been working on transplanting brains," Will stated, and the moment he said the words, he knew it was true. As if he had rung a bell or struck a minefield, he knew it was true. Suddenly it all fell into place, the grand idea of putting a superbrain into a superperson. All he needed now were the particulars.

Mara pulled her arms across her chest, as if to shield herself. When she spoke, her voice was hushed. "Taroo was involved in the process. He called himself a mechanic. It was supposed to be a joke. Actually, he was a brain surgeon."

"When was this?"

"The program started about eighteen years ago."

"So Zebarre was looking for brains to transplant into bodies—clones. But he had trouble finding smart brains. Why couldn't they use cadavers?"

"They wanted living tissue. It is difficult," Mara said, "to keep a brain alive for very long. It must be transplanted immediately."

"So they had to get the brains of living people, but of course, nobody would volunteer, so they . . ." Will stopped, his heart hammering as the certainty of it overwhelmed him. "So they abducted people—high-status people. Didn't they?"

Mara nodded, her eyes moist, hands clasped under her chin.

Will went on, as if he saw it all before his eyes. "And someone dreamed up the story that there were these criminals, dissidents, who abducted people for their brains and sold them on the black market. But it was actually our own government, our own wonderful Goodness, Hayli's people, who were doing the abducting."

Now Mara's eyes glistened, and she twisted her hands, shaking her head as if to dispel the memories. "Yes. Yes. And they even created the PAARs as a diversion, to support their claim that people of status needed protection . . ."

"But, of course, nobody was ever really kidnapped, except by Hayli's own robo-enforcers, and they can't be harmed by PAARs. How many people were abducted? How many brains were stolen? How many people died so that Hayli could try to make the perfect immortal?"

"Will, oh Will." Mara stood up, circled the room, holding herself taut, for she was trembling. "Nothing turned out the way it was supposed to."

"I know," Will said.

"What are you going to do?" she asked fearfully.

"I'm not sure yet. Someone has to stop this. Someone has to stop Hayli."

* * *

The examination lasted over an hour. Dr. Varton himself supervised the process, ordering analysis of blood, tissue, enzymes, and brain function, in addition to the usual tests.

As he lay under the test machines, Will braced himself for the news. Muscle weakness, fatigue, disorientation—yes, he had experienced all of these symptoms. He dreaded the verdict. His mind would deteriorate. His body would refuse to function.

"Extraordinary," Dr. Varton concluded.

"What?"

"Perfect," said the doctor, putting away the instruments. "You are fine. The surgery is healing well. You're a strong young man!"

"But," Will said faintly, "I've felt weak and tired at times."

Dr. Varton threw back his head, laughing. "What do you expect after surgery? The body undergoes a certain shock. And you were probably overdoing it. Of course you'd feel tired. You have nothing to worry about."

The doctor addressed Hayli on the screen. "Your boy is in excellent health."

At the sight of Hayli's face, grossly enlarged, Will felt a new rush of emotions. Inexplicably, Hayli's face conjured up the old fear and awe. Even as he understood Hayli's deception and loathed the lies, there came the memory of Hayli's one kiss, the feeling of being protected by Hayli's radiance. That was over now. He must stand alone.

"No muscle weakness?" Hayli prompted. "No impairment of memory?"

"He has a slight rash, nothing to speak of," said the doctor. "All internal organs are in excellent condition. We did a full body scan, complete blood work—I had three different medics checking the results."

"Will! Good news, my boy!" Hayli said with a robust smile. "I'll see you tomorrow, three o'clock. Right?"

"Right," said Will. He was trembling, relieved that Dr. Varton had removed the sensors from his body. He felt transparent, vulnerable.

"Tomorrow then," Hayli repeated. "Varton! You'll have everything ready for the treatments."

"Of course," said Dr. Varton. The Screen interview ended with Hayli giving his signature gesture, arms outstretched as if to embrace the entire world.

Dr. Varton turned to Will, his expression triumphant. "Hayli is very pleased," he said. "Everything he has wanted for you has been achieved. You are a splendid specimen. Splendid!"

"Thank you," Will said, keeping his expression bland, while the word *specimen* lodged in his mind. "What's this about a treatment?" he asked. "I thought you completed the examination today."

"Oh, nothing for you to worry about. We're going to inject some special supplements to increase your stamina, make you immune to diseases, like the one your poor brother is suffering from. You'll be fine. It's painless."

Will glanced about at the shining instruments, the innumerable machines with their electrodes and cables and compartments shaped to the various parts of the human body. He was almost numb with trepidation. Tomorrow. If only he could make time stop, and tomorrow would never come.

Outside, he stood for a long moment breathing deeply of the purified air, hearing the sounds of life all around him. Tomorrow, if he were dead, everything would continue as now. And in faraway Fresmofield, the birds would still feed their young, the feral cats would hunt their prey, and some people would be reclaiming the soil, trying to reclaim their lives.

Will walked and walked. At last he summoned Leora on his pulse pad. She responded immediately. "I remembered a place," he said. "It's beyond the pavilions. You'll see a large warehouse. Go downstairs to the library."

"A library!" she said incredulously. "I didn't know there was such a place."

"I'll meet you there," Will promised.

The old library was nearly always deserted. Will had discovered it years ago, quite by chance. It was after a particularly difficult day, a quarrel with one of his proctors, sharp criticism via the Screen from Hayli, nobody to talk to, nobody who cared. He had followed the paths to the Academy perimeter, that strip of land where refuse was collected and trucks and other equipment were stored. The warehouse, an enormous building with coated windows, seemed to beckon, as the sun was just setting, its golden light reflecting outward from the structure. It drew him in.

Now, as he approached the stairway, Will felt a rush of air, and as he went down into the cavernous room, the atmosphere felt pleasantly heavy, a blanket of cool and soothing stillness. Leora was already there. She stood between the vast expanse of shelves, all filled with books, and a row of tables where scholars might still be sitting, poring over the volumes and the wisdom of ages past. But no scholars, no students, nobody sat here. It was as if they had entered a mausoleum, a place where books were buried and saved until they would turn to dust.

"Someday," Will said as he walked toward Leora, "this place will be gone. They'll burn it down."

"Why haven't they done it yet?"

Will shrugged as he extended his hands to Leora. "Too busy with other mischief," he said. Strangely, he realized that he was smiling. Leora smiled back as she clasped his hands, and they stood thus, fingers linked, looking into each other's eyes.

"How are you?" Leora asked. She looked away shyly, as if she were suddenly aware of their aloneness.

"According to Dr. Varton," Will said, "I'm a perfect specimen. Except for this stupid itch."

"Oh, Will!" Leora exclaimed. "I was so worried about you. I thought . . ."

"That I'd get sick, like Berk?"

"But you're not! You're fine!" She looked happy.

"Hayli wants to see me tomorrow," he said soberly.

"What about?"

"My future, I'm sure," Will said. They sat down on either side at one of the long metal tables. Will looked at Leora, her hair with the gold lights, her smoky blue eyes. "You're so beautiful," he said. She looked older, more grown up than when he had first met her. He could imagine her five or ten years from now, in a world that was different, balanced.

She smiled, "Does that mean you want me in your future?" she teased.

"What do you think? We'll work together to bring change."

"Senna and Antone will help," Leora said. "And Reese." She paused, then asked, "How do we begin?"

"I have to get high up in the Information Ministry," Will said. "Then I can bring you with me. We'd start sifting out the lies. It's worse, deeper even than I thought. The evil."

Now Will told her about Drew. He watched Leora's face as she began to grasp the full extent of the evil surrounding them. He told her about the early experiments with S.I.s, synthetic individuals, the stolen brains and failed transplants.

"So that's Hayli's scheme for becoming immortal," Leora said, breathing heavily. "But are they still working on it?"

He hesitated. "Yes, I think so. They're looking for the perfect body." He would not say more. As he had walked that afternoon, all the information became synthesized, leading him to only one possible conclusion. He could not tell Leora. Not now. Besides, there might still be some hope for the two of them.

"Remember our plans?" he said.

"Going to live in the Desert, with the children . . ."

Will went to her side now, and they sat with their hands clasped, nothing more, dreaming of a time without edicts and enforcers.

"We can build a compound and all live together . . ."

"Plant trees . . ."

"Keep some goats and a dog or two . . ."

"Travel to the ocean . . . can we get a transport of our own?"

"Of course. Why not?" They laughed together, even while Will, in the core of his being, understood the risk of the plan that was solidifying in his mind.

It was growing dark. "We have to leave," Will said. "I'm going to see Hayli in the morning."

"What will you tell him?" Fear shone in her eyes. "Will," she said with sudden urgency, "don't go. Can't we take the transport? We can go back to Fresmofield. Reese and you and I—we can go somewhere, maybe even to the Great Desert."

"No, Leora," he said quietly. "I have to do this. I have to face Hayli. Don't worry." He managed a grin. "Look, I'll pad you as soon as we're finished. Then we'll meet at the Café. We'll sit at the senior tables. Then we'll talk to Reese."

"Yes, all right. I'll meet you," Leora said in a hopeful voice.

Will pulled at the fastener of his tunic. He pressed his hand onto his implant, felt the gold stud. Nimbly he removed the stud with its diamond at the center. "Take this," he said.

Leora shook her head. "Will, please."

Will put the jewel into her hand. "I want you to have it, Leora. Just keep it for me. Until tomorrow."

"I'm afraid for tomorrow!" she cried.

He bent down so that his face touched her hair. It was soft and fragrant. "Whatever happens, Leora," he said softly, "you have to be connected to Reese and Zebarre and the others who want to make things right. Senna and Antone, too. It's what they raised you to do."

"And you?" she asked, her voice low. "What were you raised to do?"

"You'll know," he said, "when I've done it."

CHAPTER 28

HAYLI LOOKED RADIANT. He stood at the doorway to his compound, rubbing his hands together, smiling delightedly, as if he were about to release some phenomenal new plan. "Will! Come in, my boy. Come in."

Will followed, and behind him came his PAAR, past the electronic beams, into the vast room with its mirrors and bright mosaic floors, the furniture all fabricated to surround the body with comfort and climate control. In the periphery stood Hayli's personal PAAR and enforcers, and, of course, Rondo, his face averted, hands at his sides in military stance.

Will had tried to rehearse this meeting with Hayli. Hundreds of times he had planned what to say, how to behave. Now, as he stood before the Supreme Compassionate Director, his mind went blank. There was something about being in Hayli's presence that almost smothered Will's anger and resentment. He almost believed that it was *his* mistake, that his own ineptitude had somehow caused the rift, and it was merely a difference of opinions. Something that could, by explanation, be rectified.

But he knew better.

"Sit down, here, where I can see you," Hayli exclaimed. "You're looking well! Dr. Varton assures me that you are fit, no bad effects from the surgery. What a terrible fright you gave us! But you are fine now. Fine. It's wonderful to see you!" he sounded exuberant.

"Good to see you, too," said Will. And indeed, it *was* good, the long-awaited moment was here at last.

As if he were split into two people, Will saw himself the way he used to be, with Hayli at the center of his universe, and now. So much depended upon him now.

"Your travels must have agreed with you," Hayli said pleasantly. "But even better is coming home again, isn't it?"

"Yes," Will said. "My visit to the colonies was very . . . productive. I learned so much."

Hayli leaned toward Will, his eyes gleaming with pleasure. "I was impressed with your comments and reports. You've come so far, Will! I always looked forward to this time, when you and I could plan for the future. It's come sooner than I expected, but not too soon!"

"What has changed, Father? What do you mean?"

"Things are happening quickly," Hayli replied. "You've shown yourself to be highly capable. You see, it was a good thing that you went on this trip to the colonies. It forced you to come to grips with realities, and to make decisions. It's a shame about Sileus, but between you and me, I never liked the man. Too nervous. He used to sweat too much."

"I took care of everything," Will said, seeing the delight in Hayli's eyes, and he realized that only a few months ago he would have given anything for this.

"Indeed. You were most decisive." Hayli stroked his upper lip thoughtfully. "You understand about the Compassionate Removals, the necessity for filtering information to the masses. In fact, I want you oversee the new directives that will be posted about Africa. I have decided to attach the Africa Dominion. We must begin to consolidate. We must convince the people that it is for their own welfare. And it is, Will. They don't understand how to manage. They hate details. They only want—"

"Pleasure," Will finished for him. "Simple work, leisure time, someone to make the difficult decisions for them."

"Exactly," said Hayli, taking a deep breath, satisfaction in his gaze. "You understand. Look, I feel terrible about Berk. But if I had to choose . . . I have always known you are more intelligent, more capable than your brother."

Will nodded and tried to smile, as if indeed he had achieved a victory. But his mind was racing over his plan. The PAAR had folded itself up behind him, so as to be almost invisible. Everything was ready.

What he was about to do was no small thing. No, it was the ultimate. He felt almost numb as he listened to Hayli's plans.

"The fact is," Hayli was saying, "there can really be only one Director, one head. Power divided is power corrupted. You understand that, don't you?"

"Absolutely," said Will. Once again he was aware of how large Hayli was, not only in influence, but even in body. And he was immovable. There was nobody in the entire Dominion who could challenge him. Taroo had tried and failed, had had to banish himself. Mara had probably imagined herself his equal, only to discover that she was, as she said, Hayli's pet bird.

I am to be his future, Will thought. *He can do nothing without me.* Reese had explained, after another meeting with Dr. Varton, exactly how much Hayli needed him.

Will said, "I saw Berk yesterday. He's very ill. He might even be dying."

Hayli's eyes flickered with emotion—pity? Annoyance that his experiment had gone wrong? "Oh, yes, poor boy, quite terrible, his condition. But Dr. Varton is looking after him," Hayli said smoothly. "The moment we learned of his illness, I had him transferred to my own clinic. Your brother is getting the best possible care."

"I'm sure," said Will. "But what caused this sudden illness?"

"We don't know," said Hayli. "Maybe some congenital defect."

"But Berk and I are exactly like," Will objected. "Identical twins. And, of course, you planned for us to be perfect."

"Well, never mind," Hayli said with a golden smile. "You are perfect, my son."

Will looked closely at Hayli's face. He saw no sign of aging there, no sign of decay or evil. How was it possible, he wondered, that Hayli still had that glow?

"We were given the best DNA, weren't we?" Will said, watching Hayli's expression.

"The best," Hayli said with a nod. "I've always given you the best in everything—background, training, opportunity. You have no idea what it means, to be given opportunity. Everything I have, I had to get for myself, from the moment I was born. Abandoned, cold, hungry—they say an infant doesn't remember these things." He shook his head, bit his lips together. "I remember. I always knew what it was to be alone and hungry. Always."

"Even after Mattelin rescued you?"

"Mattelin. He was brilliant, but contemptible. Coarse, without the least bit of warmth. He took me in to use me as a servant, to pump me full of his theories. I was to be the vessel for his ideas. Extreme egotist, he was!"

"And that's who raised you."

"I raised myself!" Hayli cried. "Nobody ever gave me anything."

Will sat silent, stiff, his heart pounding with dread. He wanted to shout it out, *What did you give me? The genes of a tyrant!* But he held off, pondering his next move, as if he were playing the maze game, watching his opponent, plotting the final attack. Timing is everything. He and Reese had talked about it; they had agreed: Timing is everything.

Hayli looked at him with a magnanimous expression, arms extended. "I am accelerating your rise, Will. We'll announce it soon, that you are to become Director of the African Dominion."

"I thought that was to be Berk's position. Do you consider him dead already?"

Hayli started forward, scowling. "Of course not! But we have to be practical. You said it yourself, that he's very ill—"

"But maybe he can be replaced," Will said. "I don't imagine you would create only two successors, take the risk of something happening. Aren't there more?"

"Certainly not!" Hayli said, his smile fading.

From behind him, Will heard his PAAR moving, unfolding itself. It was time for the system to be activated, the lubricating elements and the cooling fan. He heard the usual faint sounds of self-maintenance.

"I learned something else out in the colonies," Will said slowly. "Did you know, Father, that my DNA is seventy-two years old?"

Hayli's face froze. "Don't be ridiculous. Who told you such non-sense?"

"It's true. It was proven in a laboratory. I checked the results myself. You know what that means. Of course you do. You created me, Father. But not in the usual way, using your cells and a female donor. I am a clone." He watched the transition come over Hayli's face, first a flush, then a hard, fierce look. "You cloned us," Will persisted. "Me and Berk. And how many others?"

"You don't know what you're talking about!" Hayli sputtered. "I have proof of your donors . . . what makes you think you know anything?"

Will leaned forward. His tone was sharp and demanding, the way he wanted it to sound. Let Hayli know that he had indeed inherited strength and nerve. "I don't care, Father! I just want to know how many others you made. Are you planning to populate the entire Dominion with them?" It was the last thing he had to know.

Hayli twisted in his chair, his lips pressed tightly together. He glanced to the side, where Rondo stood guard, eyes averted, silent.

"Only the two of you," Hayli said, his voice husky. "The others failed. But it doesn't matter, Will! It doesn't matter at all, because I have you, and together we're going to usher in the Time of Perfection!"

"But what about all the sayings? The law? Do not condone a clone—"

Hayli waved him aside. "That law doesn't apply to you! You aren't an ordinary clone. Not at all. You're mine."

"But you lied to us. You said we were your sons."

"You *are* my sons!" Hayli shouted. "I have given you everything—background, education, the entire Dominion is at your disposal. Never in all history has anyone been so privileged. And you come here *blaming* me? How dare you!"

"You lied to me!"

"It was for your own good!"

"Just as the Compassionate Removals are good? Are you saying it's a good thing to trick people into being blown up?"

"You yourself wrote the report," Hayli cried. "I thought you under-stood."

"I wrote what you wanted to hear. I wrote what Hitler would have said."

"Hitler?" His voice rose. "Hitler?"

"My donor. My real father. Adolf Hitler. Did you think I wouldn't find out?"

Hayli stared at him, his hand uplifted, as if he would strike. But he only made a fist, punching the air in exclamation. "You don't even realize the gift I have given you," he said with contempt. "And the greater gift you are about to receive. I gave you the flesh and the bones, the ego and the energy of one of the greatest leaders of all time. If only I had such a heritage, there's no limit to what I could do!"

Hayli rushed to Will's side. "Will, listen. We are going to usher in the Time of Perfection. You and I." He gripped Will's shoulders, drew him close in a rough embrace. Will shivered at the touch. The heat and scent of Hayli's body almost overwhelmed him. Hayli went on, his breathing rapid, his words flowing. "Listen to me, Will. We are on the brink of a new era in human events. All the ministries function like clockwork, according to direction from me. It took years to integrate everything—allocation of resources, security, information. Now all it takes is maintenance. And someone to inspire and motivate the people. You are that person. You challenge me! You have the nerve to challenge *me!* Don't you see, Will? You are exactly his embodiment. You are Hitler!"

"No, I'm not," Will said, pressing his hand over his eyes. "Do you know something? I wanted to be exactly like you. All my life, I just wanted to be like you."

"You shall be!" Hayli exclaimed. "You're *mine,* my creation. I gave you the best possible DNA."

"Why not yours?"

Hayli froze, his eyes darting about as a slight whirring sound insinuated itself into the atmosphere.

"You couldn't clone yourself," Will stated. He stood his ground as Hayli came closer, so close that Will could see the slight blemishes on his face and the film of sweat on his brow. "I've made inquiries. You told me to find followers. Well, I found some very devoted comrades. One of them knows Dr. Varton. They were classmates."

Hayli's features were static, and he waved his hand, as if to brush aside an annoying bit of chatter.

"You have this terrible allergy," Will went on. "It might be inherited if you cloned yourself. You wanted someone else. You thought his traits could be duplicated."

"They have been," Hayli exclaimed. "You're perfect."

"No, I'm not. Berk is a better Hitler than I. And he's dying." Will confronted Hayli. "How do you know that I won't self-destruct? Like Berk? Clones don't do well," he added, relishing this moment before the moment. "They are prone to all sorts of diseases, premature aging, mutation."

"No. No," Hayli cried. "Dr. Varton has monitored you—"

"And provided extracts," Will said. "The blue powder."

"Yes. Supplements to make you strong, invincible!"

"But what about you, Father?" He gave the word *father* a certain twist. "If I'm invincible, made from the greatest statesman who ever lived, where does that leave you?" Will glanced at his PAAR, back at Hayli. It had finished oiling itself, and now the fan accelerated. "Time was running out for you," he stated. "Wasn't it?"

"You don't know what you're talking about. Quite the opposite! I've had scientists working on this for years. Now we're at the brink of immortality!"

"You need me!" Will said, gazing into Hayli's eyes. "You need me so desperately, don't you?"

"You need *me!*" Hayli cried. "Without me, you're nothing!"

"Your kidneys are failing," Will said. "My friend, Dr. Varton's classmate, got your medical reports. You've had all the transplants your body can take. Kidney. Heart. Gallbladder. Reese tells me your liver is damaged, too. You can't survive another surgery."

"I don't need another surgery," Hayli snapped.

"I know," Will said quietly. "You need me. My body. The S.I.s didn't work, so you decided to raise a real flesh-and-blood body, someone you could use, ultimately replacing the parts, one after the other." He shuddered. Behind him came the sound of the fan, and now there was no turning back.

Hayli came toward him, arms wide, and he was beaming. "You understand everything! We hold the future in our hands, you and I. We have perfected the technique. Immortality. Think of it, Will!"

"Absolute unity," Will said.

"Under one head," Hayli said.

"Your brain in my body. Perfection," Will said, watching Hayli's face, the very picture of triumph.

Will glanced at the time. Everything was proceeding according to plan. In the passageway outside Hayli's compound, Will had emptied the contents of his pouch into the PAAR's ventilation system. He could smell the powder being launched into the air, ever so faintly, the powder from the nuts he and Leora had brought from Fresmofield. It seemed almost ridiculous that so simple a thing could have such monumental results. Nuts.

Will could imagine Hayli's plan. News Notes would hint of Hayli's illness, and of relinquishing of power to his son. Finally a Screen message would announce it. SUPREME COMPASSIONATE DIRECTOR STRICKEN! POLICIES TO BE CONTINUED BY HIS SON, WILL. Perhaps it would be revealed, much later, that Hayli's brain still lived, that he and Will had become one, one perfect man who would live and rule for a thousand years or even beyond.

Three minutes to go. Two minutes. "It's nearly time for you to see Dr. Varton," said Hayli, clapping his hands together, a gesture of finality.

Will asked, "Is Dr. Varton going to perform the operation today?"

Hayli's eyes gleamed. "Yes, today. It will be absolutely painless, I promise you. And neither of us will be diminished. No! We will each be augmented, our brains fused together in your body. The perfect alliance."

Fusion—not his brain or Hayli's. Will hadn't thought of that, and neither had Reese known it. The new technique was to fuse their brains together in one body, Will's body, to be replaced bit by bit, like replacing worn-out parts in a machine.

For a long moment they looked at each other. Hayli's face shone with anticipation. He breathed deeply, inhaling all the potential of this day. But then he turned, perplexed. "What's that? That smell?"

Will glanced back at his PAAR. Now the sound of the fan was distinct. Will could see slight traces of the lethal powder floating in the air. "There is something you should know, Father," Will said in loud voice, covering the sound of the PAAR. "I didn't kill Sileus."

"You said you did!" Hayli cleared his throat, brought a handkerchief to his lips.

"I lied," Will said.

"Something's wrong," Hayli sputtered, coughing. "The filtration . . . air ducts. Call Maintenance."

Will moved closer. "You want to know who killed Sileus? Zebarre. A man in the colonies."

"Nonsense! Open the door," Hayli gasped, his eyes narrowed. "Open it!"

Will blocked the way. "No," he said.

"What do you mean? Will, open the door!"

"No," Will repeated. He reached inside his tunic. He took out the medal Zebarre had given him. The air was filling gradually with the powder. He saw Hayli's nostrils twitch; his lips seemed to swell.

"What's that?" Hayli demanded. He held his hand over his nose and mouth. "Rondo!" he called. But Rondo heard nothing.

Will held out the medal. Hayli's eyes widened. "Where did you get that?" he gasped. "Did Mara give it to you?"

"Taroo gave it to me," said Will. He waited for a moment, seeing Hayli's transformation from astonishment to fear, the eyes roving, like a trapped animal. "Taroo is alive," Will said. "He calls himself Zebarre now. He is part of the resistance. They are going to win, Hayli. You've failed."

"What? You lie!" Hayli bounded toward him coughing, gagging. "You! I created you! I can kill you!"

Will felt Hayli's fist against his body. He stumbled backward, his chest burning. Viciously Hayli struck, and for a moment Will thought that Mara had lied to him. There was no allergy, the idea was preposterous, murder by PAAR, poisoning the air . . . but even as Will recoiled, hands shielding his face, Hayli stumbled, clutching his throat, and now a cloud of powder settled into the room.

"Rondo! Rondo!" Hayli gasped. "Help!"

"He can't hear you," Will said, backing away.

"Will . . . listen. Stop . . . I'm . . . can't breathe. Will, please!"

Will saw himself and Hayli in the mirrored wall, reflected into infinity.

"Will!" Hayli gagged. "I'm giving you . . ." He choked, coughed. "Immortality." He fell. And Hayli's PAAR roused itself and came clambering over to where its master lay, gasping. Behind it, slowly, the robo-enforcers began to stir, and lastly, Rondo.

"I created you! I own you!" Hayli lay on the floor, his limbs twitching, lips blue.

"No," Will shouted. "Nobody owns me!"

The smell of the powder was strong, but not unpleasant. Will wrapped his arms over his chest, even as he knew it was impossible to shield himself. He thought of Leora, of Antone, of the trees. Oh, Leora! He sobbed in his heart. He had never said the words, never told her of his love. He wished that he could live to tell it, to see the cycle come round, balance restored. He wished he could be with Leora forever, or for however many years humans had on earth. Immortality is only for God, he wanted to shout, but the words caught in his throat.

The first blow came from behind, a blow so heavy that Will felt more impact than pain. He heard a sharp crack, like a tree breaking in half. His body seemed to flare with a thousand sparks. Then it grew numb. At the edge of awareness came the clear knowledge that they would strike again with all their combined force, and it would be over.

Every sense was heightened, and for one glorious moment vivid colors, golden lights burst into Will's consciousness. Purple blossoms blended with a memory of eyes that were a smoky blue, and Will heard a gentle voice, the strains of music, "I will give you honey . . ."

And then they were upon him.

EPILOGUE ▪ ▪ ▪

L EORA STOOD AT THE DAIS, looking out over the crowd. Lush green grass and shrubs surrounded the Commons. Distant fields of wheat and corn waved in the breeze, sending a delicate fragrance over the land. She breathed deeply, filled with emotions, part pride, part sorrow. Every time she came here she thought of the first time, when she and Will brought Precious to what was then called the Great Desert. How might it be if he were here now?

Leora spoke with calm determination. "I congratulate all of you who have worked so tirelessly to restore our beautiful Heartland. This library is but one more example of the wonderful changes that have come to our Dominion. I know that each of you will treasure this place, for the opportunity and the freedom it provides."

Leora paused, a rueful smile on her lips. "I remember a time when a library was a mausoleum, where books were molding and the only information people could get was highly censored. . . ."

Her thoughts flashed back over the years, her last fraught meeting with Will, the shock of his death, then the waves of confrontation as people rose up—first by the hundreds and then the thousands—to restore balance. Leora had played a role in the change, along with Reese and Senna and the others. But every advance was really a tribute to Will's sacrifice, though few people knew it.

When Leora finished speaking, several people came up to her. They pressed her hand and smiled; they thanked her for coming. But most left after a few minutes, engrossed in their own festivities, looking after their children, walking arm in arm with the people they loved. And that was enough for Leora; it was everything she had hoped for.

LOOKING AT PRESENT TRENDS, I see many attitudes and behaviors that, if continued, will lead us to a bleak and impersonal future. I see all around us the "invisible people"—the homeless, disabled, the devalued. I see "throwaway people," in relationships based only on gratification, without regard for any deeper, valuable companionship. People tell me, "Have a nice day!" while they're really busy talking into their cell phones. In the coffeehouse, on the airplane, people are absorbed with their personal computers, their Palm Pilots, oblivious of others around them. Are we becoming a society that values machines more than human beings? If we could, would we clone people to provide us with our latest whim and ideal?

As machines guide us through our daily tasks, performing faster and better than our own brains and bodies, we are in danger of imagining that they are inherently superior. Machines can be repaired or replaced. But a machine has no potential for kindness, self-sacrifice, creativity, or love. A machine has no consciousness, either of itself or of the larger world. A machine has no concern for the future of mankind.

As the study of genetics accelerates, we will once again have to face the age-old questions of which is dominant, heredity or environment. Are we born to be either good or evil? Do we have any choice in the matter? What is a human being—a mere collection of synapses and responses, an imprinted code? Or is there something more? This is where science and religion meet—in questions of ethics and morality, in questions of free choice.

Nobody knows what the future will bring. But we must ask ourselves what we are doing today that will impact tomorrow, and how to develop the kind of society that provides freedom and opportunity for everyone. This book hopes to challenge the reader to ask these questions and to seek answers.

SOURCES

──────────────────── BOOKS

Appel, Benjamin. *Hitler, from Power to Ruin.* New York: Grosset & Dunlap, 1964.

Bezymenski, Lev. *The Death of Adolf Hitler: Unknown Documents from Soviet Archives.* New York: Harcourt, Brace and World, 1968.

Brockman, John, ed. *The Next Fifty Years: Science in the First Half of the Twenty-first Century.* New York: Vintage Books, 2002.

Fuchs, Thomas. *The Hitler Fact Book.* Los Angeles: Fountain Books, 1990.

Goleman, Daniel. *Vital Lies, Simple Truths: The Psychology of Self-Deception.* New York: Simon & Schuster (Touchstone Books), 1985.

Heck, Alfons. *A Child of Hitler.* Frederick, CO: Renaissance House, 1985.

Hitler, Adolf. *Mein Kampf.* Boston: Houghton Mifflin, 1939.

Kkurzweil, Ray. *The Age of Intelligent Machines.* Boston: MIT Press, 1999.

Miller, Alice. *For Your Own Good: Hidden Cruelty in Child-Rearing and the Roots of Violence.* Frankfurt: Suhrkamp Verlag, 1980.

Post, Jerrold M., M.D., ed. *The Psychological Assessment of Political Leaders, with Profiles of Saddam Hussein and Bill Clinton.* Ann Arbor: University of Michigan, 2003.

Richards, Jay W., ed. *Are We Spiritual Machines? Ray Kirzweil vs. the Critics of Strong A.I.* Seattle: Discovery Institute, 2002.

Shipman, Pat. *The Evolution of Racism: Human Differences and the Use and Abuse of Science.* New York: Simon & Schuster, 1994.

Creutzfeldt-Jakob Disease Fact Sheet:

www.ninds.nih.gov/health_andmedic.../creutzfeldt-jakob_disease_fact_sheet.htm

The Neuropathology of CJD:

http://www.cjd.ed.ac.uk/path.htm

The UK Creutzfeldt-Jakob Disease Surveillance Unit:

http://www.cjd.ed.ac.uk/

Adrenal Crisis Health Alert:

wysiwyg://10/http://www.niddk.nih.gov/health/endo/pubs/creutz/alert.htm

ASDA Healthy Living—Food Allergy and Food Intolerance:

http://193.2011.200.19/allergy/al_type.html

Chabad.Org Parasha Articles: Why Does Esau Hate Jacob? (on the existence of evil):

http://www.chabad.org / Parshah/Article.asp?AID-63890

The Nizkor Project: Hitler as he believes himself to be:

wysiwyg://51/http://www.nizkor.org / hweb/p...adolf/oss-paper/text/oss profile-01.html

Human Cloning and Stem Cell Research:

http://apologeticspress.org / rr/rr2011/r&r0108a.htm

Summary of *The Prince* by Machiavelli:

http://www.the-prince-by-machiavelli.com/summary-of-the-prince-by-machiavelli.html

Human Cloning: The How To Page:

http://www.biofact.com/cloning / human.html

Cloning and Genetic Engineering:

http://www.biofact.com/cloning / index.html

Clonaid, the First Human Cloning Company:

http:www.clonaid.com

Inside the Santa Fe Institute (genetics):

wysiwyg:// 7http://www.businessweek.com/1996/25/ b35328.htm

EWG Nuclear Waste Route Atlas:
   http://mapscience.com/faq_radiationrisks.php
Peanut Allergy: What You Need to Know:
   http://oma.org/health/peanuts.htm
Peanut Allergy Fact Sheet, Institute of Child Health:
   http://www.ich.ucl.ac.uk/factsheets/misc/peanut_allergy/
The Philosophical Foundations of UNESCO:
   www.unesco.org / shs
Citizen Magazine—Cloning Humans: A Bad Idea:
   wysiwyg://4http://www.family.org / cforum/citizenmag / coverstory/
   a0001054.html
The President's Council on Bioethics Full Report on Human Cloning and Human Dignity: An Ethical Inquiry:
   www.bioethics.gov/reports/cloningreport

--------------------------------- INTERVIEWS

(See Acknowledgments for details)

Dr. Harold L. Karpman, M.D., cardiologist, Clinical Professor of Medicine, UCLA School of Medicine, Los Angeles, California.

Dr. Julie Korenberg, Vice-Chair of Pediatrics for Research, Cedars-Sinai Medical Center, Professor of Pediatrics and Human Genetics, UCLA.

Dr. Daniel Levitin, Ph.D., Associate Professor of Psychology and Behavorial Neuroscience, McGill University.